Michael J Moore

a novel by Michael Moore


**A HellBound Books Publishing LLC Book**
**Houston TX**

Michael J Moore

## A HellBound Books LLC
## Publication



**www.hellboundbookspublishing.com**

*Dedication*

*For my dad, Greg Murphy.*

Michael J Moore

*Acknowledgments*

*Life is a collaborative process when you're human. We're pack animals, and I just happen to belong to the best.*

*I'd like to thank God and my beautiful wife, Cait Moore, who's as much a part of my projects as I am.*

*Gabriela, Jazmin, Aston, Dante, and Carter for providing plenty of inspiration.*

*John Hovey for being John Hovey. Percy Levy for teaching me what to look for in a publisher.*

*Arthur Longworth for mentoring me in my career.*

*I'd like to thank my editor Xtina and HellBound Books for being so easy to work with.*

*My mom and dad for all the support they've shown.*

*Josh Goodman, who was the first to read this thing, and you, who were the last.*

Michael J Moore

# HIGHWAY TWENTY

# Prologue

Daryle Colombo was into women. From the time he discovered his prick in the third grade and started masturbating, he knew he liked them. He liked knives back then too. Nothing had changed. The first time he pulled one on a sex worker, he cut her deep enough to get blood all over the back seat of the rental Cadillac. It didn't matter. The company paid for the cars, the hotels—though they didn't know it—they even paid for the hookers when they sent him on jobs. There were many benefits of being an engineer.

He didn't pay that girl though, hadn't paid one since. It was more fun to use his knife. It was a big one, with a five-inch blade that folded out from a heavy camouflage handle. He always used the same one he had pulled on the first hooker back in Rochester last year. He never killed them. Why would he? They were sex workers. They weren't going to call the police. What would they say if they did?

Daryle smiled and tapped his fingers against the steering wheel to the beat of the music. He nodded his head with the bass as the singer wailed about a highway to hell.

"I don't know," a meek voice came from the backseat of the rental car.

"What was that, Chief?"

"I uh—I think I should probably go home, Daryle. My Mom's gonna be pretty mad."

Daryle wasn't into little boys. Had never been before, at least. Picking this one up had been such a thoughtless act, he had almost been like one of the many robots he had built over the years. That was a problem and he knew it. He would have to address it later. It was also a problem that he had told the kid his name. Not that it made an entire world of difference. Sedrow Woolley, Washington was so rural that even if he hadn't, it wouldn't have been hard to pinpoint a guy from out of town. Either way, he figured, the outcome would had to have been the same. It didn't take a masters from ITT Tech to figure that out.

"What? No. You'll be okay, bud. What's she gonna be mad about?"

"It's just—uh, I dunno."

"Andy. Why are you worried now? I told you, you're gonna love the surprise. Your parents paid good money for this."

For a moment, all that could be heard was ACDC. Then little Andy said, "Are you sure?"

"Does a bear shit in the woods?"

"Uh—yeah."

Daryle looked in his rear-view mirror at the boy who was wearing his company hat. It was white, with black lettering across the front, which read, "FAIRFAX." It was tilted sideways, and way too big for the kid. It made him look somehow smaller and more vulnerable. He was hard to see through the dark. The woods around the car blocked out light from the stars and moon, though it was mid-September and cloudy anyway.

"You know what this mountain's called?"

Andy nodded.

"You'll have to speak up, chief." Daryle returned his gaze to the windy road.

"Yes."

"Well, what is it?"

"Anderson Mountain."

"Very good. That's pretty impressive. How'd you know that?"

"My Dad's told me like a hundred times. Every time we drive by it." He sniffed. It was the most notable sign of panic that he had shown since Daryle picked him up that evening. It wasn't helping to alleviate his own panic.

What choice did he have though? Let the kid go and wait for him to point a finger at him? Go to prison? He was so far from home. How would Jan and the kids even be able to visit?

For the past two hours he had fought to keep his composure. Getting Andy into the car hadn't been the hard part. He just drove by, saw the kid pulling an old, beat up garbage can out to the road, stopped, and said, "Hi." It had taken all of sixty seconds to convince him that his parents had paid him to pick him up.

*"...a special surprise for ya, bud."*

There was no way, though, that it should have worked. Daryle knew kids, had two of them himself. They were his heart and soul. They were never this trusting. Only in a town like Sedrow Woolley. The boy's face had lit up, and he had jumped right in. It only made a little more sense when he learned it was Andy's sixth birthday. The panic started almost immediately when the door slammed shut and the kid spoke.

"So—where we goin'?"

The worst part was that he knew instantly he was going to kill him. He had thought—with more than a little discomfort—that he would fuck him as well. Had even taken him back to the Motel 6 he was staying in. He was relieved to find out that that wasn't in the game plan for his broken unconscious mind.

"Is your Dad a logger?" Daryle had thus far kept his cool, considering the circumstance. If the kid freaked out, though, he knew he would too. He needed to keep him calm.

"No."

"Really? How's he know the name of the mountain then?"

"He knows all of 'em. Every mountain around here. He's really smart."

"Sounds like it. What's he do?"

"All kinds a stuff. He likes to play croquet sometimes."

Daryle laughed as the song changed. He pressed a button on the radio and it went back and replayed. "No, champ. I mean, what's he do for work?"

"Oh." Andy let out a forced laugh. "He builds boats."

"No shit? Vanderpool?"

"Yeah. That's where he works."

"Really? Small world. That's where my job was."

"I thought you said you're from Cola—rado?"

"I am. I mean, I did a job there. That's why I'm in Sedrow Woolley. It's why I was here at first, at least. Then I met your parents at the Food Outlet and they hired me for this job."

"You don't even know where my Dad works though."

"Yeah, I do. He works at Vanderpool. I mean I didn't know before, but that's not what we talked about." Andy seemed to be relaxing a little. It set Daryle's nerves once again at ease. "You know what I do anyway?"

"Yeah. You drive trains, right?"

"Haha! A conductor? Naw, chief. I'm an engineer. I make stuff. Not just any stuff either. I'm in industrial automation. That means I make robots. You like robots?"

"Does a bear shit in the woods?"

Daryle couldn't help it. He burst out laughing. Had it been his twelve-year-old, he might have slapped him on the mouth.

"Yup. I make robots that can do jobs so humans don't have to do them."

"My Dad says that's what Mexicans are for."

Daryle laughed again and almost missed a corner. The car went off the road slightly and bumped under his ass as it drove on the shoulder. "Mexicans, huh?" He realigned with the road. "Your Dad's a funny guy."

"I guess."

The digital clock on the dash said it was 8:02. Daryle began to look for somewhere to turn that was concealed, but obvious enough that he could find it again tomorrow. There was no way he could have stopped locally for a shovel. He already knew he would be up most of the night driving out of town to a hardware store. He would dig when the sun came up, then catch his flight home.

"Don't like him, or what?"

"My Dad?"

"Yeah. He a meany or something?"

"I dunno."

"Don't worry, champ. I won't tell him."

"Well—it's just that, sometimes he can be a real dick."

"A dick, huh? You know, we can all be dicks sometimes." When Andy didn't respond, Daryle went on. "Haven't you ever been a dick to anyone?"

"One time, I pulled the head off of one of my sister's

Barbies."

"See? Dick move." Daryle flicked on his high beams. There had to be an opening somewhere. Some kind of a turnoff. Maybe a deer trail.

"Yeah. I guess. I used my Dad's vice and a pair of pliers. He got really mad about it."

"Wonder why." Daryle watched the sides of the road intently.

"'Cause," Andy replied. "I'm not 'spose to touch his stuff. Specially not his workbench. He beat me with his belt buckle."

"What?" Daryle paid more attention to the woods than the kid. "He beat you?"

"Yeah. Busted out three of my teeth and collapsed my cheekbone."

Now Daryle heard. "Jesus Christ. He beat you with the buckle?"

"Yup."

"A big buckle?"

"Oh yeah. My Dad has the biggest buckles in town. He's got a really nice gold one in his dresser too. It says, 'Snap On.'"

Daryle saw what he was looking for up ahead. A turnoff on the right side. If he hadn't been looking for it, he never would have noticed. He glanced down at the speedometer, which told him he was going forty-five miles per hour. Taking his foot off of the gas, he tapped the brakes. The car slowed down, and passed the turnoff before coming to a stop. Daryle put it in reverse and turned around, using the passenger seat to stabilize himself. He was a heavy man, and the motion wasn't without considerable effort. When he was facing back, he saw the fear on Andy's face.

"Relax, champ. We're here now. Everything's okay."

Andy looked at him, his eyes wide and innocent.

Daryle stepped on the gas and began to back up. The boy nodded timidly. Daryle turned the wheel as gravel crunched under the rental's tires. The night somehow grew darker. When the car was tucked far enough that he was sure it couldn't be seen from the road, he turned back around and put it in park, turning off the headlights.

"Is this the surprise?" Andy's voice was shaky, once again panicked.

"Nope. We're almost there though."

"Just tell me, Daryle. What is it?"

A cold chill ran through Daryle's body when the boy said his name.

*You're sick*, he thought. *You're sick and you need to seek help immediately. Tomorrow, as soon as you step off of the fucking plane, you find help. Find out what's wrong with you.*

The chorus picked back up, and for a moment the only sound in the car was the high pitched voice wailing about the highway to hell. Daryle turned the music off.

"If I told you, Andy, it wouldn't be a surprise." He heaved his heavy body once more so he was facing backward. "Lemme see."

"See what?" the boy whined.

"Let me see what he did to you with the belt buckle. Show me your teeth."

Andy peeled his lips back and smiled like a Jack-o-lantern. Daryle couldn't see a thing. He reached up and turned the dome light on.

"Look at that. You have all your teeth."

"They grew back."

"Your cheekbone sure doesn't look collapsed to me either, Andy. Have you been telling me lies?"

Andy shook his head, looking down guiltily at his blue polo-shirt.

"Are you sure?"

"Yes."

"I think you have. It's not good to lie about your folks, bud. My brother's kid did that and somebody came and took her away. Said she couldn't live there anymore. Want that to happen to you?"

"No." Andy's voice was some strange mixture of defeat and fear.

"It's okay though. I told you I wouldn't tell anyone what you said, and I never lie. No one'll ever know, okay?"

"Okay." Andy sniffed and Daryle knew the tears would come soon.

"Come on, Andy. Let's go get that surprise now. What do ya say?" He didn't wait for Andy to answer, just turned off the dome light, killed the engine, and stepped out into the cold night. Crickets chirped absently to their own rhythm, oblivious to what was taking place. When Andy didn't open his door, Daryle opened it for him causing the car to once again light up. "Come on out, chief. The faster we get to this, the faster we can get you outta here and get you home. You're not afraid of the dark, are you?"

Andy shook his head.

"Good. Let's get moving then."

Andy shook his head again.

"No?" Daryle asked.

"I don't want to."

"Jesus. Why not, Andy? You want your present, right?"

"I already got my present. I got Halo. You're lying, Daryle. There's no surprise in the woods. Take me home."

"What? Why would I lie to you?" Daryle slowly lowered to one knee, coming almost eye to eye with the boy.

"I don't know." Andy's voice grew high pitched.

Daryle reached up and straightened the cap on Andy's

head, causing him to flinch. "Why would I lie to you, Andy? What could I possibly get from driving all the way up here, just to play some stupid joke on you?"

Andy looked into his eyes, as if searching for any trace of insincerity.

"What else did you get today?" Daryle pushed.

"My——my grandma gave me a gift card."

"A gift card? That's cool. Where to?"

"Walmart."

"I love Walmart. But where'd we go after I picked you up, Andy?"

"To the hotel."

"No," Daryle said. "Before that. Where did we go to eat?"

"Dairy Queen." Each word came out like a question. Daryle knew he needed to cheer him up somehow.

"And what did I buy you?"

"Ice cream."

"Right. And you know what, chief? That wasn't your Dad's money. I paid for it right out of my own pocket. Now tell me, why would I buy a guy ice cream, just to trick him? What's in it for me?"

"I dunno, Daryle. I'm scared. Can we please just leave? Please?"

"Andy, you're six now. You don't need to be afraid of anything. Especially not a birthday present. Now I want you to think long and hard about what it might be. What could possibly be waiting for you out here in the woods that would be such a big surprise?"

Andy looked down at his shoes which had once been white, but were caked with dried mud. Somewhere nearby, an owl hooted in a tree. When he looked at Daryle, his eyes were wide. He opened his mouth to speak.

"Ssshhh," Daryle said. "Don't say it. Don't ruin the

surprise. Just be very quiet, and let's go to it."

A small hand unlatched the seatbelt and Andy climbed out. Daryle stood up and closed the door. The light inside the car disappeared. Something rustled in some bushes. Daryle looked around for the first time and saw that he was parked in some kind of a circular opening, like a cul-de-sac in the woods with a giant mound of rocks near the back. He knew he would have to take the boy at least a quarter mile past the treeline. He would kill him first, then carry the body.

"Gimme your hand, buddy." Daryle's head was cold. He was in his forties, and had begun to go bald more than fifteen years ago.

Andy reached up and put his tiny hand in his. It was shaking. Was he still scared, or just cold? Hand in hand, they walked around the gravel mound. Daryle wasn't a stupid man. He hadn't actually taken the kid into Dairy Queen. Just the drive through. That's when he had put the hat over his head.

As they moved around the giant pile of rocks and closer to the trees, it grew darker. Somehow it grew colder. For reasons that he didn't understand, Daryle Colombo's dick began to grow.

*Sick. Sick. Sick. Sick.* He was sick. He wasn't a paedophile though. That had been made clear to him when he hadn't made a move to violate Andy at the hotel. But something was happening that was not only wrong, but exciting and strangely sexual.

Andy's hand in his left, he reached his right into the pocket of his blue jeans and wrapped his meaty fingers around the cold metal handle of the camouflage knife.

"I don't see anything," Andy said.

The owl hooted again, closer now.

"Just a little further, champ."

Daryle brought the knife out. He had become very

efficient at opening it swiftly with one hand. There was an elbow on the bottom of the thick blade, with a notch of steel that could be pressed, causing it to fly out with leverage.

His heart began to race and his body grew light. What he did next, was as automatic as it had been to pick the kid up in the first place. He released his grip from the boy's hand and pulled the hat off of his head. In his other hand, the knife snapped open with a "click" that seemed to echo into the night.

*Sick. Sick. Sick. You're a sick fuck and you need help, Daryle Colombo.* His wife's voice inside of his head made him eager to get on with the deed.

His body tensed. He took a deep breath and as if to confirm to himself how fucked up and sick he was before doing it, he looked down into Andy's bright, young face. The boy was smiling. Looking up at him. But those big eyes were different. Horrible. How? There were no words for it. And the smile...Nobody ever smiled like that. It was the most merry, happy, terrifying smile he had ever seen.

Daryle froze. A tremor began in his chest, and expanded out in all directions. He felt hair that he didn't have stand up on top of his head.

"Uuuhhh," was all that would come out of his mouth.

Andy reached up with both hands and lifted Daryle's shirt. Cold instantly nipped at his belly, which hung over his own large, chrome belt buckle. The boy took a roll of his stomach lard in one hand and sank his teeth in. There was pain only for a second, then nothing. Daryle stumbled back, pushing Andy with his fists, the hat still in one hand, the knife in the other. He landed on his back in a tangled mess of sticker bushes which tore at his skin and clothes.

*Don't drop the knife*, he thought. *Don't you even dare drop the fucking knife.*

His eyes had to refocus to get a good look at Andy.

But Andy was gone. Where he had stood only seconds ago, was a giant insect in a little boy's polo-shirt and jeans. It was four feet tall—the same height as Andy, in the kid's dirty white shoes. Its eyes were big and black. Sharp teeth wrapped around its head in a horrible smile. Its arms were thin, with spikes running up the side. They ended at hands with three fingers and sharp pointed claws. The bug just stood there, staring down at Daryle. Smiling. Then its mouth opened.

"Daryle? You okay?"

Now the clothes were gone. All that stood in Andy's place was the insect. Its skin was dark and lumpy. Daryle used his hands and feet to crab walk backwards, still clutching the hat and knife. Sharp thorns dug into every inch of his body. Into his fists. Into the top of his head. The huge bug took a step toward him.

"No!" Daryle screamed.

The owl took flight, flapping loudly away from the rude disturbance. The crickets fell silent. Daryle lifted his knife, then the hand plopped back to the ground. He attempted to raise it again. It wouldn't move. He tried to roll onto his side. Still nothing. His entire body collapsed. From his back, he stared up at the cloudy sky. The insect appeared, standing over him, looking down into his eyes, smiling.

"Oooh." The noise came from deep in Daryle's throat, but his lips and tongue wouldn't move to form words. "Oooh."

"Ssshhh," the insect said. Its voice was a calm, soothing whisper. "Relax. It's gonna be okay, Daryle."

Daryle was paralyzed. He tried to wiggle his fingers. Nothing. Then his toes. Without trying, he blinked. A tiny ray of hope crept into his heart. He tried to close his eyes. Nothing. It seemed only his involuntary systems were functioning.

*It was the bite*, he thought. *The motherfucker poisoned me.*

The insect disappeared. Then the sky moved. No. Daryle was moving. He was being dragged. His head and back tore into tiny rocks, probably leaving a trail of blood behind. Though he couldn't move his neck to look, he knew that Andy had him by his ankles. It grew darker. The bug boy was taking him into the woods.

Daryle tried to moan. This time nothing happened. His cheek caught in a thorn, and flesh tore from his face, but there was no pain. Twigs cracked under Andy's feet. Trees and bushes passed over Daryle, and the last bit of light from the moon trying to shine through the clouds disappeared.

Though he was completely numb, it didn't escape his notice how effortlessly the boy was able to drag him. Daryle weighed two-hundred-forty pounds. Andy couldn't have weighed eighty-five, soaking wet. He stopped moving and listened as Andy came around to stand over him once again. If he could have screamed, he would have.

"Here we are." The voice was no longer a whisper, nor was it the voice of a boy. It was inhuman. Unreal. The sound of a fly's wings flapping, yet somehow forming words. The sound of somebody whispering through a fan. Andy was only a silhouette. It was too dark to make out anything tangible. The silhouette moved down to Daryle's abdomen. A few moments later there was noisy rustling. Digging.

It grew harder to breathe. Andy had done something to him. Something terrible. He had ripped him open. Had violated his insides. Though Daryle couldn't move his neck to see, nor could he feel, he knew he had been ruined. He grew lightheaded as dirt landed on his face—in his eyes.

Then he was moving again. Being dragged. He plopped into the earth. He was in a hole, looking at dirt on his side. His hand landed in front of his face, and he saw that it still clutched the camouflage handled knife. Dirt began to fall around him. Daryle Colombo was being buried alive. He would die soon anyway. The little fucker had maimed him. Why? God knew.

Daryle prayed silently for death. That he would stop breathing before he was completely covered in the cold earth. That didn't happen though. Instead, it filled his mouth. His ears. His nostrils. He couldn't taste it. He could only feel the dizziness as he choked on it. Then he saw bright red flashes. Before he was completely covered, he heard the horrible insectile voice again.

"Come home soon, Daryle. You know where to find me."

Before he had time to consider what it meant, his body attempted to convulse. It was impossible while crushed between heavy dirt on all sides. He took his last breath and the world went black.

# Chapter One

Conor Mitchell opened his eyes and looked up at the ceiling. The alarm was blaring. He glanced toward the noise and saw a nipple. Shelby slept high up on the pillow, and her breast pointed into his face. Her dark-brown hair was a tangled mess that rested over her mouth as she drooled into it. The noise didn't seem to be affecting her in the least. He squinted as he sat up, reached over her, and pressed the snooze button.

The digital clock told him that it was 6:00 AM. That meant it was 5:50AM. He kept his alarm set that way, had since he used to wake up as a boy to work on the farm at tortuous hours of the morning. Laying back down on his side, he looked into Shelby's face.

"Don't stare." Her mouth opened, but not her eyes. "It's weird."

"Thought you were asleep."

"How, with that annoying alarm in my ear?"

"Well that's what it's for."

"To wake me up every time I stay over? Get rid of it."

"I suppose I should get rid of my job too." He smiled. "Then I could just move in with you and your parents."

"Ugh. Shut up, dude. I'm going back to sleep." She scooted her petite body down so only her head rested on the pillow, and pulled the blanket over her chest. Then she rolled over to face the other direction. Of course she was going back to sleep. She was hung over.

Conor rolled onto his back and stared up once again at the ceiling. The studio was small. The bedroom was his living room. The living room was his kitchen. The only thing in the modular structure that had its own space, thankfully, was the bathroom. It worked for a twenty-two-year-old though. Shelby shifted again, next to him.

"You gonna be here tonight?" he asked.

"You want me to be?"

"Well—yeah."

"Fine. Leave your key so I don't have to stay all day?"

"Sure. Want me to pick anything up on my way home?" He already knew the answer.

"Vodka. Oh, and some cranberry juice. If you want, you can just leave some money and I'll pick it up while you're gone."

"Cool," he said.

"Cool?"

"I think I have a few bucks in my wallet."

"Twenty should be fine."

"Let me see what I have."

She moved slightly, burrowing deeper into the nest of pillows and blankets. "What time are you off tonight?"

"I should be back by six-forty."

"Mmm."

Conor yawned. He thought about work. It was Saturday, which meant not only did he have to finish the transmission job he had been working on, but he would be filling in as manager, taking calls, and catering to customers at the shop.

The studio was dark. He kept blankets over the windows that functioned as curtains. Even if they hadn't been there, it was still pitch dark and cloudy outside. The only light came from tiny bulbs, telling him that his electronics were connected to outlets.

"Cranberry," Shelby repeated, her voice tired.

Conor considered asking her if she felt like maybe spending a night over sober, even opened his mouth, ready to form words. But what were the words? How did you ask a girl who you had only been dating (or fucking, as she liked to refer to it) for three months why she didn't change everything about herself? He closed his mouth and continued to lay silently, ready to get up.

Shelby snored—not loud, and it was only once—as if attempting to rev her own engine, then bottoming out. "We could..." she mumbled. "We could... Goodness I'm tired."

What time had they fallen asleep? Conor tried to remember what the clock had said the last time he looked at it. The memory was a blur. Not because he had been drunk—Shelby had, but not him—but because she had been riding him. Hard. The bed had been squeaking so loud that he wondered if his parents—almost seven miles away—could hear. She had been loud too. Much louder than usual, and the red numbers on his alarm had refused to hold still. Twelve-forty-something. That was it. How long after that had they finished though?

The alarm went off again, and Shelby growled. Conor looked and saw 6:00AM. He had fallen asleep again. He reached over, knocking her pack of Marlboros off of the nightstand, and killed the noise. He planted a kiss on her cheek before returning to his spot on the bed. She pulled the comforter back over her face.

*Up*, he thought. *You can do this. One foot, then the other.*

Somehow, almost automatically, his body obeyed. Once he stood by the side of the bed, all six-foot-four of him, he was hit by how cold it was. He quickly pulled on the clothes that lay at his feet, and turned on the portable heater in the middle of the room. Shelby's hand crept out from under the blanket and found her cell, which sat on the nightstand charging. Her head popped out next and looked at the screen. Then she collapsed onto her side once again.

"I was thinking," Conor said as he made his way in the dark. "Ow! Son-of-a-bitch!"

"You okay?"

"Fine. I kicked some—" He turned on a lamp. "I need to put this fucking battery somewhere else."

"Put it in the car," Shelby offered.

"I know. I know. I need to take that thing out for a drive soon too. I was thinking tonight. We could go out and do something." When she didn't respond, he went on. "Like a movie or something."

"In the goat?"

"Well, yeah. I need to run her anyway. It's been over a month." He got into the refrigerator and began to bring out everything he would need to make his lunch.

Shelby yawned, stretched. "Don't you have to put the battery in first?"

"It'll take me three minutes. That's not a problem."

"That's it? Three minutes, and the thing's been sitting on your floor for a month? Lazy much?"

"Spend eight hours a day putting shit in cars, and tell me if it's what you feel like doing when you come home at night."

"What about your days off?"

Ignoring the question, Conor slapped two sandwiches

together. He could buy a soda from the machine at work.

"You really wanna take that car out tonight?" she went on. "Don't you wanna spend time with me?"

"I'd like to take you both out. Just think about it. Send me a text before I get off, so I know whether or not to pick up food. Go ahead and go back to sleep."

"I'm up now. For now at least." She climbed out of bed and walked naked across the studio, into the bathroom. When she came back out, Conor had finished packing his lunch. Shelby dove back into the bed and twisted her tiny body into the covers. "Oh! It's fucking cooold in here." She unplugged her phone and began to press keys. The light from the screen illuminated her face, and Conor saw her smile. Her eyes, which often caused people to ask if she were mixed with anything oriental, were tired slits.

"It'll heat up soon. Try and turn the heater off if you're awake, or you'll roast."

Conor knew there would be no date. There never was. Though he liked to believe he was dating Shelby Metcalf, at the end of the day, she was probably right. They were fucking. And as much as he often wished that she were wrong, what would that mean with a girl like Shelby? She drank. He rarely did. She smoked. (And though she claimed to never do it in his home, he knew she lied.) He couldn't even stand the smell of cigarettes. And the pot? He would leave the twenty dollars that she asked for. He would even pick up the bottle that it was supposed to pay for. Money wasn't an issue. But it was becoming clearer every time they were together that the two of them had little in common outside of his bed.

They had met in college, where he studied for two years to become a heavy-duty-diesel-mechanic. He graduated first. She still attended with no clear direction or plan for graduation. Liberal Arts. That was her study.

He had been catching up on credits with a vocational writing course near the end of his degree. She sat next to him most days. It wasn't until close to a year after he graduated when she called him one night, drunk out of her mind.

"Conor! I need your address!"

When she pulled up twenty minutes later, and scraped the side of his old green Buick, he knew that he couldn't let her drive home. He considered calling her an Uber. And he would have done it, too, but then she dropped her clothes onto his floor.

"You can't let me drink home like this Conor."

Since that night he had been in a perpetual state of blissful confusion. Was she the third girl he had ever dated, or the second girl he had fucked? Did it really matter? Maybe, but he never asked.

Once he finished his morning rituals he went to the nightstand, fished two tens out of his wallet, and set them next to Shelby's phone, which announced that she had received two text messages. He picked up her Marlboro pack and set it on top of the bills, then put his one and only house key off to the side. Shelby smiled up at him, her eyes tired.

"Don't lock me out if you're not here," he said.

"I'll be here, dork."

"Just making sure. I don't wanna get stuck sleeping in my car."

"Shut up. You'd like that. I'm sure you'd sleep in the goat. Probably make love to it all night."

Conor laughed. "Sometimes I wonder what it's like living in that sick mind of yours."

"Oh, you should see the visuals."

"I'll go ahead and pass on that one, thanks. I'm managing the shop today, or I'd try to get off early."

"All good. Just get here when you can. My day's

gonna be sooo boring already. I think I'll go home and pick up a change of clothes. Maybe I'll get lucky and my Mom won't be there. The last thing I need to hear is her shit talking."

"About me?"

"Tsh. About everything, dude." Her phone flashed and caught Conor's attention. It was set to silent, and announced that she had just received another text. "Do we really have to go out tonight?"

*No*, he thought. *We can just sit around here all night, while you get drunk or stoned, or whatever it is you need to be around me.*

"You really don't want to?"

"It's not that. It's just, well, I wanted to stay in and spend the night with just you. I like being here with you. Isn't that okay?" She looked up at him with a pouty face.

"Fine," he said. "I'll bring food."

"Bring tacos. From one of the trucks in Mount Vernon."

"Sure. No problem." There was a taco truck on just about every street in Mount Vernon. He could go to the one right next to the shop.

"And a torrrta." She exaggerated the rolling of the "r," sounding like a tiny, naked lawnmower in his bed.

"'Kay."

"Kiss me before you go?" She puffed out her lips. They were thin little things and the effect wasn't cute. He leaned down and kissed them anyway. She grabbed the back of his head, taking a handful of his hair and pulling him into her face. He tasted raw liquor and cigarettes.

"Okay," he said when she finally released him. "I'm outta here."

"See you soon?"

"Soon."

"Want me to stop by for lunch if I'm in town?"

That wasn't going to happen. He knew it and he knew she knew. "Naw. Probably not. It's gonna be a busy day. I have to finish that trany-job or I'll lose commission. I might not even take lunch. Just text me."

"Fine," she said. "Are you mad?"

"About what"

"That I don't wanna go out tonight?"

"Why would that make me mad?"

"I don't know. You look a little pissed. We can go next week if you want. It's just that—I don't know. I think I'm about to start my period or something. You understand, right?"

"Of course. Christ."

"Tsh. Of course you don't. We can still bone though. Even if I bleed. We can totally fuck up your sheets. Wouldn't that be fun? I could mark my territory in case you bring any other bitches over."

"Like that would happen." He meant to just think it, but it spilled out of him like water.

"You never know. You're a handsome man. For all I know you're a player. Maybe you've fucked every skanky bitch in Sedrow Woolley."

This made Conor laugh. Before Shelby, there had been Amber. Amber Wilson, who was slightly overweight, but had pretty features. He knew from the time they started dating senior year that he wasn't in love with her. But she had let him make love to her. Until they parted ways after graduation. Before that, Luna Rosas in the fifth grade. She had been one of two Mexicans in the entire school. She and her brother, Pedro. Conor could never quite pronounce her last name, but he had been convinced that he loved her.

"You're the only skanky bitch for me." He regretted the joke as soon as it left his mouth. His heart began to speed up as he looked down at what might have been his girlfriend. She gasped and opened her mouth and eyes in mock appal. Then the expression morphed into a smile.

"You're stupid!"

Relief came over Conor. He leaned down and picked up his lunch box.

"Maybe next weekend?" Shelby asked.

"Yeah. Why not?"

"Seriously. Where would you wanna go?"

"I don't really know. Let me think about it."

"We could go to Seattle. There are some pretty nice clubs. Me and Edith went once to this place called, 'Boom-Boom.' It was pretty classy."

And just like that, she had blocked him. Shelby knew as well as Conor or anybody who knew him that if she gave him the choice, there was no way he would opt to go into some nightclub two hours away in Seattle. Or any nightclub for that matter. Drinking, dancing, mingling with drunk college kids hadn't even been his idea of a good time when he was in college.

"We'll think of something," he lied. It was official though. There would be nothing. Sometimes he wondered if she just didn't want to be seen with him. Most of the time, he chose not to care.

"Yeah. For sure. I'll check out some other places too." She yawned. "As soon as you leave. I think I'm gonna sleep 'til noon. Maybe even later."

"Shit." Conor looked at the clock. "I have to go."

"See you tonight." She smiled lazily.

Conor didn't kiss her again, just left.

It was cold and dark outside. A car whished passed on the highway, which his home was positioned ridiculously close to. Ever since moving off of the farm and into the place, he had expected some drunk redneck to plough a pickup through his living room one night. Or worse, into the goat.

Conor's 66 Pontiac GTO convertible had been a graduation gift. Half of it at least. His parents had helped him buy it upon finishing high school. He kept her under a thick blue tarp in front of the modular, the only part visible being the shiny wire rims. He had personally rebuilt the engine. All of his friends and family had insisted that it would be a chic-magnet. It hadn't, but it didn't matter. Conor loved the car anyway, and only drove her once a month, just to keep the pipes clean.

Next to the goat was his old, beat up Buick Skylark. Next to that was Shelby's car. Conor's breath turned to fog as he made his way down the porch steps. The metal handle on the Buick was cold and painful to touch. With some effort he opened the door and stepped inside, setting his lunch box on the passenger seat. When he turned the ignition, the car complained momentarily, then growled as it came to life.

It was 6:26am. It only took twenty minutes to drive from Sedrow Woolley to Mount Vernon, two towns over. John would probably be there already, working off the clock.

Conor turned on the car's stereo. It was an old one that matched the old car. Not that he couldn't afford a nicer one—or a nicer car for that matter—but what was the point? Sedrow Woolley was a town of farming and logging. A town of two-lane streets and back dirt roads. The Skylark was functional.

The Mark and Thomas radio show came through the speakers.

"...now that's a cause I could get behind."

"I'd get behind her, but..."

"Hahahaha! And this is a family show?"

"Don't worry kids. Daddy'll be right back."

"And the weather?"

"The weather. The weather. How 'bout that weather?"

A semi passed on the highway, so close that the car rocked. The engine began to idle smoothly, and Conor put it in reverse. He used his rear-view to back out into the fog, as Mark and Thomas continued with "your number one pick when you want a weekend morning show, but you're not a weekend morning person."

* * *

Sedrow Woolley, Washington was small. Cute. Some might even dare to say closed-minded and racist. Others knew better. It was 2019. Times were different. Stereotypes didn't die easy though, even if old fashioned ignorance did take on new forms.

The place was surrounded by woods. In just about every direction, if you could somehow see past the trees, you would have seen mountains reaching to heaven like giant, hairy tits. On the side of those tits, foresting crews thinned out young growth, logging crews ate up old growth, and perfectly square patches were laid bare.

The town itself wasn't exactly honky-tonk. More like hoity-toity. At the edge, just before you entered the land of no return and headed into the woods toward Concrete, off of Highway Twenty, was Vanderpool. It was the biggest corporation in town, and employed some of the finest middle-class that Sedrow Woolley had to offer. Then, in the middle of town, was Brown's Auto. Steve Brown and his son owned dealerships all over the valley. Though they only had the one in Woolley, (a Honda lot) their corporate office was local and both of their mansions were out on Mosher road.

ABC-123 Thrift Store sat in an old building, which rented to other small businesses as well. The only ones making any real money in the whole structure were the Chinese, who ran their restaurant. (What was it called?

*Wong-Tong Chicken* or something like that?) They didn't live in Sedrow, of course.

There were a couple of grocery stores, the largest of which was the food outlet. That franchise wasn't always small, but since 2000, every outlet in the state of Washington had disappeared and been replaced by a Safeway or an Albertson's—except the one in Woolley.

The outlet sat along Highway Twenty on the right, on the other edge of town. Keep going for a few more minutes, and the world began to come to life as you entered Burlington.

Across the highway from the grocery store, was the train. That's where Percly slept most nights. It was an old steam engine with three cars behind it. The cars would have been ideal, had they been boxcars. They weren't though. They were logging carts. Not just that, but they held logs. Always. The freshest, roundest logs Percly had ever seen. Not that he paid much attention to logs, but the last four years in Sedrow had made it impossible to not notice them sometimes.

The train was painted black, and sat on tracks that began a few feet behind the last car, and ended a few feet in front of the locomotive. There was an old-fashioned self-serve gas station nearby, and statues of eagles, Indians, and the like scattered about. Even a wooden bear who stood on its back legs, watching traffic hungrily. It was all for decoration, of course.

To the side was a giant sign, about twelve feet across, and as tall as a man. It had been carved by a chainsaw a very long time ago, and announced, "Town Center."

The locomotive was home. It was cold too. Especially this time of year. In twenty plus years of being homeless, though, Percly had learned to ignore the cold. He had a pretty decent sleeping bag anyway. The weather, however it chose to present itself, had become a part of him. The early morning chill was his alarm. It let him know that it was time to get up. Get a move on. City crews may, or may not be through today to maintenance the square, clean the train, mow the grass, weed the garden, and kick him out.

They never cleaned the inside of the locomotive. Once, during the summer, he had slept in and woken up to the sound of lawnmowers and weed whackers, and the smell of freshly cut grass. He had lain there, holding in his urine for about two hours, and they had never noticed him. The first night he had slept in the thing, (what was it, two years ago?) it had been a fun house of spider webs and dirt. He had made it liveable though, and only been kicked out once. That was so long ago that it was doubtful anybody even suspected a black man with an eye patch still slept there.

It was dark. Percly stretched out in his sleeping bag and yawned. He had to piss. His breath was a cloud of fog that travelled out the open windows that may have had glass at one point in history. Who knew? He didn't shiver. He never did. Next to his face was the empty Sisco bottle from last night. He wondered briefly if he could just relieve himself in it and go back to sleep. Of course he couldn't. He needed to go, needed to get his bags out of the train and hide them in the bushes up the road. Then he could peruse the ashtray across the street at the Food Outlet for cigarette butts, and catch the 7:20 SKAT bus into Mount Vernon in time for breakfast at the Friendship House.

He brought one hand out of his bag and glanced at his watch. It was a cheap one from the dollar store, but it kept the time. His one good eye took a few seconds to adjust. 6:34am. He rubbed his face, and the black patch that he wore over his bad eye—more to keep from freaking people out than anything—moved to the side. A chill nipped at the top of his head, which unlike the sides and his face, was smooth and balled. He needed a new beanie cap. Today he would find one.

Percly slowly sat up, unzipping the top of the sleeping bag. He heard movement right outside of the locomotive.

*Who would be here at this time?*

He couldn't climb out with somebody there. The train was the best place he had found to stay in, in years. He didn't want to draw any more attention to the spot than necessary. They would start showing up early in the mornings to kick him out. Though stray kids and runaways sometimes passed through, Percly was the only homeless person who lived in town. People were nice to him, even gave him change. There was no reason to make himself a nuisance.

Outside, there was rustling in the wood chips that surrounded the train. Something being dragged?

*Fuck.*

So they were going to work here today. It was early though. They never started this early. And what were they dragging? A lawnmower? There was clearly only one of them, or he would have heard them talking to one another.

But why hadn't he heard the truck pull up? Was he that tired? Was he growing sloppy? That wasn't it though, and he knew it. The answer was obvious. It wasn't them. There were no city workers outside of Percly's train. It was somebody else.

Wood chips continued to rustle.

Who, then? A kid? What in the hell was a kid doing out here? It was a weekend. Maybe some teenagers had been out partying all night. Well, one teenager. What was he dragging though? It didn't matter. Whoever was outside, Percly couldn't get up until he or she left. He couldn't be seen leaving the train. People would talk. Word would get around. He liked Sedrow, and there was nowhere better in town to sleep.

More scraping. More rustling. Then scratching.

Scratching? Wood chips began to hit the side of the locomotive in a rapid, tapping rhythm. Somebody was digging. Not somebody, it was an animal. It had to have been a dog.

Percly felt stupid as he climbed out of the bag and stood up, looking out through the side window. He looked down at the dog. It wasn't big. It wasn't small either. Some breed of mutt, digging frantically into the chips with its front paws, tossing them between its back legs. The thing was ugly, too, with mangy brown hair and muscular legs.

*Wait.*

Percly blinked to get a better look through the darkness and the fog. The hair was gone. Then it was back. Then gone again. It took all of six seconds to realize that he was looking down and seeing two different scenes at the same time. They were cutting in and out and blending with one another. In one was the crazy, ugly, digging, digging dog. In the other was something else. What was it?

Muscular legs. Dark, bumpy skin. They were frog legs. But they weren't. They were too big. The dog continued to dig, oblivious to Percly. He moved to the side for a better look, then saw what it was about to bury.

Another dog.

The other dog wasn't a mutt. It was a white pit bull, with dark splotches on its fur. An American pit. A big fucker, too. It lay on its side, motionless, aside from its midsection, which was heaving heavily up and down. It was open like a fur coat. Not ripped open, but cut, almost surgically in a perfect line that went from the animal's chest, down its abdomen. Its mouth lay open, its tongue hanging loosely out to the side over its teeth.

That's when Percly saw that the dark splotches on the dog weren't all spots. Some of them were blood. The butchered dog's head didn't move, but with only its eyes, it stared up at Percly and whined.

"Hey!" Percly yelled at the ugly dog-thing, almost automatically. "Get! Go on! Get!"

The dog stopped digging, and looked back over its shoulder. Percly gasped. It wasn't a dog. Not even close. Its eyes were blacker than the train's thick coat of paint. They were big, too—no huge. It had what must have been hundreds of pointed, razor sharp teeth that curved around its entire head in a terrible smile. It looked slimy. Lumpy. Evil. Like some kind of a giant insect, the size of a dog. It turned all the way around and stood up on its hind legs. The front, which Percly now saw, had dug a three foot hole, the size of the pit bull impossibly fast, had long, dangerous claws on them.

The bug barked. Then it barked again. It sounded like a fucking dog.

Percly yelled. He pissed himself. Then the thing took a step toward the train and he stumbled back. He dove out the door opposite the monster and ran right into the bear, causing it to rock. Percly didn't stop. He recovered, ran around the sculpture and right into the highway.

When he made it to the empty parking lot of the Food Outlet, the fog was so thick that even if he had looked back, he wouldn't have been able to see the thing. He just kept running.

* * *

It was 6:53am when Conor pulled into the parking lot of Skagit Break and Muffler, and killed the Buick's engine. John's car was parked near the back of the lot. He used the customer entrance, checking the computer to make sure John wasn't clocked in yet. Then he took his lunch to the break room. When he came back out, the smell of grease and metal filled his nostrils. John was just lifting his welding helmet. He was a short, stocky man and the helmet added a few inches of height.

"Late night?" He flashed a smile that revealed a missing tooth on the left side of his face.

Conor tilted his head. "Why?"

"Dunno. You tell me."

"What makes you ask?"

"You look like hell, bud."

"Good to see you too, John."

"Should a told me, man. I could'a opened for you. You could a come in later."

"I'll manage," Conor said, moving to his toolbox, which was almost as tall as him.

"Guess it's yer job. You're early anyway. Can't imagine why. Don't have a wife to run from."

Conor laughed. John was early nearly every day and went home as late as possible. It wasn't about money either. Even if it had been, Pauly, who owned the shop, wouldn't have let any of his employees work an extra second on the clock.

"Is it Denise, or the kids, though, that you run from? That's what I haven't figured out yet."

John pulled off his gloves and wiped his hands on a rag. "Depends on what time a'the month. Wanna hear what the oldest did this time?"

"Do I have a choice?"

"Course you don't, you fuckin' lug. Cute you ask though."

"Thought so. Shoot."

"So I get a call from the high school——excuse me, *Denise* gets a call. I'm at work. I gotta come home to this shit. So she gets the call and it's the fuckin' principal or guidance counselor or some shit. Turns out Livia got busted smoking."

Conor opened a drawer and began removing wrenches, setting them on the bench. "No shit?" He didn't look at his co-worker. "Well, what is she? Fifteen?"

"*Six*teen." He emphasised the first syllable.

"Shit. At Sedrow Woolley High there's a corner for kids to go off grounds and smoke. When I went to school the staff all knew about it too. Probably still do. I guess it made more sense to not have them sneaking around."

"Yeah. Makes a lot more sense. Keeps 'em off the other shit, right? You ain't even let me get to the cream filling though. It wasn't cigarettes she was smoking."

"Weed?"

"Huh! I wish. The little bitch was behind the gym with some boys smoking crystal."

"Jesus. Meth?"

"Crystal fucking meth. Believe that shit?"

Conor had been in high school, himself, only a few short years ago. He considered telling John that he was lucky it hadn't been heroin. Instead, he asked if she had been arrested.

"Naw," John shook his head. "By some fucking miracle, the boy with the dope ran off and there was no proof. Little bitch is lucky, too, 'cause I'm telling you, I wouldn't a bailed 'er ass out. Be glad you don't live in this shit hole town, Conman. Fucking spics aren't happy fuckin up their own country. They seem to think they need ta send 'em up here to fuck up ours too. I guess it's not a whole lot better in Sedrow lately though, huh?"

"What did you do?"

"About Livia? Shit, what do ya think? Beat her brains in with a monkey wrench."

Conor snickered.

"Seriously though. What *can* you do these days?

You're young. You may not know this, but there was a time when you could discipline your kids without worrying about going ta jail."

From the look of him, John knew plenty about jail. Conor never asked though. He also refrained from telling him that his Stepfather had practically written the book on disciplining young children.

"Ah, anyway, what's it matter? Ground 'er, she goes out anyway. Lock 'er in 'er room, she climbs out the window. Throw 'er out, the wife leaves too. That might not be so bad though." He once again flashed his missing tooth. "I figure you let 'er run 'er course an learn the hard way. Sooner or later she'll fuck herself over real good and come on home begging for help. Enough about that though."

Conor finished arranging the tools he would need, transferred them over to his carrying box. "I'd move to Woolley," he said absently.

"Right. That would go over great. You know we just refinanced the house last year? Plus, it's not a whole lot better out there lately. People goin' missing a shit."

Conor flashed him a questioning look.

"You ain't watched the news, or what?"

"No. Not lately."

"You'd think you'd a seen all the damn camera crews in yer town. Some old guy from out a state disappeared from that hotel you got out there."

"The Motel Six?"

"That's the one. How 'bout you though?"

"What about me?" Conor made a mental note to watch the news tonight.

"Wanna talk about your wild night a lustful depravity? You probably got some shit ta confess."

"I don't know what you're talking about."

"Haha! You dirty little pup. I knew it. She come over

every weekend?"

"Pretty much." Conor hoped his tone would end the conversation. Not that he had an issue with the idea of talking about sex, but a conversation like this could easily lead to questions that even he couldn't answer, didn't want to put too much thought into.

"She always drain the life outta you? No. I never seen you this beat up. Must've been a special night. Anal?"

"Come on, man." Conor wrinkled his forehead.

"Not on you, bud. I mean did *you* give it to *her*?"

Conor shook his head, meaning it as a dismissive gesture, but realizing too late that he had inadvertently answered the question. He picked his box up off of the bench and began toward the already hoisted station wagon.

"I'm just fuckin with ya, bud." John followed him laughing. "When we gonna meet this little firecracker though?"

"Maybe I'll bring her into the shop sometime," he lied. Conor always played it cool with the men he worked with. He was well aware of how they felt about the fact that Pauly had recently given the coveted weekend manager position to the shop's newest and youngest employee. And though he wasn't crazy about pissing them off, who would've turned it down?

It had always been that way. He hadn't tried to overachieve in school. Hadn't set out to be every teacher's pet. It just happened. The grades kept coming back, and in turn he didn't get his ass whipped black and blue at home so often. The adults tended to have better conversation anyway. That hadn't attracted girls. (Though he knew he wasn't an unattractive boy.) It was the only thing that saved him from the wrath of his co-employees, however. Every one of them was much older than him, yet they all liked him most of the time.

Conor set his toolbox down under the wagon.

"Naw, ya big lug wrench." John stood off to the side looking up at him. "Don't bring yer fun ta work. Bring 'er over ta dinner sometime. The wife'll talk 'er to death, but who knows? That might just be doin' ya a favor."

"Yeah." Conor tried to sound sincere. "Why not?"

"Seriously. We have a jacuzzi, and Denise can cook— believe it or not. That's one thing the woman's good for. Learned it all from 'er fat Mom. Mull it over, man. We don't bite. Not very hard, at least."

Just then a primer grey hatchback flew into the parking lot. Heavy metal music radiated so loud that even inside the shop, the ground seemed to vibrate. It was Jake Prescott, who was notorious for showing up five minutes late every morning, but could talk an owner who just drove off the lot in a brand new BMW into getting a brake job and a tune-up.

"Well," John said as both men looked instinctively up at the clock, which displayed a picture of two women in swimsuits that belonged on an early nineties beach show. "Seven oh four. Time to clock in with our cocks in, Conman. That mortgage sure as shit ain't gonna pay itself."

* * *

The day dragged on. They always did on the weekends. Even though Conor was manager Saturday and Sunday. He supposed it was partly because he knew he would be going home to Shelby. Why did that make the days feel so much longer? Who knew? Even if he did get off early, she wouldn't be there. She didn't wait at his place until right before he showed up. And if she wasn't fucked up on vodka or weed already, she would be soon enough.

Still, he sometimes wondered what it would be like to

come home every night to Shelby Metcalf. He wasn't sure, but he thought he might love her. Conor Mitchell wasn't a particularly emotional man. His Stepfather, who had been the only Father he had ever known, only knew how to express affection with his bare knuckles. Conor hadn't learned violence. No, that wasn't who he was. He had been in one fight in his entire life, with Pedro Rosas, over his fifth grade girlfriend. When they broke up over it, he had been heartbroken.

Conor's mother was a quiet, coolheaded woman, who sometimes snuck treats to him and his sisters that were deemed "forbidden" by her husband. She did it with devious eyes, but Conor knew that she told him everything. She never would have lifted a pinky without Brett's permission. Cindy and Catey were both younger than Conor. They were the man's blood daughters, and even though Conor had received the blunt end of Brett's wrath, they had both moved out of town with men the second they were legal. They were quiet girls like their Mom. Like Conor. When Brett Mitchell yelled, it seemed even the roosters didn't crow at dawn.

One morning during his twelfth year, the old man woke him early and drove him down to the courthouse. That day Conor's name was legally changed from Carter, to Mitchell and he forgot about his broken heart, and learned what true love was. Brett became Dad.

Now it was Shelby. She was a very attractive girl, only a year younger than him. She wasn't perfect, by far, but who was? Not Conor. Not Amber Wilson. Not Luna Rosas. And surely not Brett Mitchell, who he knew he loved. So why not Shelby?

Classic rock played from a small stereo system in the shop all day as Conor's co-employees laughed and made idle talk while working. Business went as usual on a Saturday. Slow and easily paced. He finished the transmission job and made himself busy straightening the break room before closing. His mind drifted at some point to the conversation with John that morning. He decided that he would ask Shelby if she wanted to go over for dinner next weekend.

One by one, the guys came in and picked up their lunch boxes, joking and saying their goodbyes. Conor considered telling John that he wanted to take him up on his offer, but decided against it. Better to see what Shelby said first. It was just past 5, and already dark out when he closed up shop. The taco truck next door was still open. He stopped by and picked up six tacos, a burrito, and Shelby's "torrrta."

When he checked his phone, he was mildly surprised to see that she hadn't texted him all day. No request for him to pick up vodka. Once back in Sedrow, he stopped at the Food Outlet for cranberry juice anyway.

It was 5:43pm when he finally pulled off of Highway Twenty, in front of his home. Shelby's red Mazda was parked in his place next to the goat. He parked where her car had been that morning and stepped out. The fog was accumulating early tonight, and it was getting colder, and colder by the minute. He hurried up the wooden steps leading to his front door. The small modular sat on blocks a couple feet up and sometimes vermin would scurry out and surprise him. His hand was on the handle when he heard a noise which was alien to his home. He stopped short, taking time to process what it was.

"Woof! Woof! Woofwoofwoof!"

*A dog?*

That didn't make sense though. The noise was coming from inside of his house.

"Woof! RRRWoof!'

*Son-of-a-bitch.*

There was a dog in Conor's house. But Shelby didn't

own a dog. That could only mean one thing. Who the hell had she let into his place? He twisted the knob. It didn't move. Even though he knew she had his key, he reached into his pocket. Before he could wrap a finger around the chain, however, the door opened. A brown, mangy beast appeared, barking obnoxiously at him. Shelby was behind it, holding it back by a black collar. The dog wasn't big, but neither was she and it was almost comical to see it nearly overpowering her. She stood wide in black leggings and a blue shirt, tottering as it barked and pulled. Light radiated behind her, and noise blared from the TV.

"Come on! Come on! Come on! Come on! Get in! Quick!"

"What the hell is this?"

"Just get in before he gets away."

The dog stopped barking and straightened its back, pointing its nose like an arrow at Conor's crotch. It had big ears that flopped lazily on the sides of its head. Its tail wagged as it sniffed and pulled. Conor took a step back and its head came up, finding the Mexican food in his hand.

"Whose dog?"

"Just come in, Conor! Hurry."

"Jesus." Conor shoved the dog with his knee, and stepped around it. It continued to sniff him maniacally.

Shelby shut the door. "Isn't he cuuuute?"

"Sure." He took a good look at the thing. It was light brown, almost golden, and had wavy hair on top that didn't blend with the straight hair near its belly. It was a medium sized dog. It was energetic, sniffing every wall, every corner, every surface, as if looking for a lost treat, then finally standing up on its hind legs and seeking out the covered food with its wet nose.

"Whose is it though?" Conor pushed the dog down.

Shelby's eyes shone like stars into his as she

exclaimed, "He's ours!"

"Oh-kay." Conor spoke slowly, attempting to process the situation. "Where did he come from?"

"I found him. Today. He was all alone. I couldn't leave him." The dog made its way to where she now sat on the couch, and put its face in hers. She took it in both hands, and nuzzled it with her nose. "Could I? No I couldn't. No, no, no." Her voice took on a goo-goo-ga-ga tone. The dog sat down and stared her in the eyes adoringly. Its tail moved back and forth like a rudder, thumping on the floor.   (Are you gonna feed me? Walk me? Pet me? Throw a ball?)

Its mouth opened and its tongue flopped out. Its breath was heavy. Shelby puckered her lips and the dog licked them. She wiped them on the back of her forearm and made a sour face. Then the dog walked in a small circle and plopped down at her feet.

Conor took a deep breath, let it out slowly.

*Ours, huh? Well, there's only a few ways this could go.*

"Okay—" he began.

"Really, he found me. At the store. Come over here and sit down." She looked up at him and ran her hand over the couch cushion. Taking the food with him, Conor took a seat next to her. Her phone, which sat on the armrest opposite him, vibrated, indicating a text message. On the other side of the dog, was his cluttered coffee table. He set the food on it. The dog stirred, but didn't look. It appeared on the brink of sleep. Some reality show played on the TV.

"The store, huh?"

"I was just coming out. I saw your Mom there, by the way."

"At the outlet?"

"Uh huh. She said to tell you 'hi,' and you should stop

by sometime."

Shelby hadn't officially met his parents, and he hadn't met hers. She hadn't met his friends, either, aside from Dale, who had been his closest buddy since elementary school. He only knew hers from college. She had asked him once, only a month ago, if it bothered him that most of them were guys. He had sensed that his answer wouldn't make a difference one way or the other, and said, "No."

Shelby had only met his mother because she managed the Food Outlet, and they had been in together multiple times.

"She should have had the day off," he said.

"She was shopping."

"Gotcha."

"So was I. I went in to pick up the vodka, and when I came back out this dog just walks around the back of my car and jumps in. I was like, 'Hi there.'" She laughed. "I didn't wanna touch him at first—because, you know, rabies or whatever? But he wasn't growling or foaming at the mouth, so I was like, 'Come on, dude. Get out.' So I grabbed him by his neck hair and pulled him out and he just jumped back in. He got in the passenger seat and looked at me like, 'Let's go home.' What else could I do?" She shrugged.

"So you stole somebody's dog from the store."

"No! He didn't belong to anyone. Look at the poor baby. He probably hadn't eaten in a month."

Conor looked down at the dog, who was now sleeping at Shelby's feet. It looked well fed to him.

"Plus, he was dirty. I mean, like really dirty. I had to give him a bath."

"So you brought a stray dog over and bathed it here?"

The dog stirred and looked up tiredly. His expression seemed to say, "Fuck you." He licked the roof of his mouth twice, and collapsed once again onto his paws.

"Conor, what else was I supposed to do?"

"I don't know," Conor replied. "Call the Humane Society?"

"The pound? They would've killed him! Plus, look at him. Isn't he just adorable? He can be our baby."

Her phone buzzed again. She leaned over, checked the screen, and a smile crossed her lips as she typed a text and sent it.

*Our baby*, Conor thought. *Right. Because we're such a power couple.*

How often did they even see each other? Two nights a week? And how many of them did she spend *not* intoxicated? That's when something occurred to him.

*She's not intoxicated.*

He looked back toward the counter, and didn't see a bottle sitting anywhere. "You're not drinking tonight?" He realized after asking the question that he had almost sounded disappointed.

"You wanna drink?" she responded.

"No. I just thought you picked up vodka today."

"Tsh. Do I have to get blasted every time I come over to spend time with my boyfriend?"

There it was. Conor felt his heart rate pick up. She had used the "B" word. Did that make it official? They were no longer just fucking?

"I did buy it," she went on. "But when he jumped in the car, I took it back in and returned it. They almost wouldn't do it either. But your Mom helped. I bought dogfood instead. And some weed. Your Mom got him the collar."

"Jesus." Conor tried to pretend that his heart wasn't doing flips.

"Oh yeah. Dude. Your Mom was laughing her ass off. She thought it was a great idea to bring him here."

Shelby said "their baby" could stay at his place. She lived with her parents, and didn't work. They were paying to put her through school. There was no way that they would let her bring a stray dog home. Conor didn't say yes. He didn't say no either. Just sat and looked at the wall behind the TV set. Finally, when she had finished, he spoke.

"I got you your torrrta."

"Oh good. I'm starving. But go shower first. You smell like a grease rag."

"Does it have a name?"

"*It's* a *he*. And I thought we could think of one together." She smiled, looking deep into his eyes.

Conor looked down, once again, at the mutt, sleeping peacefully on his floor. Its chest heaved up and down with every breath.

"Fine," he said. "But I'm taking him in for shots."

"Yay!" She clapped her hands lightly, then threw her arms around his neck, planting a kiss on his lips. "Our baby! Now go shower so we can eat."

Conor couldn't help but feel like he had just been played. But wasn't that how relationships went? Plus, he and the dog just might hit it off, even if he and Shelby didn't take things any further. He liked dogs anyway, had always had them growing up on the farm. Even when Brett moved him out into his own room in the garage, he had a German Shepherd to keep him company. This animal seemed nice enough.

He stood up, and the dog growled. His eyes didn't open. He was still sound asleep. The movement had just startled him.

* * *

He expected the bathroom to be a mess. It wasn't too bad, though. Surprisingly enough, there was no dog hair anywhere in sight. So the thing didn't have a shedding problem. Score one for the beast. There was water on the floor, however, and the towel that Conor had been using, had been used to dry off the dog. He used it to soak up some of the water—pushing it back and forth with his foot—then fetched a clean one from under the sink.

The shower was hot. He ran it that way intentionally, placing his palms on the wall and letting the scolding water hit his back like a flogger. It hurt and it felt good.

She had called him her boyfriend. Was it nothing but a manipulation tactic to get him to keep her new dog at his place, or could it be that something had actually developed between them? He had only recently begun to hope for the latter. Not because he hadn't been attracted to Shelby Metcalf since Vocational Writing, but because even since they had been hooking up, he still had trouble believing that she could actually want him.

For the first two months, he had played it cool, refused to even entertain the thought of love. He thought of her as his girlfriend whenever his logical mind would allow it, because...well, what else was he supposed to think of her as? But on those rare occasions, which had mostly occurred in the past month, when Conor Mitchell stepped outside of the box and examined his life, himself, their relationship, all he could see was a college girl who came over and fucked him on the weekends because he supported her habits.

Tonight, though, Shelby wasn't intoxicated. She had sat in his living room, perfectly sober, and called him her boyfriend.

The water ran down his back, burning his skin, as his tolerance adjusted and the sensation became normal. The bathroom filled with fog. He considered how to approach the topic of dinner with John's family, then decided to just leave good enough alone. Why spoil what had been said?

He could ask some other time.

The dog was named Benji. There was no reason in particular. He had floated "Conan," and she scrunched up her face and shook her head. She had suggested "Goldy."

"He's not gold, though," Conor said. "He's brown."

The dog seemed to know that they were talking about him. He kept lifting his ears—sometimes his whole head—and looking at them from where he still lay in front of the couch. Then Conor said it. There was no thought involved. It just spilled out of him.

"Benji?"

Shelby's eyes lit up. "That's right! He looks like a Benji, doesn't he?"

Benji didn't bark much. Only when a loud truck passed on the highway and startled him. He didn't even get into the tacos when he woke from his nap, and saw two of them left over, sitting on a cardboard plate atop the coffee table. He didn't seem to have a humping problem. (Though he still had his balls.) And he didn't jump up on people.

All in all, Conor could tell he was a good dog. He knew how to sit, lay down, shake hands—even knew to bark at the door when he had to go. Under his fur, he couldn't have weighed more than seventy pounds. His only vice, it seemed, was sniffing. The dog sniffed, and sniffed, and explored the world with his small black nose as if it were a metal detector. Conor and Shelby cuddled up on the couch, and spent most of the night watching him. He almost forgot that he had planned to watch the news. When he turned to channel 4, the story was already airing.

"—of a man who went missing in Sedrow Woolley Thursday night." the male anchor said. "New details have police scratching their heads."

"Really?" Shelby asked.

"Yeah. I heard about it today."

The screen changed, displaying a tall, neon sign by the side of Highway Twenty, which announced, "Motel 6." Then it moved down into the hotel's parking lot, where a small, attractive woman stood in front of a door marked, "11," holding a microphone.

"Video surveillance taken from this hotel parking lot reveals that Daryle Colombo, who went missing Thursday night, had a companion."

A black and white image filled Conor's TV screen. A round man in a black T-shirt, wearing a white baseball cap walked side-by-side with a young boy. The picture was blown up, but it was still difficult to make out much detail. The boy looked away, but Conor could vaguely see the man's face. He had a dark goatee.

"This boy, who police are saying is between the ages of four and six, is seen getting out of the car with Colombo, and entering the hotel."

"Hey!" Shelby stiffened on Conor's arm.

"A half hour later the two exited the room and got into this 2017 Chrysler." A picture of a silver car filled the screen.

"Go back! Go back! Go back!" Shelby jumped to her feet. Benji stood up from where he lay in front of the TV, and looked at her.

"I can't," Conor said. "It's not DVR."

"Investigators believe that the boy, who has yet to be identified, is still with the forty-six-year-old native of Boulder Colorado."

A scene from earlier that day popped up. The reporter held a microphone to the face of a middle aged Sedrow Woolley sheriff, who spoke over the sound of traffic in the background.

"This just gets weirder and weirder, the more we learn." He looked into the camera. "We just hope to figure out who this boy is so we can be sure of his safety."

Then the reporter was once again alone on Conor's TV. "Daryle Colombo has no noted criminal history, or history of mental illness." A picture of Colombo standing next to an overweight woman and two children, a boy and a girl, came on. They were in a living room with a brightly lit Christmas tree behind them. Conor could see now that the man was bald on top, with short stubby hair on the sides. "Police are not calling this a kidnapping investigation at this point, but ask that if you have any information on the whereabouts of Colombo, or the identity of this boy, that you call in at one-eight-hundred..."

The black-and-white image once again filled the screen.

"Dude!" Shelby picked up her phone and began to dial frantically.

"What is it?" Conor pointed his remote at the TV as the story ended, and pressed 'power.' A half-second later, the screen went black. Benji sniffed it.

"Shit. Shit. Shit. Come on. Where's that stupid number?"

Benji whined. Conor started toward the front door, then realized the dog didn't want to be let out.

"Got it," Shelby said. "Just be quiet for a minute, okay?"

"Sure." Conor sat back down. Benji walked over and looked up at him, his head tilted sideways. "Okay." Conor patted the couch cushion.

The dog wagged his tail, his body gyrating along with it. His mouth opened into what almost resembled a smile, and he jumped up on the couch, laying his head in Conor's lap. Conor pet him lightly.

"Come on." Shelby began to pace. "Pick up—Hello! Aunt Betty? It's Shelby. Yeah. Yeah. I know. I know,

Aunt Betty. Okay. Yeah. Listen, is Andrew okay?" There was a long pause in which nobody seemed to breathe, and Conor began to piece the situation together. There was no way, however, that Shelby could have recognized the boy from the surveillance. The picture hadn't been clear enough.

"No—It's just, I was watching the news, and—yeah. Isn't it crazy? Yeah. Oh my God. Thank you. Yes.

"Hey, little dude. How you been? Oh yeah? Good to hear. What grade are you in now? First? Wow!"

She talked for close to six minutes. When she finally hung up, she turned her phone off and sat next to Conor and Benji. "Wow. Fuck *me*, dude. I thought that was my cousin."

"Who?" Conor asked, even though he already knew. "The kid on the news?"

"Yeah." She shook her head 'no.' "Tsh. It looked just like him."

"Wow," Conor said. "Crazy. I wonder why nobody's filed a report on that kid."

Who wouldn't report their child missing? There was no way they didn't know by now. Or maybe the kid wasn't missing. Maybe he had just been with the guy briefly, and now he was back home. Maybe the parents knew. That wasn't right either, though. The guy was from out of town, and the news didn't mention he was visiting anybody. Who would've just let their kid go in some hotel room with him?

Shelby just sat next to him, seeming to try and regain her composure. That night, even though she had all but expressed her love to him, they didn't *make* love. They fucked. They fucked, and passed out in each other's arms. Sometime in the late hours, he dreamt that Benji was crawling on the walls and walking upside down on the ceiling.

# Chapter Two

A truck growled hungrily up Mosher Road. The animals in the woods on either side of the old streets didn't mind. They were used to the sounds of early morning traffic. Though it was still dark out, they all knew on some level that it was close to bedtime. It had been a long night of hunting, of lurking, of competing with one another in a nocturnal singing competition. The crickets, it seemed, had had enough. The owls were well fed. No coyote had howled in hours. Still, most of the forest nightlife was awake and alert.

The woods weren't regularly maintained. No thinning crew had been through to assure that the trees were spaced a good distance from one another. They grew that way naturally. In this particular patch of woodland, sticker bushes and other troublesome weeds were scarce. The property belonged to Walter Murphy.

Murphy owned ten acres, which until recently, he had rarely explored. He had been too old to be stomping around in the woods. In the middle of the lot, however, was a five acre clear-cut, with a yard that took all day to mow. At the edge of that yard, sat the double-wide that Murphy and his wife, Luann, had lived in for twenty-two years.

This morning Luann wasn't in the trailer. She was in the earth, three feet down. Murphy moved around trees, stomped over ferns in his heavy boots toward the spot where he had buried her days ago. Though it was pitch dark, he saw the man-sized plots of dirt scattered perfectly about his forest. There were close to a hundred of them, and a few empty holes.

Walter Murphy moved with purpose. A tall, young man in a sheriff's uniform stood leaning against a tree, smoking a self-rolled cigarette. The cherry lit up as he sucked on the thing. The two men paid no attention to each other.

Murphy's boot landed in one of the graves, leaving a deep indent and smearing dirt as he passed over it. In some bushes, a raccoon scurried away. Murphy stomped and he stomped, and he made his way deep into the woods until finally he was there. He could see the street, only fifty yards away, but no other vehicle passed. It was four in the morning.

At his feet lay Luann. In the earth. Waiting for him. He looked down at the dirt plot, sure that it was the one. How could he forget? Walter had only been married once. For a man of sixty-six, there was something to be said about that. He and Luann had had their ups and downs. Sometimes it seemed the downs couldn't go any lower, and there was no foreseeable way back up, but they had always worked through them.

She had an affair once—well, once that he knew of— with a man from work. Walter didn't work, hadn't since his back injury almost thirty years ago. He collected SSI, and hadn't had any opportunity to get even. Not that he would have had co-employees kicking down his door to lay him if he did work, but he liked to think he retained his Elvis-like good looks, even at his age.

All in all, Luann was a good woman, and though Walter Brady Murphy didn't often tell her, he loved her. That's why he was here now, at four in the morning, standing over the grave that he had left her in. He fell to his knees, and looked down at the soil. Only a few feet to the right, was another. And to the left. There were so many buried in Walter's woods, that the ground was hollow.

"Luann. Daddy's here, you beautiful bitch."

The sheriff walked quietly to where he knelt. He leaned up against a tree and lit another cigarette, looking intently at the short grave. Neither man acknowledged the other. Walter began to dig. No shovel. He used his hands, first one, and then the other, scooping dirt aside. He dug, slowly at first, looking down into the earth with an intensity that may have frightened a lesser man.

"Luann." He spoke softly, melodically. "Luann, I love you. Daddy's here now, sweet thing. Daddy's here to take you home."

The earth began to harden as he made his way closer to her body. Then a finger emerged. It was an old, pruned, pale thing, with a nail so short that it could have been a man's. It was followed by the rest of the hand. Murphy took it in his, wrapping his own fingers around it. They had long ago quit wearing their wedding rings. He leaned down, and kissed the hand. Then he let it go, stood up, and took two steps back.

The Sheriff puffed his cigarette and pulled it away from his face, blowing out a long stream of smoke. Both men watched silently.

The hand was followed by a forearm. Then another

hand. The dirt collapsed on itself and wrapped around Luann's face, pouring down her cheeks like water. Her eyes were wide, her mouth open like she had been screaming. She sat up, stretched out her wiry arms, and closed her jaw. She wore one of her favorite dresses. It was yellow, with sunflowers stitched on it. Her hair would have been grey had she not kept it dyed jet black. Tiny chrome studs sat in her ears.

She looked at the sheriff, then at Walter. She smiled. He smiled back. Every animal that had been lurking nearby fled in different directions. This caused other beasts—nocturnal and those that had been sleeping—to scare and run as well. For the next six seconds the woods were noticeably active as bushes shook and branches snapped.

Luann stood up and every speck of dirt fell from her dress, leaving it as clean as if she hadn't just been buried for the last two days.

"Daddy." She threw herself into Walter's arms.

Somewhere in the distance, another woke up and crawled out of the earth. Something snapped and some unlucky animal squealed, then fell silent.

"Luann," Walter whispered. "How do you feel?"

"Alive," she said. "Never so alive."

"Did you sleep well?"

*Crunching. Slurping in the woods.*

"Never better."

Walter kissed her forehead. They embraced long and hard, then she pulled away and looked into his eyes. "I missed you."

"I know you did, you beautiful bitch."

She looked around at all the graves. Then at the sheriff. "Hello, Phillip."

"Missus Murphy."

"How long?"

"Have I been awake?"

She nodded.

"Few minutes."

"Thought so. Will you be leaving soon?"

"Figure I will."

Luann Murphy nodded again.

Phillip took a long puff of his cigarette, turning the last bit to ash, then tossed it to the ground and stepped on it. "Be seeing you then?"

"I think you will," Walter responded.

"'Kay then. Have a good one." He turned and walked toward the road.

"Nice kid," Luann said once he was out of hearing range.

"Yup," Walter agreed. "A lot like his old man."

"Walter?" Branches snapped in the distance, as somebody made their way through the woods.

"Yeah, dear?"

"Can we go home? I'm terribly hungry."

"Yup. I suppose we can go out and eat later."

"That sounds lovely."

With that, the two walked side-by-side through the forest toward their double-wide trailer.

* * *

Conor woke up before his alarm. Something was off. A noise. It took a few seconds for his brain to come to life and register the slurping sounds.

*Benji.*

The dog was into something. He sat up, his eyes began to adjust, and he saw him chewing the sheets on Shelby's side of the bed. She didn't even stir.

"Benji," he didn't yell, and the dog didn't seem to notice. Of course he didn't. He didn't know his name yet.

Conor reached over his naked girlfriend, who was wrapped in a baby-blue blanket like a sushi roll, but he stopped short when he saw that Benji wasn't chewing his sheets at all. He was licking them.

*What the hell?*

Then his eyes fully adjusted, and he saw why. Blood. A dark crimson puddle that he instantly knew would have been a dried stain had Benji's saliva not been keeping it moist. Shelby had started her period.

"Benji, stop." He shoved the dog away.

Benji hunched his head between his shoulders and looked wide eyed at Conor. Then his tongue came out and he began breathing heavily.

"No. Go away. That's disgusting."

"What?" Shelby's voice was strained.

"The dog." He lifted the blanket and saw the mess on his side as well. So she had started last night, during their sex.

Benji made himself busy, sniffing around the studio.

"I think we're both gonna need a shower."

"*What*?" Shelby's voice came instantly to life. "Fuck." She sat up and looked under her own blanket. "Fuck. Fuck. Fuck. I'm so sorry, dude." She let out a long breath and collapsed onto her back, stiff as a board, looking up at the ceiling.

"No problem." Conor tried to sound comforting, but didn't really know how. "Lemme ah—I'll go grab ah—"

"Ugh. I knew this was gonna happen. How bad is it?"

"I have more sheets."

"Oh-em-gee! I'm so sorry."

"Don't be. I'm sure you're not the first girl to have her period in her boyfriend's bed."

"Ugh. Not now, Conor."

He smiled. "Well the dog cleaned most of it anyway."

"What!"

"The thing licked it up. Right where you're lying."

Benji whined at the door.

"Fuck!" Shelby exclaimed. "Fuck, dude. Put him outside. Please. Oh. I'm gonna be sick."

Conor chuckled as he got up and walked naked to the front door. When he opened it, the cold nipped at his face, his chest, and his genitals. Benji ran out and down the steps. Conor flipped the switch next to the door, causing the porch to illuminate, giving him a full view of the damage. A small area of dried blood circled his penis, reached up his pelvis like tiny fingers. It covered the top portion of his inner right thigh as well. The left side was pale white. His next thought made his stomach turn.

*The fucking dog.*

Benji had licked him clean at some point in the night. He quickly dismissed it though. There was no way he would have slept through the dog's tongue that close to his genitals. Somehow he had just managed to not get blood on that side. He was sure a closer examination under better lighting would reveal at least some mess there.

In his peripheral, he saw Shelby climb out of bed and walk quickly to the bathroom, the blue blanket wrapped tightly around her. He glanced out at Benji, who was squatting in the small yard in front of his house. The dog stood up and looked back at him, tilting his head.

"Sorry." Conor looked away.

Shelby was in the shower by the time Conor had the linen off of his mattress, and in a hefty bag. He set it on the counter out of the dog's reach, then joined her, leaving the bathroom door open.

The blood was cleaned from her body. Moving aside, she let him under the water, which turned bright red as it poured down his legs like a scarlet avalanche. It hit the floor, where it lingered for what seemed like too long.

When it all finally washed down the drain, and they were left standing in a clear, shallow puddle, Shelby didn't speak. She took the washcloth in one hand, soap in the other and stared down as she rubbed them together.

Conor reached out and took them from her, then dropped to his knees. He gently washed her entire body, starting with one foot, working his way up, then back down, and ending with the other. When he was finished he washed her hair, massaging her scalp. She closed her eyes, tipped her head back. Her lips curved up in a subtle smile. Conor grew unexpectedly aroused.

When Shelby's eyes opened, they landed on his manhood, then slowly traveled up his body, coming to rest on his. Her ribcage moved up and down as her fingertips found his chest.

They didn't fuck again. They made love. Until Benji started barking.

Conor caught his breath, pulled away, and looked down at Shelby's face. Then at her naked body, pressed into the wall. Then her face again. She giggled.

Conor said, "I'm gonna neuter that dog myself."

"Go see what it is," she whispered.

"Fine." Conor stepped out of the shower and poked his head out the door. His alarm was blaring. The clock read, '6:00.' Benji stood beside the bed, barking. "Okay. Okay." He walked across the room and hit the snooze button. The dog stopped immediately, and began to sniff his crotch. "Go away." He shoved his head.

When he made it back into the bathroom, Shelby was just stepping out of the shower and wrapping a towel around herself. "Get in and finish getting cleaned up."

Conor shook his head, forced a grin as he stepped under the water.

"I'll take the sheets and blankets to the laundry mat after you leave for work," she said.

"You don't have to. I can just do it on—"

"Shut up, dude. I'm gonna do it. Benji, stop!"

"What's he doing?" Conor scrubbed his body.

"Nothing. It's fine. I'm gonna take the bedding in, okay?"

"You sure?"

"Of course I'm sure, you goober. I'll take them in and leave them here before I go home. I don't have anything planned today anyway."

"I'll leave money," Conor said.

"Don't worry about it. I have money left over from the dogfood. It shouldn't cost more than a couple bucks anyway. Don't forget to feed Benji when I'm not here. He has to eat at least twice a day. There's instructions on the bag. They base it off the weight of the—"

"I've had dogs before. We should be fine."

After a brief pause, she said, "You don't have to be a dick about it."

"I wasn't trying to be a—I was just saying—"

"I'm kidding. You think he'll be okay here while you're at work? Like, by himself? What if the poor thing has to go to do a tinky-poo-poo?"

Conor hadn't thought about that. "Just make sure you put him out before you leave. I'll have to talk to the landlord about putting in a dog door. Or we could just build a doghouse out back and get him a chain."

"What? Noooo! You can't leave him outside all day! It's cold out there."

"Sure you can," Conor replied. "That's why dogs have fur."

"Oh. Okay. So as long as you have clothes on, it's fine if I put a chain around your neck and leave you out in the cold all day?"

Conor laughed. "Why? That something you'd be into?"

"Maybe. If you do it to my baby. Don't worry, Benji. I won't wet dat meany weave you outside awe day. No I won't. No- I- won't. He tinks he can just tweet you wike one of is farm animals, doesn't he?"

"Yeah," Conor replied. "We never ate the dogs."

"I'll bet you left them outside to freeze to death, though."

"Not all of them. The ones who did, all lived though."

"Well," Shelby's voice came from outside the bathroom now. "Benji's an indoor dog. Right, Benji? Right? Good boy. Who's a good boy? Who's an indoor doggy? Hey, hon?"

At first, Conor didn't answer. She had never called him 'hon' before. She had rarely called him anything besides 'dude.'

"Yeah?" he finally asked.

"When they drag their butts across the rug, doesn't it mean they have worms?"

He shook his head, rinsing shampoo out of his hair

Shelby giggled. "Just kidding. Benji, sit. Can you sit? Good boy."

Conor reached for the knob, then stopped, letting his hand rest there a moment. He pulled it back and took a deep breath, waiting for Shelby to stop talking to the dog. When she had, he let it out. "Hey, Shelb?"

"Yeah?" Her voice was far off. "It's freaking cold in here."

"Turn on the heater."

"I just did. What's up?"

Conor stepped out and began to dry his body. "You still wanna do something next weekend?"

"What was that?"

"Next weekend. A friend of mine invited us over for dinner with his family. His, uh, wife and kids."

She appeared in the doorway in her black leggings and

a bra. Her blue shirt hung at her side. She just looked at him.

"It's just a friend from work. I mean, if you wanna—"

"Which one?" Shelby had never been to the shop, but he sometimes talked about the guys.

"John."

"The old one?"

"They're all old."

Shelby pulled on her shirt. "The creepy one who hates his kids or whatever?"

Conor laughed. "Yeah. That's the one. He doesn't hate his kids though. He's just joking. I think."

"Funny."

"Well he thought we might wanna come over sometime."

"Oh-kay." She spoke slowly, cautiously.

"Well?"

"Is that something you would wanna do?"

"I don't know. I guess I was thinking—"

The alarm went off again and the dog went crazy.

"Hold on," Shelby disappeared. "Benji! Chill dude! Ugh. How do you shut this thing off?"

The dog continued to bark. A few seconds later, the noise stopped. Conor heard the sound of Benji's rapid breathing. He wrapped the towel around his waist, and stepped out of the bathroom. Shelby sat on the couch, looking down at her phone. The light shone up into her face, illuminating an expression that he couldn't quite read. He went to the bed and began to dress. "So?" he asked.

"Yeah?"

"What do you think? Dinner at John's place? I think he said something about a hot tub or—"

"Is it something you want?"

"Well, yeah. I was thinking it could be fun."

"With me?"

"Who else would I go with?"

"I don't know. Whoever you wanted."

"I wanna go with you."

"Okay."

"Okay?"

"Okay." She didn't look up from her phone. Benji jumped onto the couch and laid down next to her. She put one hand over the dog, using the other to press keys with her thumb.

"All right. I'll tell him then. Next weekend?"

"Sure. If that's what you want."

He pulled on his work jeans and looked at her for a long moment. She pretended not to notice, though he knew she did.

*Don't stare*, he heard her in his head. *It's weird.*

He opened his mouth to speak, then realized there was nothing more to say. He went back to getting dressed as Shelby continued to focus on her phone and her dog like nothing else in the world existed.

* * *

It had been a hot summer that seemed like it would never end. Since Conor's goat was a convertible, he had taken her out a time or two with the top down, speeding up back roads, strangely turned on by the way Shelby's hair danced in the wind. He had even pulled over into a field and fucked her in the open once. If the smell of grass and fertilizer had bothered her, she hadn't shown it. It was so familiar to Conor that he guessed it had added to the nostalgic sense of a future with her that was terrifyingly similar to his childhood. A childhood, which wasn't so bad, but hadn't by any stretch of the mind, been good either.

Now it was looking like it would give way to a cold winter. The mornings were dark and foggy. The days were gloomy. The nights were chilly. This morning the fog was so thick that in spite of the streetlights running along both sides of the highway, Conor could only see a short distance in front of the car. Even with his high beams on, which didn't seem to be a problem, since he hadn't seen any other vehicles out. This was only part of the reason he hit he girl in the street.

The speed limit was forty-five. Though Conor felt he could have driven any street in Sedrow with his eyes closed, he was going thirty. He had briefly listened to Mark and Thomas, then turned the stereo off. His head was in a strange place and he couldn't quite put his finger on why.

Before he left for work, he had sat on the couch next to Shelby sipping coffee and watching the news. He found himself oddly interested, waiting for the story about his town to air again. But it wasn't about his town, was it? It was about a missing man and a boy. For all anybody knew, one, or even both of them, were buried high up in one of the nearby mountains. The story never played though.

Benji had laid at their feet. To be exact, he had lain *on* their feet. Even though Conor had been wearing his work boots, the dog had plopped his petite body over Shelby's bare toes and the thick dirty leather, and made himself comfortable. He was unusually at ease for a dog in a new home. Maybe he *had* been a stray. A dog which had been abandoned by his owners and left to sleep outside and fend for himself. In a town like Sedrow Woolley, it wouldn't have been difficult for an animal to escape notice by spending its nights in the woods. Plenty of domestic dogs roamed the streets anyway. Pets that Conor had had growing up used to leave the farm and explore all the time. Nobody batted an eye unless they were sneaking away from somebody's property with a chicken. He had lost a blue healer once to a neighbor's 22 rifle.

The whole scene inside of his apartment that morning had been like some kind of a modern rendition of a Norman Rockwell painting. It was all too perfect to be right. He knew it was only in his head, but he felt it in his chest. An uneasiness. Like his heart was no longer comfortable in his ribcage and might fall into some black hole in his abdomen at any second. He had even considered leaving early. Showing up, to work off the clock with John.

Up ahead, a roundabout came into view. There was a streetlamp installed in the middle of the concrete island, which had been put in a year ago and served no purpose that Conor knew of. Even with the extra light, he only had a gritty view in front of the Buick. He slowed down and took the roundabout at just under ten.

The unease hadn't gone away when he left for work. It wasn't Shelby either. It couldn't have been. This is what he had wanted. For how long now? He had only become aware of it recently, but he sensed it had been there for much longer. That it stemmed from places inside that he had no interest in exploring or even acknowledging.

He stepped on the gas and brought the speed back up to thirty.

That's when he remembered the dream. It was one of those that felt so real that he thought he had woken up in bed. Then he saw the dog high up on the wall, crawling, its legs bent impossibly, its movements unnatural and spiderlike. It had moved slowly onto the ceiling and taken a couple steps before it stopped. It lingered upside-down, and though it was dark, Conor knew that it was looking at the bed. Watching them. Smiling. Then the dream had ended and there was nothing but darkness and rest.

Conor didn't often dream. If he did, he didn't remember them. It had been years, and that one had been equally unsettling. A visit from his dead grandfather, a rotting corpse who wouldn't stop talking about the war.

And now this. A dream that was clearly some kind of a psychological metaphor for what he was experiencing in his love life. And he had woken up, all thoughts of it gone, only to find the dog licking menstrual blood from his bed. The combination had had some unconscious effect on him. He had inadvertently filed the dog in his mind alongside talking corpses and other creepy-crawly shit that had potential to turn his stomach sour.

That had to be it. The object of his unease. Not the dog. Not Shelby. It was him, and some fear of everything that he thought he wanted, actually materializing in a relationship. He had a girlfriend. They had a dog. Everything was okay and because it was, he began to relax and hit the girl in the road.

She just appeared through the fog, and then it was too late. He slammed on the brakes. The tires slid. The blacktop screamed. He turned the wheel and the car began to fishtail, the back end moving toward the front in what seemed like slow motion.

Conor only had time to catch a short glimpse of her. She was walking in the middle of the highway, oblivious to the car coming at her and all he saw was curly blonde hair drooping down the back of a pink sweatshirt. It was just enough for him to know that she was a teenager. The passenger side of the Buick slammed into her. There was a hollow "thud" as she went down. The car didn't jump, which meant that it hadn't passed over her—that she was being dragged, scrapped against the concrete.

Conor's heart seemed to stop as he tried to realign with the road. It all happened too fast though. The Buick turned and slid the other way. Then the passenger side slammed into the curb and the car stopped moving. The smell of burning brake fluid blew out of the heater, into his face and at first he just sat there trying to register what the hell had just happened.

He had to get out of the car. His hands shook as he attempted to unlatch his seatbelt. Finally, it came loose. He opened the door and cold instantly filled the car. It may have been the coldest air Conor had ever breathed. He almost forgot to put the vehicle in park before taking his foot off of the brake.

*It's okay. She's okay. She's not hurt too bad. She's not...*

The Buick continued to growl as he stepped out. He couldn't help but be grateful for the sound of the V-6. He imagined if it weren't there, he would hear the cries of a teenage girl, crushed between his car and the sidewalk.

*Move*, he told his feet. But they didn't seem to hear or care. Then, before he knew what was happening, he was in motion. Not running, but walking around the front of the car almost reluctantly. His thoughts came in rapid succession, seeming to smash into him, each one hitting more violently than the last.

*Look what you did. You killed a girl. Or maybe you didn't. Maybe you just broke her spine into pieces. Have fun cleaning her blood off of your car.*

Then, d*on't worry about the mess. You're going to prison. You're going away for a long, long time. Can you do that? Can you survive prison?*

Time seemed to hold still as he made his way around the boat of a car. Then a man in a black trench coat stepped out of the fog and Conor froze. It only took him a second to recognize Percly Valentine. Everybody in town knew about the black man who lived in the train in the town center, but never gave anybody any trouble. Percly was unusually nice for a transient. He walked purposefully toward Conor, a large revolver hanging at his side. His eye patch rested in the middle of his forehead.

Percly wasn't a tall man. He was wide though. He raised the gun and pointed it at Conor's face. Conor felt his consciousness lift out of his body for a fraction of a second, then without thinking he said, "It was an accident. I didn't see her. The fog—"

Percly looked into Conor's eyes and though Conor had often seen the homeless man around town, even given him loose change from his ashtray a time or two, it occurred to him that he had never seen him without the black patch over his eye. It was mostly white, with a trace of baby blue behind the surface.

Conor raised his hands, palms facing Percly. He felt like he would tip over. He knew in that moment that he was going to die. Then Percly lowered the gun, walked to the side of the car, and pointed it at the back wheel.

POP! POP! POP!

Conor opened his mouth to yell. To tell the transient to 'get,' the way one might shoo a raccoon from the back porch. Then his entire body tingled, starting with the top of his head, and moving down like water pouring over him as he became aware of Percly's angle. He wasn't positioned right to shoot out the tire.

Then he was walking again, moving around the car. Percly's head snapped up. The gun followed a second later as he pointed it once again at Conor's face. Conor took a step back.

"Go." Percly's voice was low and cold.

"Please. I—"

Percly raised his voice. "Go!"

"Just try and relax."

"GET IN YOUR FUCKING CAR AND DRIVE AWAY, MOTHERFUCKER! YOU HEAR ME? NOW! BEFORE I BLOW YOUR FUCKING HEAD OFF

YOUR SHOULDERS!"

"Okay." Conor snapped out of it. "Okay. I'm going." He walked slowly backwards, refusing to lower his hands or take his eyes off of the homeless man. He stumbled into the car, closed the door, and put it in drive without putting his seatbelt on. He slammed his foot down on the gas, and the car took off. Conor grew sick to his stomach as the wheel scraped the curb. He looked in the rear-view mirror and saw Percly disappear into the fog.

Conor's knuckles turned white as he gripped the wheel like he might float away if he let go. He clenched his jaw so tight that his teeth hurt. What had he just witnessed?

What had he just done?

*You didn't do anything. It was an accident.*

But then what? Had it been an accident when Percly Valentine walked up and shot the girl? What would it look like to the police? He hit her with his car, then the bum blew her head off before Conor drove away.

*Who cares? Who cares? Who fucking cares? What difference does it make? Why are you still driving?*

Conor looked at the speedometer, which told him he was going just over sixty. He couldn't see a thing. The short distance of visibility in front of the car was coming at him so fast that he was practically driving blind.

Still, he knew the next turn was a right onto Bradshaw Drive. Conor let off the gas and took it, driving for under a minute along the residential street with trees in yards before pulling over. When he looked in the rear-view, what he saw wasn't himself. It was a mess of stress and sweat. His face and hair were drenched. He turned off the heater and stuck a shaking hand into his pocket, finding his cell phone.

*You killed someone. You murdered her, then you drove away. You're going to prison. You and that bum'll be cellmates, and you can reminisce about what you did for the rest of your lives.*

Conor tried to ignore his thoughts. He had to use both hands to dial. Almost instantly, a female voice spoke into his ear.

"Nine-one-one Emergency. Name please."

Conor took a deep breath. "Conor—ah, Conor Mitchell."

"Location?"

"I just witnessed a murder."

"Please state your location, Conor."

"Yeah, I'm uh, I'm at," He looked toward the closest house. It was still dark and he couldn't see the numbers through the fog. "I'm on Bradshaw Drive, in Sedrow Woolley."

"Can you give a street address?"

"No. I mean, I don't know. I'm in my car. It's dark out."

"State your emergency."

"I just told you. I witnessed a fucking murder."

"Conor, go ahead and stay where you are, please. Can you give me a description of the car you're in?"

"Yeah." His throat was dry. "I'm in a green Buick. Seventoo-seven. It's a Skylark. I just turned off of Highway Twenty."

"And can you tell me what you saw?"

All he could think of was the girl slamming into the Buick, dropping to the street where he had dragged her across the pavement. He found himself grateful that he hadn't seen her face before he crushed it between his car and the curb.

"Conor? You still with me?"

His voice was grew weak. "Just send someone. Please."

"That's what we're doing, Sir. In the meantime, if you could—"

Conor hung up.

* * *

He sat in the driver's seat, his hands on the wheel. A porch light came on across the street and somebody peeked around a curtain. He kept the headlights on so the police would see him when they arrived.

His phone vibrated in the seat next to him. He looked at the screen and saw, "Unknown Number." Knowing it was the dispatcher calling back, he ignored it. He also tried to ignore the scene which refused to stop playing and replaying in his head. It was impossible, though. Not just that, but another scene, one from his childhood, kept playing somehow right alongside it.

Brett Mitchell grew up in Seattle. He wasn't what anybody would call a hick. However, when he had gotten out of the Marines and married Conor's mother, he moved the three of them out to the farm in Sedrow Woolley. The transition into the country had seemed as natural to the man as taking a shit in the morning.

They hadn't lived in town a whole year when a deer ran out of the woods one night and met the front end of Brett's truck. Conor had been sitting in the middle seat between Brett and Mom, watching wide eyed as his Stepfather got out and stood over the animal which flailed from its side, unable to stand up. The whole ordeal had been illuminated by the bright headlights like a nineteen-forty movie set.

A few moments later, Brett had come back and pulled Conor out of the truck. "Come on out here. You should see this."

Conor hadn't spoken, just followed as his stepdad retrieved a heavy tire iron from the back of the old pickup. He was a smart boy, but it wouldn't have taken a genius to figure out what was about to happen. He didn't dare protest. Though many of the trucks in town had gun racks with rifles in the windows, theirs didn't.

Conor avoided the deer's eyes as Brett beat its head in with the lug wrench. He had felt hot tears building up behind his own eyelids, but knew better than to let them out in front of his Stepfather.

When Brett was done, he dragged the lifeless animal by its antlers into a ditch on the other side of the road, and he and Conor climbed back into the truck. Conor's mother had thrown a fit. That was one of the only times Conor remembered his mom ever talking back to the man.

The phone continued to buzz. Conor reached over and picked it up. He rejected the call, and got into his contacts. He found the number quickly, knowing that as soon as the operator called again, the screen would change. Selecting it, he pressed "send."

After the third ring, a tired "Hello," came through and he remembered too late that it was John's day off.

"John?"

John yawned. "Yeah? Conor, that you?"

"Yeah, it's me. Look, sorry to wake you."

"No problem, bud—Nothing. No. It's nothing. Go back ta sleep Denise. Jesus Christ—Sorry 'bout that, Conman. What's up?"

"No, I'm sorry, man. I thought you'd be at the shop."

"Day off, brother."

"I know. I know, I just—"

"You cool, Conman?"

"Yeah. Jake's working today, right?"

"Uh, yeah. I think so. Why?"

"Well, I'm gonna have to call and have him cover for me for a while at the shop."

Another yawn. "What time is it? Lemme—I think could—you sure yer cool, man?"

"I'm good. There was an accident on the highway though and I don't know how long I'm gonna be. John, I gotta go—"

"Fuck." John cut him off. "An accident? Were you in it?"

"Yeah. I'm fine. I think the police are gonna want a statement though."

For a moment all he heard was a raspy voice in the background, then, "Denise! Would you shut up for a second? Yeah! Shut up. Thank you. I can be there in half an hour tops, Conman. Don't worry about coming in. If you need to, go ahead and take the whole day off. I know how ta run the place. I'll cover for ya. Yer car okay?"

"It's driving. Look, you don't have to—"

"It's no problem, man. Jesus Christ. An accident? It's that fucking fog. I can barely drive through Mount Vernon in the mornings. Sure you're okay?"

"I'm sure. Thanks, man. I'll try to be in as soon as I can. I really appreciate it."

"No problem, bud. You'd do it for me. Is anyone hurt?"

Conor took a deep breath. Then the inside of the Buick lit up as red and blue lights flashed behind him.

"I have to go, John. The police are here."

"Course. Keep me posted, Conman. Lemme know yer okay—'kay?"

"No problem." Conor hung up and looked into the rear-view to see a cruiser parked directly behind his car. The overhead lights made it difficult to make out any detail. He killed his headlights, then reached for the door handle. As an afterthought, he stopped and waited for the cop to approach.

Returning his gaze to the mirror, he saw the cruiser's door open. Then a leg swung out, followed by another. Then a tall, lean body. Conor could only make out the cop's silhouette, which approached slowly, hand positioned near the gun. He rolled down the old manual window, and cold air touched his face.

Gravel crunched under feet, and a woman in a tan sheriff's uniform appeared just outside. Conor found himself wondering why it surprised him that it wasn't a man. It only lasted a second, though, then the thought passed. She was in her late twenties—possibly early thirties—with dark hair, which was pulled back into a tight ponytail.

"Hey there. How ya doing?" She looked first at Conor, then examined the inside of the car. "You wanna go ahead and kill the engine?"

"Uh, yeah." Conor turned the key, causing the world to fall uncomfortably silent.

"Conor Mitchell?"

"Yeah."

"Good to meet you. I'm Officer Sims. As you probably know, I'm here because of a call we received a few minutes ago. Did you call nine-one-one?"

"Yeah. Yeah, that was me."

"Okay." She smiled. "No problem. Mind stepping out and talking?"

"Yeah. I mean, no. I don't mind."

"Great." She opened the door for him. He stepped out and closed it harder than he meant to. Sims was tall. Not as tall as him, but at 6'4, neither were most men. She had sharp features, high cheekbones. She wore some perfume that had a relaxing effect on him. "Mind if I have a look at your license, Conor? You're not in any trouble or anything."

"Uh, lemme see." He reached into his pocket, brought out his wallet and offered her the license.

She eyed him curiously for a moment. "You don't have to be nervous, man. Take a breath." Accepting the card, she looked at the picture, then back at him. "So what's going on?"

"Yeah, uh, where do want me to start?"

"Well generally when you call us, we show up, and you tell us why you called." She smiled again. "So I guess you could just start there."

"With the call?"

"How about the reason for the call, Conor."

"Jesus. I'm sorry. This is just—"

"No problem, man. Just relax. I told you, you're not in trouble. You told the dispatcher you saw a murder. Is that right?"

"Yeah. Well, a shooting."

Sims didn't bat an eye. If what he said had any effect on her, she gave no indication. Her face remained pleasant. It suggested that no matter what he had seen, (what he had done), everything was going to be okay. "Somebody got shot?" she asked.

"Yeah. I mean, I think. I'm not sure."

"Listen, Conor." She spoke slowly. "Go ahead and relax, okay? This is what I want you to do. Take a deep breath, then I'm gonna ask you a few questions. If there was a shooting and somebody was hurt, then we need to be able to get to them as soon as possible. Agreed?" She looked up into his eyes, and he found himself nodding almost involuntarily. "Good. Now I don't mean to be pushy, but you can understand why a situation like this could be urgent, right?"

He nodded again.

"Okay then. Go ahead and take a deep breath."

He did, and her perfume filled his lungs and seemed to expand into every cell of his body. It was the smell of summer. He considered asking her what the fragrance was, buying a bottle for Shelby, then her voice interrupted his thoughts.

"Now let it out. Good. Now try and remember for me, Conor. Did you see anybody get shot?"

"No." Conor shook his head. "Not directly. I mean my car was in the way. I was up by the front and it happened on the passenger side. I'm sure he shot her though."

"Who?"

"Which one?"

"You said he shot somebody. Who was it?"

"No. I know. I get that. Are you asking about the shooter, or the victim?"

"Either one'll do, man."

"Jesus. I'm sorry."

"You're doing fine, Conor. Just answer the question the best you can."

"It was Percly. Percly Valentine."

Recognition registered all over Sims's face, she nodded and said, "The shooter." It wasn't a question and she didn't wait for an answer. "And you were out of the car?"

"Yeah. I mean, I pulled over because I hit her." It occurred to him how it sounded, but there was no other story to tell.

Sims didn't seem to notice. She handed him back his license and brought out a pad of paper, which she scribbled on. "And the woman?"

"Girl."

The sheriff tilted her head.

"It was a girl," Conor said. "She looked like a teenager."

Sims paused a moment, thinking. "You don't know who she was, then?"

He told her he didn't.

"Okay." She asked him to go on. He didn't want to anymore though. In fact, in that moment, he couldn't remember ever wanting anything less. All he wanted was to go home and lay in his bed with Shelby before she left his house. That wasn't an option, though, and he knew it. All there was to do now, was face what had happened. What he had done.

He told the sheriff everything that had transpired that morning. About the accident. About the shooting. He described the girl he had hit, the best he could—though he had only seen her for a fraction of a second before she was thrown to the pavement. Sims took notes and nodded as he spoke. At some point, a light blue Sedrow Woolley Police car showed up and parked in front of the Buick, boxing it in. A male officer came and stood by, listening straight faced. People began to open doors and look out, as the police cars lit up their neighborhood.

When he was done, Sims put her notepad away. She nodded to the city cop, and he jogged to his car and took off. Then she addressed Conor. "Can you take me there?"

"Of course."

She put a hand on his arm, looked into his eyes. "Cool. You're doing great, Conor. Let's hurry. For all we know she's still alive."

"Yeah," Conor nodded. It was a lie though. He knew the girl was dead. Not only could he feel it, he had seen it in Percly's eyes. Sims seemed to know that he knew. It showed on her face for a fraction of a second, then she shoved him lightly.

"Come on. We'll take my car." They walked quickly to the sheriff's cruiser. She made it first and opened the back door. "Can't let you sit up front, man. You're not under arrest or anything. It's just a policy."

Conor had seen plenty of cop shows. He paused a moment, then asked, "Am I being detained?"

"Come on, Conor. Let's try and move quickly. We can talk on the way."

He felt his heart rate pick up again. An old couple

stood in their doorway staring. The woman had what looked like a knitted blanket wrapped around her. The man's arm rested over her shoulders. They didn't speak or move, just watched silently, smiling. Why the hell were they smiling? He knew why though. They were judging him, assuming the worst. Conor's phone vibrated against his leg, but he didn't reach for it. Just climbed into the back of the cop car. A second later, the door slammed shut behind him.

* * *

"Why'd you hang up?" Sims didn't look back at Conor as she pulled on her seatbelt.

The back of the cruiser was cold. Up front he heard the heater blowing on the officer. The seat had no cushion. It was crafted from some kind of hard plastic. There was a plexiglass window between him and her, and no handles on the inside of the doors. Conor Mitchell was locked in. He was a prisoner.

Sims killed the overhead lights, brought the car to life, and flipped a U-turn.

He considered asking again if he was being detained, then thought it better not to rattle the cage. He had gotten into the car voluntarily. But what would have happened if he hadn't agreed to get in? But the other cop had left her alone with him. That had to mean he wasn't a suspect. A suspect to what, though? For all the police knew, no crime had really been committed.

He brought his phone out of his pocket, looked at the screen.

Missed call from: John.

"I don't know," he responded.

"Gonna have to speak up. Take a right up here?"

"Yeah." He raised his voice. "I don't really know why I hung up. I was freaking out, I guess."

"Fair enough. Hey, Conor? You're sure it was Percly Valentine you saw?"

"Yeah. I'm sure. I've seen the guy enough around town to recognize him."

"Cool. Just making sure. And you have no idea who the girl was?"

"No."

"But you know her age?"

He looked up into the rear-view mirror and saw her almond shaped eyes staring into his. They gave the impression that she wasn't just fishing for details about what he had seen. "What? No. I don't know her age. I just said she looked like a teenager. She was young."

His phone buzzed again as the car turned onto Highway Twenty. The sun was beginning to come up, and the fog had cleared a bit.

"You can get that if you want," she said as casually as if he weren't locked in the back of her car.

"Yeah, I should probably, ah—" He answered the phone, pressing the speaker button so she could hear that he had nothing to hide.

"Conman?"

"Yeah. What's up, John?"

"Jumpin' in the car right now, bud. I should be at the shop just in time ta open up. Everything cool?"

"Yeah. I shouldn't be too much longer. Just gotta—"

Sims spoke some numbers into her radio, and said something about being en-route. A reply came almost instantly, but he couldn't make out what was said.

"Jesus." John shrieked. "Are you in a fuckin cop car?"

"Yeah," Conor answered.

"Son-of-a-bitch. Are you cracked?"

"What?"

"In trouble, man. Are you in trouble for something?"

In spite of everything, Conor had to suppress a laugh.

"If I were in trouble, I don't think I'd be calling you from my cell right now. Well, not my cell *phone*."

"Tell him not to talk on the phone and drive," Sims called over her shoulder.

"Who the hell is that?"

"Officer Sims," Conor replied.

There was silence for a moment, then John said, "Let 'er know I'll be sure an not do that. Listen Conor, you sure everything's okay? Yer not in any kind a trouble?"

"Not in trouble. I just need to answer some questions about the accident. Look, I should be in soon, so—"

"Don't worry about it, man. Take the day off. We can manage without'cha."

"No. I think I wanna come in."

"Okay, bud. But if ya can't make it, it's no problem." The sound of John's car coming to life rang from the speaker.

"You just want the hours," Conor said.

"Fuck." John retorted. "I'm going in to work off the clock. Fuck the hours. I gotta get away from the woman before I end up in that car with you."

Conor laughed. "Go ahead and clock in, John. I gotta let you go. Talk to you soon."

"'Kay, man. Sounds good. Keep me posted, you understand?"

"No problem. I really have to go, though."

"'Kay. Bye."

"Later." Conor hung up. "Right up here." He raised his finger and tapped the plexiglass, pointing at where the accident had happened. "On the left."

"There?" Sims pointed. The fog was still thick, but the emerging sun provided a slightly better view than when Conor had last been here. There were no police cars in sight.

"Yeah."

Sims leaned forward in her seat, as the car slowed down. Conor took note of the pink band, holding her ponytail in place. Then he squinted, bracing himself for what he was about to see. The fog, however, hovered low, concealing the patch of cement where he knew the girl lay. The Sedrow Woolley Police cruiser passed on the left, going the opposite direction.

"Turn around," Conor said.

"You sure?"

"I'm sure. You passed it."

Sims flipped another U-turn, and he told her where to pull over. She parked a short distance back and stepped out of the car. He watched as she walked away from the headlights, disappearing into the fog.

Everything that he had felt all morning came flooding back, filled his stomach. The sense of unease. The irrational fear. Even the dream of Benji staring from the ceiling like a spider while he slept.

*This is it. You're going to jail now. As soon as she sees what you did, she'll come back and put you in handcuffs.*

Conor felt he was going to vomit. His hand touched a hard surface and he became aware that he had unconsciously reached for the door handle which didn't exist. Not knowing what else to do, he pressed a button on his phone, bringing the screen to life. He opened his texts and found the last message that he had received from Shelby.

Almost there. 20 min :-)

He selected it and pressed "send."

The seat began to sink under him. He willed himself not to vomit as the phone rang. He had hit that poor girl, then just drove away. It didn't even matter that Percly pointed a gun at him. How could he prove it? Even if there was a camera nearby, there was no way it had picked up a clear image through the fog.

"Hey, handsome." Shelby's voice appeared in his ear. He could hear the smile on her lips.

"Hey, ah—" He felt a tornado tearing up the inside of his abdomen. "Something happened and I was in an accident."

At first she didn't respond. Then, "What?"

"An accident. I hit a girl." He took note of how fast he was speaking. "On the highway. She just came out of nowhere and I tried to turn, but I hit her. Then, uh, well somebody shot her."

"Hold on, hon. Slow down. Benji! Stop! You hit someone, then... Wait... *What?*"

"Somebody fucking *shot* her. I'm in the back of a police car, Shelby."

"What? Not funny, dude."

"You think I don't know that? I'm not joking. I'm in a fucking cop car."

"Are you in trouble?"

"I don't think so. I don't know."

"Okay. Are the cops there with you right now?"

"Uh-uh. She's outside the car. I just thought I'd let you know—"

"Dude, someone shot somebody?"

"Yeah."

"Where?"

Conor's imagination went wild with images of the teenage girl's head exploding, as a bullet destroyed her skull. Of thick blood decorating the top portion of her pink sweeter like some experimental designer brand. "I don't know. I didn't see." Then realizing she wasn't asking where on her body the girl had been shot, he said, "On the highway. Just up the street from the house."

"*What?* Benji! Fuck off! I'm coming right now, hon. How far up the highway?"

"No, no, no, no. Don't come here. Just chill.

Everything's all right." He didn't believe his own words and knew there was no way she did either.

"Fuck, Conor. Why would somebody shoot someone? That's whack, dude. Why would you hit someone with your car?"

"It was an accident, I told you. She was walking in the middle of the street and the fucking fog—and the roundabout—Jesus, she was just—"

"Okay, okay, okay. I get it. Just listen to me, Conor, okay? Are you in handcuffs right now?" It was a stupid question. How would he be calling her in handcuffs? But it only took him a second to realize that it was rhetorical.

"No," he answered anyway.

"Benji! Dude! Go away! Right now! This fucking dog is crazy. All right. Listen, hon. If it sounds like they're trying to accuse you of anything, don't answer their questions. You tell them you want a lawyer. Do you hear me? Don't answer anything."

"I didn't do anything though."

"I know that, sweetie. I know that and you know that. But they don't. They'll try and trick you up with questions to get you to confess to something you didn't even do. That's how cops work."

"No. I don't know—"

"Conor. Listen. To. Me. Remember Cody?"

"You mean that guy who went to jail for DUI?"

"My *friend*." She emphasized the word. "Who went to jail for vehicular assault. And it was an accident."

"He was drunk." Conor heard his own voice come out as a whiny shriek, and fought to get it back under control. "Jesus."

"It doesn't matter, sweetie. It was still an accident. And you know what? They still locked him up. In prison, not jail."

He opened his mouth to object, knowing that she was

wrong, but not knowing how, or what to say. The words were right there, in the back of his throat, but what were they? His tongue even moved, eager to form them. Then he let out a breath and deflated in his seat.

Sims appeared through the fog, walking purposefully toward the car. The Sedrow Woolley cruiser pulled up next to it, and the nausea returned.

"I have to go."

"Wait. Hon. Promise me."

"Shelby, I have to hang up now."

"Are you listening? Conor, promise me if they start asking too many questions, you'll ask for a lawyer. I don't wanna lose you. Don't fall for their bullshit."

Something stirred in his chest, travelled up his neck like a volcano, threatening to spill out of his eyes. He blinked it back and said, "Okay. Yeah."

"I *love* you." It was almost a question, but she still said it. It was in the open now. Vulnerable. Not just that, but it was exactly what he had thought he wanted, yet now he had no clue what to do with it. He hung up and put the phone in his pocket.

Sims walked between the two cars, stopping outside of Conor's door. She opened it and looked down at him. At first nobody spoke and the moment seemed like it would go on forever. Conor wasn't sure how long he could take it. He considered just sticking his wrists outside of the car to be cuffed. Then she broke the silence. "Why don't you go ahead and step out, Conor."

He heard the other vehicle's door open, then close a second later. His legs were weak as he climbed out into the cold. The cop walked over and stood next to Sims.

"Can you show us?" she asked.

"Show you what?"

She tilted her head, squinted as if trying to read something complex on his face. "Conor, can show us exactly where it happened?"

Something came over Conor that he had never experienced before. A terrible chill, like a million tiny spiders crawling out the top of his head and scurrying down, down, down, stopping in his gut to nest. It wasn't so much what he knew he was about to discover, but the fact that he had already suspected it somewhere in the part of the mind that entertains impossible ideas. And that's exactly what it was. It was as ridiculous a notion as dogs walking upside-down on the ceiling. He was dreaming again. He had to be. He considered pinching his own arm, but found himself instead pointing, almost involuntarily to the spot where the girl had to be, but he knew she wasn't.

"Right there." Then his feet were in motion. He didn't have to look back to know that both cops were exchanging glances behind him, or to know that they would follow.

With every step the path ahead cleared a few more feet until it came into view. The place where the girl had to have been crushed between his car and the sidewalk. Where Percly had shot her. Had to have. There was no other version of the truth that was acceptable.

*So where is she? Where's the mess? The blood?*

Conor stopped, looked down at the green paint where the Buick had scraped the curb. Sims and the other officer stopped on either side of him. For a moment nobody spoke. Then Sims said, "There's nothing here, Conor."

"I don't know," Conor's voice shook. "This is where it happened. It was right there." He pointed to the paint.

"And you're sure there was a girl?" the male officer asked.

"I'm sure." Conor nodded. He should have felt relieved. No girl meant that nobody was hurt. No crime had been committed. Nobody would be going to jail. But there was no relief. He wasn't crazy. He knew what he had seen, and somebody *needed* to go to jail. Somebody had shot a teenage girl in the middle of the street.

*And somebody else ran her over, didn't he?*

"Conor," Sims spoke softly. "Is there any chance you may have mistook what you saw? I mean the fog's been a real pain in the rear lately for drivers. Hell, just the other day we had an accident out on Blackburn. Girl on her way to school drove right off the road and into a ditch."

"No," Conor said. "I know what I saw."

"Gotcha. Then let me ask you again, just to be sure. You were driving thirty-five—"

"Thirty," he said.

"Why don't you relax, champ," the Sedrow Woolley officer cut in.

"It's okay," Sims flashed him a look that was clearly meant to back him off. Then back to Conor. "You're doing fine, man. I just have to ask one more time, or I wouldn't be doing my job. So you were going thirty miles-an-hour, and a teenage girl in a pink sweater was walking in the middle of the road. Tell me again what happened after that."

Conor took a deep breath, let it out slowly. "I tried to swerve out of the way. My car fishtailed and the back end of the passenger side hit her. She fell to the road between my car and the—" He took another breath and pointed to the curb. "See that paint? That's where it hit."

Sims nodded, examining the curb. "And you're positive the girl was between your car and the sidewalk?"

"How could you be, if you didn't see her after the crash?" the other cop asked.

"Because," Conor tried to keep his cool. "I saw Percly Valentine. He walked up from right there," he pointed, "and shot between my car and the curb."

"How many shots?" Sims asked.

"Three. I told you. Three. He fired three shots from a huge revolver. I think it was a forty-four."

"You know a lot about guns?" the male cop asked.

Before Conor could answer, Sims cut in. "You're a smart guy, Conor. I can tell. But you gotta level with me, man. There's nothing here. No body. No blood. There's really no reason to believe anybody was shot. I'm sure there was a girl, and you probably did hit her—"

"Why would I lie?"

"I don't think you would. But that doesn't mean you couldn't have mistaken what you saw. It happens all the time in high stress situations like car accidents. The mind just doesn't have time to process everything that's going on, and things get all mixed up. Normally I'd just take your statement and sort through it all later, but you're talking about a potential murder here. You have to understand how serious that is."

Conor opened his mouth to tell her that it seemed like he was the only one who *did* understand. That she, and the other cop didn't get it because they hadn't been there, hadn't seen the determination in the homeless man's walk, the cold look on his face as he pulled the trigger. But before he could form the words, she touched his arm for the second time that morning.

"Look, Conor, we'll get somebody out here to check everything out. Make sure there's no traces of blood, see if any cameras caught anything. But in the meantime, would you mind coming to the station with me?"

"Am I in some kind of trouble?"

"Not at all." A girlishness, which he hadn't notice before was accentuated as she looked up into his face. "I just need you to put your story in writing. Shouldn't take more than a few minutes."

"Yeah," Conor responded. "Yeah, I can do that, no problem." He glanced at the sidewalk again, then back at her. "I'll just follow you?"

She smiled. "We'll take my car."

"What about mine?"

"You think anyone's gonna steal that thing?"

Conor shook his head.

"It should be fine, but if it gets towed, I'll have it out before you even knew it was gone."

Conor tried his best to return her smile, feeling only half of his face comply.

"Awesome!" Sims finally removed her hand from his arm. "Back to the car, then. You can go ahead and sit up front."

* * *

Daryle was hungry.

There was no denying that his forty-six years on the planet had been what some would call strange. Once, as a young man with no clear career path in sight, he had spent close to a year living in an alley in South Park. He had lost more than forty pounds, and hardly moved until Mom had come, took him by the hand, and led him home. Technical School had not only been her idea, but her treat shortly after. However, not even during that year of slothing, had he been this hungry.

It had little, if anything, to do with the fact that he had just spent the night treading down Anderson Mountain, where Andy had left him days ago. He had felt it the second he woke up in the earth. In fact it was the hunger which had awoken him, stirred him to dig his way out and walk the countless miles down the mountain, along Highway Nine, and finally onto Highway Twenty.

Though he didn't feel it, he was aware that it was cold out. His breath didn't make fog the way another man's might, because it came out of his body the same temperature as the world around him. Daryle's steps hadn't slowed a beat since last night, when he had crawled out of the dirt and began his journey. Before turning onto the Twenty, only six vehicles had passed him all night. None had stopped, or even slowed down. He reached up and straightened his white FAIRFAX hat. The sun was just beginning to shine timidly through the grey clouds.

The highway was mostly empty, but a couple small stores had begun to open for business. Daryle had considered walking into K.C.'s Auto Glass, to alleviate his hunger, then decided that it would be better to wait. Daryle Colombo had never eaten another person before, but it didn't take a masters from ITT Tech to figure out that the best way to go about something like that would be very sneakily.

Andy's house was just a few more miles anyway. If he didn't find food on the way, the boy would feed him. He didn't know, nor did he care how he knew this. It was irrelevant. All that mattered was finding Andy and eating—and not necessarily in that order.

So Daryle continued to walk. His right hand was balled into a fist, the blade of his camouflage handled knife sticking out the top. He had folded and put it into his pocket multiple times throughout the night, but kept looking down to find it back in his hand.

Yeah, something was different. *He* was different. It didn't escape his notice. However, the thought evoked no more attention than a twig, floating down the Colorado River. It passed quickly and naturally. Folding the knife once more, he let it drop into his pocket where it landed hard on top of his keys.

The fog was thick, had been every night since he arrived in Sedrow Woolley. He noticed, but it had no effect on him today. Daryle could see perfectly through it. He had seen perfectly all night, even in the pitch dark woods. In fact, he could see further and more clearly then he had ever been capable of. That's how he saw the two police cars and heard the voices up ahead. His first thought was obvious. It was only the natural order of things.

*Food.*

He could probably lure one of them away, or even find his way into the back of one of the cop cars. That wouldn't be too difficult. Men of much lesser intellect were able to do it every day. It didn't even matter that he would be handcuffed if he went that route. He could easily slip out of them, maybe even break them.

But would he be able to eat without leaving evidence? Not the mess—that would be cleaned up, of course. But any indication that he had been around when somebody disappeared. If he were still who he used to be, he might have searched his memory for everything that he knew from TV about police investigations. His thoughts didn't work that way anymore, though. As he came closer, (not close enough to be seen), he heard their voices.

"There's nothing here, Conor." A woman said. An attractive woman, by the way she spoke.

"I don't know." The voice of a younger man responded. It was weak and afraid. Vulnerable. The hunger cried out and Daryle wasn't sure he could take it much longer. "This is where it happened. It was right here."

Lights flashed from atop both cars, which were parked in the street. The people were on the other side of them. Daryle wasn't able to get a good view of them through the cars. Only days ago, he wouldn't have been able to hear them either. They were too far away. Like his sight, however, his hearing had improved.

Then there was another voice, one that caused him to stop walking for the first time in hours. "And you're sure there was a girl?" It was different. Familiar. Before, he would have considered it alien. It was the voice of the boy, standing over him as he dropped dirt into his grave.

*Come home soon, Daryle. You know where to find me.*

It was the voice that, at the time, he had associated with the buzzing of a fly, or somebody whispering though a fan. The voice of an insect.

"I'm sure," the young man said.

The woman told him about an accident that had happened because of the fog. She assured him that she knew he wasn't lying. She was though. Daryle was able to read her tone like a schematic. The scared, weak little treat of a man spoke again and Daryle grew hungrier with every word. He once again began to walk toward them.

Then all three of them came into view. A cop, a tall man, and somebody—no, something—else. Something that looked almost how Andy had looked in the woods. Only bigger, standing upright and addressing the other two as if it were no different than them. And like Daryle, it had once been one of them. A young cop. He saw it not only how it now was, but how it used to be, simultaneously.

Daryle wasn't a stupid man, never had been. He knew that the people were clueless. He also knew that if he were to look into a mirror, he would see something very similar staring back. An instant sense of comfort fell over him. Suddenly, the hunger was nothing compared to the longing that he felt just to speak with it. He picked up his pace.

But the other turned—not completely, it was a subtle shift of the neck—and his huge, black eyes met Daryle's. His teeth were curved into a giant smile. He didn't have to speak. His body language communicated more than any words Daryle had ever entertained.

*Stay put.*

Daryle stopped walking. He stood just outside of the people's visibility, paying little attention to what they said. Soon, they all got into vehicles and left. Only then did he resume walking, noticing that the knife was once again in his hand, blade open. He folded it and stuck it into his pocket.

Andy's house was close. The sun was emerging more with every minute that passed. Maybe something to eat would meander out for a morning stroll. In spite of his hunger, Daryle had a feeling that today was going to be a good day. He found himself singing along with the song which was still playing in his head.

"I'm on a highway to hell—"

# Chapter Three

Conor couldn't help but glance periodically at the laptop that sat open between he and Sims. He wondered if he was supposed to be able to see it. It announced something about a traffic stop on Woodchuck Lane. Every so often, a voice would come through her radio, speaking in cop code, which he didn't even begin to understand. He had made his statement short.

*At 6:30 AM on 9/17/2019 I was driving on highway 20 in Sedrow Woolley. It was very foggy and I thought I saw a teenage girl on the road. I swerved out of the way and my car hit her and the curb.*

*I thought I saw Percly Valentine fire a gun at the girl and I was afraid so I drove up the street and called 911.*

He hadn't originally intended to write about Percly. Not because he wanted to protect the man, but because he was beginning to doubt what he thought he saw. Then Sims had read the statement and asked him to elaborate, so he had added the second paragraph. He guessed that solidified it. If he was delusional, it was on record now.

He had expected to be put in some kind of cold holding cell, but instead Sims led him into a warm, carpeted room with a rectangular table and three chairs. There were no chains, no handcuffs, and no locked doors. The only indication that he was even in a police station was the mirror, which he guessed was a two-way.

She had left the room while he wrote, then returned and left again for him to write the rest. That had all been at the city department.

"You guys share the station with the city police?" he asked from where he now sat, once again in her passenger seat, feeling the need to make conversation, mostly to stay out of his own head.

"Ah, no. We have our own office. Well, we have our own—what do you call those classes they put on the sides of schools?"

"Portables?"

"Portables!" She laughed. "We have a small precinct in one of those things up river. You wouldn't even know it was a police station, really. Only reason I was called along with the city boys was because you reported a shooting on the highway. I figured we could just get your statement at their station, though. Easier than dragging you all the way into Lyman."

The day was as bright as it was going to get. The fog had cleared up. It was already nine, and he found himself wondering how so much time had passed. Once she finally returned him to his own car, he could be at work within a half-hour, but wasn't sure he would stay.

"Makes sense," he replied.

Sims's eyes were bright as she looked briefly at him, then returned her gaze to the road. The highway had filled with Sunday morning churchgoers. Though Sedrow Woolley seemed to have a church on just about every street, Conor had seldom been inside of one. His Dad was the kind of religious man who took his family to church for weddings and baptisms, and said prayers before meals on holidays. Conor had often watched him curse as he wadded up envelopes that came in the mail from the church, reminding the family that the only Roman Catholic Parrish in the county was two towns over in Mount Vernon.

"You going in today?" Sims asked casually.

He flashed her a questioning look.

"Sorry." She seemed to repress a smile. "I just heard you tell your friend you'd be at work later."

"Oh." He forced a smile of his own. "No problem. Yeah, I think I'll be going in."

"Well, can I make a suggestion?"

"I don't see why not."

"I mean, do you need the money? Is that why you wanna go in?"

Conor sensed that Sims didn't miss much, and she had a pretty good idea of what was going on in the madhouse that was his mind this morning. "I don't—well, not particularly."

"I thought I heard you mention a shop Mechanic?"

He nodded. "Yeah."

"Really? My Dad was most of his life. Still is. You know Kyle's?"

"Kyle's Tires?"

"Yeah! Right there in Burlington. Surprised you know it. It's such a teeny little place. Yeah, that's where he's working right now. Needless to say, I didn't have a college fund put aside."

He wondered briefly if college was a requirement to become a cop. He thought about asking, then told her instead that he had applied at Kyle's Tires once.

"Really? My Dad's been manager there for a few

years now. He probably did your interview."

"Big beard? Bald on top?"

She burst out laughing. "Decade old coveralls? That's him! He wasn't rude to you, was he?"

"No." Her laugh was contagious, and he couldn't help but return it. "Not at all. Actually he tried to hire me."

"Wow. I've seen the breed who work there. Bunch of hillbillies, just like him. You must've made quite an impression."

"Yeah, I guess. It probably doesn't hurt that I went to school. You don't see that too much in shops."

Outside the car, a teenage couple walked hand-in-hand on the sidewalk. They had already passed the place where Conor had apparently hallucinated being an accessory to murder. A couple blocks up, was Bradshaw, where he had left the Buick.

"College?" she asked.

"College."

"Okay." She nodded approvingly. "Auto Mechanics?"

"Basically. Heavy Duty Diesel Mechanic."

"Wow. Impressive. I take it my Dad's boss wasn't gonna pay you enough then?"

"Correct."

"Yup. Story of his life. Where'd you end up?"

"Skagit Brake and Muffler. Over in Mount Vernon."

"Nice. Benys and all?"

"Benefits? Uh, yeah. Now that I'm weekend manager, at least."

Another dramatic nod. "Not bad at all for your age, man." The words didn't seem to flow naturally from her mouth. Probably because Conor was sure that she wasn't much older than him. She turned onto Bradshaw, and gravel crunched under the tires. "Well, it is the weekend and all, but think they could get by without you for a day?"

His first thought was that he was being hit on. "Well, I don't ah—"

"I was just thinking," she interrupted, "that you might consider taking the day off, man. You've had a crazy flipping morning and it wouldn't be the worst idea to just try and relax. Set your mind at ease, you know?"

"Yeah. I guess. Maybe. I'll have to think about it."

"Really, man. You may not know it, but your mind and body'll be grateful to you for looking out for them. And just for the record, I don't think you're crazy."

Of course she did. *He* thought he was crazy.

She pulled up behind the Buick and put her car in park. "I'm serious. Even if we don't find any evidence that you hit a girl, I wasn't B.S.ing you, Conor. Sometimes memories get all mixed up in crazy situations. Happens all the time in accidents. And I believe Mr. Valentine *does* have a gun. Doesn't surprise me a bit to tell you the truth. I've been meaning to do something about that guy sleeping in the town center for a while now. Only reason I haven't, is because the city boys leave him alone for some reason."

Conor unlatched his seatbelt. He didn't move to get out of the car, though, and Sims looked into his eyes.

"Take the day off, Conor. Trust me. Go home. Relax. Spend it with your girlfriend. The last thing you want is to go in and get hurt because you're not focussed. Here —" She reached into the breast pocket of her uniform and produced a small, white card. "It's the number to the precinct and my cell. If you remember anything else, or you just need to talk, don't hesitate. And if you see Mr. Valentine anywhere, keep your distance and call nine-one-one immediately. Cool?"

He heard everything she said, yet only processed two words.

*Your girlfriend.*

He was sure he hadn't told her about Shelby. Was she just fishing? *Was* she hitting on him? He told her that he would call if he saw Percly, then offered his hand. When she took it, all perceived girlishness vanished—crushed by her firm grip.

He stepped out, looking around at the houses, thankful that nobody was outside. It had been bad enough, people seeing him put into the back of a cop car and taken away. He expected Sims to pull out before he reached his vehicle. She didn't, though. When he was at the door he turned and looked one last time to see her watching him, presumably making sure the car started. She didn't know the Buick. It had belonged to his Grandfather. Conor had got it when he passed, and the bitch was loyal.

He nodded. She waved as he climbed into the seat, put his key in the ignition. He looked in the rear-view, seeing the cruiser finally in motion. It passed on his left, disappearing in seconds. Conor didn't wait for the Buick to warm up. He put it in drive, turned around, and headed back toward the highway.

He had already made up his mind. He wouldn't be going in to work today. Not at all. The cop was right. Too much had happened. He needed to think. Or maybe not to think. To clear his mind. Relax. Regroup. He needed to not stew on the bizarre morning that he had had. Most of all, he needed Shelby.

It didn't escape his notice that he was exhibiting co-dependent behavior. And all of a sudden? Why now? His nerves (and possibly his mind) were going crazy. As he turned onto the highway, he began to make plans to throw her onto his bed the second he walked in the door, mess up another set of sheets. He shook the thought off though. There was something that would have to be dealt with first, and he knew it.

She told him she loved him.

And he hung up on her. All the times he had gone in circles in his head, trying to conceptualize how he felt about Shelby Metcalf, and he hadn't had one word to offer in exchange for her love. Did he love her? He had *made* love to her in the shower—even let her leave a fucking dog at his house. Of course he loved her. He loved her in some way that made little-to-no sense even to him, and that's why he had choked. Why he had hung up.

Coming up on his left was the terrible spot. The place where reality had become a blur, and Conor no longer knew what was real and what wasn't. He couldn't get a good look anymore, through the heavy traffic. Sims said she would get somebody to test for traces of blood. Had that been done already?

That's when reality began to knock again, asking to be let back into focus, and a wave of adrenalin surged through Conor's body. He squeezed the wheel almost automatically, letting out a long breath.

*Blood. Fucking blood.*

Why hadn't he thought of it earlier? Why hadn't the police? If he had crushed the girl between his car and the curb, if Percly had even shot her next to his car, then there should be blood on the Buick. Maybe the transient *had* somehow cleaned up the sidewalk, but there was no way he could have known where the Buick was parked.

HONK! HONK!

Conor looked in his rear-view and saw a black SUV riding his tail. He glanced down at the speedometer, saw that he had slowed down to thirty. Waving his hand apologetically, he picked up his speed, looking for a place to pull over. He had already passed K.C.'s. Up ahead, on the left, was First Vineyard Presbyterian Church. Conor didn't know what time services started, but First Vineyard seemed to be the most popular church in town. The parking lot was only half full right now. His place was just a few minutes away, though. He decided to wait and look there.

* * *

Lori Sims yawned as the light at the edge of town turned green. She stepped on the gas, lightly at first, then let the cruiser pick up speed. The limit on the highway would turn to fifty-five in a couple minutes and she would make it to the precinct before 9:30am. She decided she would take an early lunch.

Thankfully, the call from Cranston had come in after Conor Mitchell was out of her car. She had silently been praying that it would, sure of what would be said, and not wanting Mitchell to hear.

There was no blood. No camera footage. No reason to believe that he had hit a girl, let alone that somebody had been shot. She had still collected as much information as she could about the kid, however, including where he worked and his license plate number.

Now all that was left to do was to bring Valentine in for questioning. The city boys had let that transient rot the town for long enough. It didn't matter if he hadn't shot anybody. The fact that people were afraid of him to the point of thinking that he had, was the last straw.

She knew exactly when and where to find him, too, and she just happened to work the right shift to do it. Tomorrow morning she would go to the locomotive. She would wake him up, cuff him, and bring him in. She would charge him for loitering, trespassing—for any and everything she could or even couldn't make stick. He would be booked and released before he even had a warm meal in the county, but it would allow her the opportunity to give the dirty SOB the incentive he would need to pack up and move out of the town center. Hopefully leave Sedrow altogether.

Outside of town, Highway Twenty was barren of just about everything but trees. There was no slow transition from civilization, into no-man's-land either. Once she passed the light, then the last gas station on her right, the cruiser was instantly surrounded by forest. They always seemed to reach for each other over the road, giving the impression of driving through a conifer tunnel. Today, however, was grey, rather than green, with a smooth layer of clouds spread across the entire sky. It looked like it might even sprinkle later.

Her radio buzzed about a possible shoplifter at the Food Outlet. Had she wanted, she could respond. The outlet was located on the highway, which was sheriff jurisdiction. It was also, however, inside of city limits, and the city boys could deal with taking teenagers to juvie for stealing cigarettes.

She had only responded to the call this morning because she was in the area and dispatcher had mentioned a possible murder. She guessed the boys could probably use another gun, and Lori was very good with her gun.

All in all, it hadn't been a terrible morning. The Mitchell kid was nice. He was the same age as Harris. She had meant to ask him if they had attended Sedrow Woolley High together, but forgot.

His statement hadn't been necessary. Not pertaining to the accident at least. That just amounted to an insurance claim, not a police investigation. She did, however, need it for another reason. It gave her probable cause to look for Valentine without anybody crying about illegal arrests or racial profiling.

She slowed down, took a corner at twenty five. A dark green pickup, pulling a trailer full of equipment, passed on her left coming down river. A John Deer hat rested atop the driver's head. Lori waved with her fingertips, leaving both hands on the wheel. The man in the truck saluted her.

She smiled as the vehicle disappeared in her peripheral.

The precinct was positioned in a lot on the right, which people often drove by never knowing it even existed. She slowed down and turned in without using her blinker. In front of the portable, two cars identical to hers, sat side-by-side. That meant both Harris's were here, and nobody was on patrol.

She parked and got out of the car, then climbed the few steps and walked into the station. The inside always looked bigger, somehow, than the outside. The first thing anybody saw, was a service desk. Behind that, were small personal desks and a flat screen TV mounted on the far wall, which announced all the activity in the area. It was the same activity displayed on the laptops in their vehicles. The walls were light brown, giving off a country vibe that always made Lori feel at home.

Young Harris sat behind his desk, reclining in the seat and watching as she entered.

"Sup?" she said, shutting the door and walking around the service desk.

"Sup," he responded.

She looked around. "Where's the old man?"

"Out."

"Out?" She got into the office's mini-refrigerator and brought out a Pepsi. "What? He went for a walk?"

Young Harris and his Father worked most of the same shifts. Lori didn't know how they did it. If she had to work with her Dad, she would have hung herself a long time ago. Or him.

"Nah," Harris responded. "Out sick."

"Tsh." She laughed. "Hung over? His car's right out front."

"Yep. Had Janet come by'n pick him up." He took a long drink from a bottle that she hadn't noticed before, then slammed it down on the desk.

Sims blinked, just to be sure she was seeing correctly. "Jesus Christ, Phil. Is that a fucking beer?"

"Yep."

"What the hell are you thinking? Hide that thing for Christ's sake. If someone comes in—"

Phillip Harris laughed. "Nobody's coming in here, you big pussy. There's more in the fridge if you want one."

"What? No, I don't want one." Lori bent down, opened the refrigerator, and took another look. She was grateful not to find any beer inside. "Could you at least hide the fucking thing? Who's filling in for the old man, anyway?" When she looked back, the beer bottle was gone.

"Me." He smiled.

Phil wasn't an unattractive man, by any means. Plus, he was Navy, like her. A few years younger, but that hadn't stopped Lori from imagining what it would be like to manhandle the kid when he joined the force last year. Then she got to know him. That was the story of her sex life, though, and the reason she hadn't been intimate with a man in close to a year.

She smiled back, and shook her head. "Funny. Seriously though. Is it Bobbitt? Tell me now, so I can spend the rest of the day on patrol."

"Nah." Harris brought the beer out from behind the desk, and took another drink. When he was done, he opened his mouth wide. "Ahhhhh. Me, baby. I'm filling in for the old sack a dust. Filling in everything today. El Sergente, right here."

Lori looked at him unbelievingly, then at the beer, hoping he would get the message. When he didn't, she gave up. "He left you in charge? Must be going senile. So nobody's filling in yet, or what? I'll get someone in here to cover the shift." She went to her own desk and sat down, placing the Pepsi in front of her and bringing out her cell phone.

"Nope," Harris said casually. "What happened this morning?"

She opened her contacts, and began to scroll. Technically, protocol would be to call Bobbitt in, since he was a regular at the Lyman precinct, and lived just up the street. But the man was disgusting and intolerable, and his eyes never seemed to stop undressing her. She cherished the two days a week that she didn't have to work with him like a precious gem. She decided that she would call headquarters in Mount Vernon and let them decide who to send in.

"An accident," she said absently, as she found the number. "Hold on." She selected it, bringing the phone to her ear.

"Hang up," Harris said.

She looked at him, tilted her head.

"Lori, hang up the phone."

Something about the way he said her name sent a chill through her body, down her spine. Something about it, she recognized with a bit of regret, almost turned her on. His demeanour was laid back. He just sat there casually looking at her, slouching in his desk chair, legs open, beer resting in one hand. He gripped the neck with his middle and forefinger, letting it swing ever-so-slightly back and forth. Their eyes met and she was sure that he was drunk.

"Why don't you go park your car around back? You can lay down in it for a while."

"Skagit County Sheriffs," a man's voice said into her ear.

"Are you deaf, or just stupid?" Harris's bottle was no longer in sight. Lori just looked at him. She didn't speak. Was he screwing with her? Maybe he wasn't drunk. How could he be? From one beer? Maybe Old Harris wasn't out sick after all. She was merely falling victim to some sophomoric prank.

"Hey, Patrick," she said into the receiver. "I must've butt-dialled you. Sorry about that."

"Lori?"

"Yeah, absent minded and ditsy, at your service."

The man on the other end of the phone laughed. "Yeah? Men like absent minded and ditsy. So why can't you land one?"

"Eat me. I have to go."

"Fine. Don't talk to me."

"Bye, Patrick."

"M'bye then."

She hung up, then addressed Harris, forcing a laugh. She was displeased that it came out cute and girlish. "Okay. Stop playing. Where is he?"

"Who?"

She became aware that he hadn't taken his eyes off of her in an uncomfortably long time. And now she was sure that she was aroused. She didn't like it one bit. "Okay, Phil. I'm not in the mood to be fucked with. If the old man's out, and we don't get someone to cover his shift, Doss'll have both of our balls in a mason jar."

Harris burst out laughing. He laughed long and hard, then slammed the palm of his huge hand down on his desk so hard that the wood seemed to cry out. It echoed through the small precinct. Lori tensed up.

"Christ sake, woman. You sound like you're on your fucking rag."

She opened her mouth to snap on him, but as the words formed, even she heard the lack of conviction behind them. "What did you say to me?"

"Rag. Rag, rag, fucking rag." He moved his head from side to side. "Need me to say it again, or did you get it that time?"

"Know what? I don't need to put up with—"

"I will enter you," Harris interrupted her.

"Excuse me?"

He broke into another fit of laughter. Lori just stood dumbfounded, not knowing what to say or do, until finally he spoke again. "I have your attention now? Good. Here's what I need you to do then—try and relax, okay? Take some deep breaths for me. Today," he began to speak very slowly, "my old man's out. I'm covering his shift as sergeant. That means I'm in charge. El jefe. Cop-ee-tone, right fucking here. If I wanna call someone else in, that's what the fuck I'll do, understand?"

"You're drunk."

"I sure the fuck am not." He smiled. "Not even a little. Now why don't you go ahead and answer my question before I send your cute little ass home on suspension."

Lori felt her heart pound against the inside of her ribcage. She suddenly had an almost uncontrollable urge to either punch this kid in the mouth, or fuck him on his desk. Or both. "I'm outta here." Her chair slid back as she stood up. "Get some help, Harris."

"Not until you answer my question, bitch. You're not going anywhere."

"Watch it, Phillip. I've put up with a lot of shit from you and your Dad. But don't think I won't report your ass quicker than you can say 'harassment claim.'"

"Harassment claim, huh?" His face lit up, and suddenly the joke was over. His cheeks were rosy-red, protruding beneath his dish water hair. Something dark and dirty began to stir in Lori's stomach. She had to go. She had to go now. "You gonna sue me, Lori? Is that what you're gonna do? You think I don't see the way you look at me? The way you strike a pose every time you bend over to pick up a fucking pen? I don't think that's what you're gonna do at all, is it? Matter-a-fact, why don't you come on over here and sit on my lap while we talk?"

"Sleep it off, Harris!" She started toward the door, first walking, then picking up speed. Her feet seemed to have a mind of their own, and before she knew it, she was running. Sprinting. Then something caught her by the neck and she knew without looking that it was him and he wasn't drunk.

Her back slammed into the service desk and she looked up at Harris. Only it wasn't Harris. The face protruding from his uniform was horrible and lumpy. She didn't have to touch it to know that it was slimy. It was some shade of grey, or dark, dark green. It was ugly and insect-like. Huge, black eyes stared down at her. And the teeth...there were so many of them. They stretched from one side of the face to the other in a sick, twisted smile.

Sims's hands came up automatically, and wrapped around its bony wrist. She couldn't breathe. Without thinking, she released one of them, let it drop. When it came back up, it held her service pistol. Sliding the safety off with her thumb, she raised it to the monster's head. She tried to speak, to say something clever before sending it back to hell. But all that came out of her mouth was choked gargling.

As she pointed the 9 millimeter at the thing's face, another hand wrapped around hers and the gun, forcing it away. It went off, and a tiny slug slammed into the wall. Her wrist snapped as the creature bent it unnaturally, ruining the bone. Pain shot up her arm. Lori tried to scream, still only able to choke. The thing released her hand and the pistol crashed onto the floor. It stared down at her the way a hunter might eye a small animal caught in a trap. It never stopped smiling.

Then its grip loosened and Lori could breathe again. Her throat burned as she took in a long breath, then another. The thing, which still had her pinned to the desk, no longer wore Harris's clothes. They had somehow disappeared. What stood over her was unreal. It laughed. The voice was Harris's. She closed her eyes, refusing to look any longer.

"Open them," Harris said.

"No." She felt tears trying to push their way out.

"Now." The voice began to change.

"Eat me.

The thing, which couldn't be Harris but had to be him, burst into hysterical laughter, the voice morphing rapidly into something terrifying and alien. It was unlike anything she had ever heard. It was as if it spoke without a voice box. "Poor choice of words, sugar."

Every bit of courage drained from Sims's being. She squeezed her eyes as tight as she could, yet somehow felt the tears now pouring down her cheeks. "Please," she said.

"Open them, Lori."

"I don't want to."

Harris's grip once again tightened and a helpless squeal escaped her throat. Her mouth and eyes came wide open at the same time. She pulled at his wrist with her good hand, only now noticing that it was like touching a reptile.

"That's it." He stared down at her, still smiling. "Good girl." The tension released and she could breathe again. "Now get a good look at me, baby. I don't think you wanna piss me off, do you?"

Lori's breath, coming in and out shakily, made her aware that her whole body was trembling almost to the point of convulsing.

"Do you?"

So many teeth. Not huge. They were small, like human teeth, only they weren't human teeth. They were sharp, each one pointed and identical to the rest. They seemed to never stop. A thin black tongue moved behind them. She just shook her head, trying to blink back the tears.

"Good," he said. "Then I'm gonna go ahead and take my hand off of your neck. You're not gonna run, are you?"

Sims took in a shaky breath and let it out slowly.

"Lori, we'll get a lot further if we learn to understand one another. That's how relationships work. Now I'm gonna ask you questions, and you're gonna answer them. If you don't, I'm going to cause you the worst pain and suffering you've ever experienced. You're a smart girl. Use your imagination. Can you think of any ways that I could do that for you?"

"Please."

Harris didn't hesitate. He reached his free hand up to her face. Then there was pain. There was ringing, which echoed inside of her mind. She screamed and she screamed and the throbbing, which started on the side of her head, seemed to travel over her face—to wrap around the back of her skull. Harris brought his hand back, and she saw her ear, pinched between two razor sharp claws.

"Ssshhh," he said, dropping the ear and stroking her hair with his horrible hand. The fingers were long and bony—three of them in all—and each one had a claw, which couldn't have been less than two inches long. "Ssshhh, baby. Try and relax."

The pain somehow took her mind off of the panic. It was in her hand, in her wrist, shooting up toward her elbow. It was where her ear should have been.

"Now let's try again." Harris continued to stroke her hair gently. She was horrified that she found the gesture soothing. "When I take my hand off of your neck, are you gonna try and run?"

"No. No. Jesus, no. Please. Harris. I don't wanna die.

Please staaaahhhh—"

He squeezed again, then released his grip altogether. Sims's first instinct was to roll off of the desk and run. Some part her mind that trumped instinct, however, seemed to know better. She would never get away from the son-of-a-bitch. This was it. Today, she would die. The best she could do for herself was to try and make it as painless as possible. She clutched at her neck with her good hand.

Harris continued to smile. Not because he was happy or joyful, she knew, but because he had no lips. "Good," he said in his horrible insectile voice. "Now come on down and take a seat. I wanna talk about that accident."

* * *

Conor parked next to Shelby's car and got out of the Buick. Inside the house, Benji was going crazy. He walked around the front of his car for the second time that morning, bracing himself for what he would see, or maybe more for what he wouldn't see. No blood meant no girl had been crushed, no transient with a gun had went Dirty Harry on anybody, and essentially, he had hallucinated the whole thing. When he made it around, an involuntary smile crossed his lips. There was nothing. No sign of anybody having been hurt there. Only a small dent and scratched up paint.

It was official. He was losing his mind. The smile faded as he tried to remember the morning differently. If he could recall even one detail out of order, or slightly obscured, it might not pull him completely out of the rabbit-hole, but it would be a step in the direction of sanity. However, everything was the same. There was no escaping what he had seen. What he had done. Even if it hadn't been real, it was real to him and it didn't seem to be going anywhere anytime soon.

Benji continued to bark on the other side of the door. Conor turned to look at the tiny structure which currently housed his girlfriend, his dog, his entire life. As long as nobody was hurt, who gave a shit what was real and what wasn't? He would go inside, tell Shelby that he loved her too, and call the insurance agency.

Turning one last time to the Buick, he looked closer at the dent. It pressed inward at multiple angles, but the metal hadn't broken anywhere. Leaning down, he ran his fingers over it, felt the damage. When he brought his hand back, he saw one tiny piece of chipped green paint. Then he touched higher up on the car. This time, his fingertips came back covered in dust. His first thought was that he needed to clean the thing more often, take some pride in his shit. He knew the words were his stepfather's, though, and not his own.

But it only took a second for the implications of what he was seeing to sink in. He stood up straight, looking down at the dent, wondering why he hadn't noticed right away. The entire section that had hit the curb, and about a foot radius around it, seemed to have been wiped clean. He ran his whole hand over it, looking down at his palm. It *had* been wiped clean.

*Bullshit*, he thought. There was no way. How could Percly Valentine have known where he was parked? He had driven too far away before pulling over. For fuck's sake, the fog had been too thick.

And what about the neighbors? Plenty of people had watched him as he was taken away by the police. They would have seen if the transient had tampered with the car after he was gone. Somebody would have called it in.

But somebody *had* cleaned it. Not the whole car, either, but the part that just so happened to be the only thing left standing between Conor and sanity. He wondered if this was what going crazy was like. Not having proof one way or the other. Not knowing you were crazy because that would defeat the purpose. There was no escaping his next thought.

*Call it in. You have to report it.*

And what if he did? If there was no more evidence of a crime having been committed, then he *was* crazy, plain and simple. He belonged in a nuthouse, and they might just put him there. Or maybe in jail for making a false statement.

But what if there was evidence? What if they found camera footage, blood, even a body somewhere, and he didn't report it? They would come back and check his car. They would find it wiped clean, and assume that he did it. And how would he prove otherwise?

Benji continued to bark. Conor found himself wishing Shelby would just open the damn door and let him out so he could see it was him and shut up. Or maybe not. Maybe he would crawl up the wall like a fucking spider, and bark some more.

He took a deep breath, remembering almost unconsciously a conversation he had overheard as a child between his mother and a school counselor. Conor was damaged. Something to do with his biological father not being around, and it would manifest in one way or another eventually.

But why now? Twenty-two years of sanity, of levelheadedness, of good grades and responsible decision making, a kid growing up in the 21st century who had never even tried a drug, and his mind decided to run off this late in the game?

He let his breath out slowly, making his decision. He would show Shelby, let her examine the dent. If she thought it looked like it was wiped clean, he would call Sims and report it. Turning, he made his way up the porch steps. On the other side of the door, he heard Benji scratching the wood maniacally.

"Damn it." He turned the knob and slowly opened it.

The dog's head fished through the small crack and barked once. Then he saw Conor and stopped. He stuck his tongue out, breathing heavily as he wedged the rest of his body through. Forcing the door open, he ran into the yard and squatted.

Conor left it open as he entered the studio. It was like stepping into an oven. Shelby must have had the heater on full-blast since he had left. The TV was on as well, but the volume was low. When he didn't see her, his eyes travelled to the bathroom door. It was wide open. He walked over and looked in. The light was off and it was empty.

"Shelb?" He glanced at his bed. The blankets that he had put on this morning were flat. Had she gone for a walk? He looked at the counter and saw the bloody linen sitting in the hefty bag where he had left it.

Benji came back, sniffing the doorway on his way in. His tail wagged and his mouth opened, forming an expression that resembled a smile. He trotted over to where Conor stood, and looked at him.   (Are you gonna feed me? Pet me? Throw a ball?)

Ignoring him, Conor fished his phone out of his pocket and pulled up his texts.

Almost there. 20 min :-)

He pressed 'send,' and a second later, reality crumbled in just a little further as her phone vibrated from where it sat on the couch. Shelby didn't go anywhere without her phone. Not just that, but she didn't take walks, let alone along the highway. Even if she did, why wouldn't she have taken the dog? He hung up, looked at Benji. The dog just stood in front of him, continuing to wag its tail and smile. Conor's insides once again began to dance.

*No. Don't you fucking do this. Don't you go crazy. Stop it right now. You can think rationally. You just have to want to.*

But he did want to. He wasn't sure he had ever wanted anything more in his life.

Benji sat down and closed his mouth. He tilted his head, but didn't break eye contact. Conor looked away first. Walking around the dog, he closed the front door, then turned off the portable heater.

*You're not doing this. Not now. You just need to think. Think. Think. Think. Fucking think.*

He plopped down on the couch next to her phone. The screen announced one missed call from him, and six text messages. That didn't mean anything. Shelby sometimes received six texts in a minute. The screen slowly faded to black as Benji jumped up on the couch next to him. Conor tried to ignore him.

On the television, some kind of fashion gurus battered an overweight woman about her wardrobe. He picked up the remote and turned it off. Benji breathed heavily into his face.

"Stop it, Benji." He didn't look at the dog.

But the dog didn't listen, didn't even move. Conor reached over absently to pat him. Benji slowly sank, until he was laying down, his head in Conor's lap. Conor continued to stroke his fur. It was soft and thin. He felt the ridges of his spine, and wanted to pity him. Wanted to feel compassion for the thing because somebody had loved him once, then abandoned him. But he couldn't. All he could do as he patted the dog, who he was sure now that he didn't like, was entertain one irrational thought after another. Finally, he looked down.

"What did you do with her?"

Benji shifted ever-so-slightly, his body slowly going limp, and Conor knew that he was sleeping. He continued to pat him, in spite of the fact that the dog's head in his lap was beginning to make him sick to his stomach. He knew that it wasn't Benji's fault. Conor was the one losing it, not him.

Maybe it was because of Shelby. Maybe his mind wasn't ready for everything he was feeling for her. Who knew? Conor fell asleep with the dog and he dreamt again. He dreamt that Percly Valentine was outside of his house, tapping on the door with his revolver, smiling. He didn't know how he knew he was smiling, or that it was even Percly. He was on the wrong side of the door to know any of it. He knew, though.

He didn't wake up until Benji jerked in his lap, his claws scraping the cushion loudly as he jumped off the couch barking.

"Son-of-a-bitch." Conor looked around for something to tell him what time it was as the dog ran to the door. Grabbing Shelby's phone, he brought the screen to life.

10:23

He wasn't sure when he had gotten home, let alone fell asleep, but it occurred to him that he hadn't slept nearly enough this weekend. Benji continued to bark at the door. Somebody was outside.

*Shelby.* How long had she been gone? Where the hell did she even go? He sat up, and waited for his eyes to readjust to the light.

Then there was knocking and he knew right away that it wasn't her. She would have just came in. He was sure he left the door unlocked. Could it be Sims? Maybe she had discovered something new, and needed another statement. Maybe she would see the side of his car wiped clean and take him into custody.

The knocking was soft, almost a tapping, which he barely heard over the dog. The dream still fresh in his mind, he was sure for a second that Percly was outside.

He shook the thought off, stood up, and walked to the window, moving the blanket that served as a curtain and looking out. A black and white sheriff's cruiser sat parked by the goat. Benji just kept barking.

"Benji! Shut up!" He made his way to the door.

Benji flinched, ducking his head and squeezing his eyes shut the way a dog who had been abused might have. For a brief second, Conor *did* feel a hint of sympathy for the animal, who backed up a couple of steps and didn't bark again.

"Sorry." He lowered his voice, then opened the door, taking a deep breath and preparing himself for what waited outside.

"Mitchell!"

At first, he didn't speak, just stared at the person on his porch, who definitely wasn't Sims. The sheriff was male, with dishwater blond hair, and stood as tall as him. It took Conor a moment to recognize him.

"Phillip Harris?"

"Yeah! Fuck yeah. What's up, man? Haven't seen you since high school."

"No. No, it's ah—it's been a while."

"Still hittin' the books'r what?" He stuck his head inside and looked around. "Nice place you got here, man. Like a—bachelor-pad or something? Live here alone?"

Conor had talked to Phillip Harris maybe a handful of times in all the years they had gone to school together. Something about the way he spoke—like they were old friends made him uneasy. "Yeah." He said, trying not to let it show. If anybody had been hurt, it was an accident. Could he really be arrested for that? Shelby seemed to think so. But that was insane. If he did what she said, if he requested a lawyer, it would just make him look guilty.

"Nice," Phillip said. "Recon you bring a whole metric shit ton of sweet tail back here, huh?"

"I ah—I don't—So you're a cop, now?"

"Sheriff." He smiled and flexed his pectorals, causing his badge to jump.

Conor nodded. "Nice."

"Pays the bills." Phillip Harris reached into the breast pocket of his uniform, bringing out an unfiltered cigarette. "How 'bout you?"

"Mechanic, actually."

"No shit?" He spoke through gritted teeth as he cupped his hand around his face and lit the cigarette. Taking a long drag, he pulled it away from his mouth. Smoke came out as he spoke. "Thought you'd be a scientist or some shit by now."

"What can I do for you, Phillip?"

Phillip smiled. "Catch you at a bad time?"

"Uh-uh—well, maybe. Kind of. Is there something new?"

Phillip took another pull from his cigarette, and when he was done, smoke floated up in a thin stream from the cherry. He turned his head, blowing out a dense cloud, then looked back at Conor. "You mean about the girl you hit this morning?"

Conor felt the ground begin to sink beneath his feet. "So there *was* a girl?"

"Isn't that what you said? You know, in your statement?"

"Yeah. I mean—I saw her, but—"

"Relax, bud. I'm not here to haul your ass off to jail or anything. Just have a question for you. Can I come in?"

* * *

Phillip smiled as he took another drag of his cigarette, waiting for Conor to respond. He was hungry as shit. Had been since he finished with Lori back at the station. It was the same hunger that had awakened him from the earth out in Walter Murphy's woods this morning. Unlike anything he could ever remember experiencing before today.

The craving was specific. He didn't just need something to eat. He needed something in particular, and though he had only had it once, he had done a damn good job getting it.

Sure, it would have been easy to just walk into a random house, kill everybody, and eat one of them. But that's not what he had done. He had chosen like a fucking pro. Esther Murdock. She was old. She lived alone, (if you didn't count her yapping little shitzu) and her relatives didn't visit often. Phil knew, because he had dated her granddaughter, Brenda, during senior year. And Esther just so happened to live on Highway Nine, which just so happened to be on the way.

So he had walked out of the woods, moseyed up Mosher Road, taken a right onto the highway, and into her house. Not that it would have made much of a difference, but the door had even been unlocked. He would have bit her before she even woke up, but the dog had barked. It even ran out as if it could have done anything to stop him, and it died in the grip of Phil's brand new claws.

Then he walked into the room and bit Esther. Just like he knew it would, the bite paralyzed her. She had been unable to move, or even protest as he sliced her open and chowed down on her insides. She stopped breathing before he was finished. He discarded the rest of her, burying her and the dog in the woods out behind her house.

Not like he had been buried, though. Esther wouldn't be coming back up. The hunger had only returned after he laid his eggs in Lori, and buried her behind the precinct. There was a correlation between these actions. He knew before his Momma even explained it to him. He didn't know how he knew; the knowledge was just there. Not in his mind, but somehow in his being. He hadn't cared how he knew either. There wasn't much that Phillip Harris cared about anymore.

Conor Mitchell hesitated at first. He looked from Phil's eyes, down to the cigarette in his hand. "Uh, sure," he finally said. "Mind leaving the smoke outside?"

Phil brought the cigarette, pinched between his thumb and index finger, to his lips and took a long pull, causing the end to turn to ash and fall to the porch. Then he flicked it into the wet grass and blew out a cloud of smoke that expanded as it floated away. He smiled at Conor and for a second a shadow crossed Conor's face. He knew something. The same way Lori had known at the precinct. Phil braced himself in case Mitchell decided to try and run. But instead, he took a step back, inviting him in.

As Phil stepped inside, his eyes fell on a light brown dog, with medium length wavy hair. It stood on all fours, its back arched, its teeth bared. It stared at him and began to growl. Phil smiled again.

"Benji!" Conor shut the front door, and turned to the dog. "Cut it out. Stop!" He looked at Phil. "Sorry about that." He shook his head.

"No problem, man." Phil took a step toward it. "Handsome little devil, isn't he?"

The dog took a step back, lowering its front half and bracing its back legs as if ready to attack. That's what Conor Mitchell saw, at least. Phil had known instantly otherwise. He looked closer and saw something that looked exactly like him, only smaller, with a dog collar around its neck. It stood on two feet, smiling and growling like a dog, only in its true voice. He reached out and pat it on the head. It swiped at him with its clawed hand and barked like a dog without a voice box.

"Benji!" Conor yelled. "Shut the fuck up! What's your

problem, man?" He walked fearlessly to the dog, which wasn't a dog at all, and grabbed it by the collar. "Come on! You're going outside!"

Benji stopped growling, but continued to stare at Phil as Mitchell led him to the door, opened it, and shoved him out. He closed the door behind him, readdressing Phil. "Fucking dog. My girlfriend brought the thing here yesterday. Really sorry about that."

"No problem." Phil was aware that he was smiling as if amused. He wasn't amused, of course. It seemed he wasn't capable of that anymore. He hadn't felt anything aside from a desire to eat and reproduce since digging his way out of the dirt this morning. Even when he had done the deed with Lori Sims. Even though he had done it with her because he had always wanted her, he hadn't felt it the same way as before. He wanted without wanting, He felt without feeling. And though what he had just witnessed with 'Benji' was quite amusing, all that truly mattered was how it affected his agenda.

Why had the dog let Mitchell push it around? Why hadn't it eaten him yet? Or changed him? It was clearly acting territorial over the guy. That, Phil knew, was because it had been reborn as a dog—therefore had the mind of a dog—but what was it waiting for? Harris decided that he wouldn't be eating Mitchell after all. Not now, at least.

"No shit? What, from the pound?"

"No." Conor walked over to his couch. "He was a stray, I guess. Found him in the parking lot at the outlet. Get you something to drink?"

"Nah. I'm okay." Only now did Phil look around. The place appeared bigger from the outside. He would have expected more than one room. It had looked like a small house. But inside it was more like a studio, with a kitchen area, a bed, a couch, and a TV. "You said you got a girlfriend, huh?" He walked over and they both sat down on the couch. "Not bad, Mitchell."

Conor laughed. "Thanks."

"I always wondered about you, man. You know most of those science club dorks were fucking rope-suckers, right?"

Mitchell didn't respond at first. Just looked at him. Then he laughed, and Harris knew it was as phony as a wooden pony.

"Remember Blake Vanderpool?"

"Yeah," Conor replied. "I guess he's managing the business for his Dad now."

"Managing to take a banana up the tailpipe every night, is what he's doing. Married to a fucking man. You hear about it?"

"No shit?"

"Shit you not, compadre. Some nigger from Seattle. They live together in a big fucking house out on Thomas Road, where they pack each other's lunches *ever-ee-fucking-night*. Believe that shit?"

Conor seemed to consider this bit of information. "Yeah. Guess I can see it."

"All legal as a fucking beagle. Thank Obama for that shit. You, though." He reached out and patted Conor on the back. "Got yourself a chica, huh?"

"I ah—I do."

"Fucking science club." Harris shook his head.

"I never joined the science club actually," Conor said.

"No shit? I could've swore—"

"Nope. Shop."

"Right! You were a greaser, weren't you? Well that makes sense then. Personally, I always thought you would've made a hell of a running back. How come you never tried out for the team?"

Conor laughed again. "Oh, I don't know. I thought

about it."

"Shit, you could've wrestled or something. Would've at least got you some tail. Not that there was a whole lot to choose from, but they sure weren't hanging around the shop, I reckon."

"No," Conor agreed. "Not really. So ah, you said you have a question?"

"I do. Wanted to ask about that girl."

"The one from the accident?"

"So there *was* a girl, then?"

Conor's mouth hung open for a moment, as if he didn't know what to say. Harris, however, had never been so sure of his words. He didn't even have to think about them before they came out. He remained quiet, though, waiting for Conor to choke out any bit of information which might be useful.

"I'm not even sure," he said at last.

"Bullshit." Phil raised a bottle to his lips, took a drink. When he was done, he let it rest between his legs. Conor Mitchell looked questioningly at the beer, which a moment ago, hadn't existed. It had appeared multiple times throughout the morning, the same way the cigarettes kept coming from his pocket in a seemingly unlimited supply. His clothes had changed as well. During the fifteen minute drive from the Lyman precinct to Mitchell's, Phil had looked down to find himself in the suit he had worn to his brother's wedding, two years ago. He knew instinctively, however, that this was a result of how he perceived himself. It had merely taken a thought to return to the sheriff's uniform.

The beer was unintentional, but he could get rid of it just as easy. Instead, though, he held it as if it had been with him all along. Conor Mitchell seemed to buy it, concluding that he had just overlooked the bottle before. His eyes traveled up to meet Phil's, but didn't speak.

"I know if I ran someone over with my car," Phil went on. "I'd be damn well sure."

Conor opened his mouth and the front door swung open, letting the sound of highway traffic in. Both men turned as Benji stepped inside. Phil used his body language to let the dog know that he was no longer a threat. Benji seemed to understand. He came in slowly, cautiously, no longer growling, only eyeing Harris.

Conor stood up, looking hopefully at the door. Then his eyes fell on the dog. "What the hell? I could have—Benji! Outside!"

"It's okay," Phil said, smiling at the mutt. "Why don't me and him give it another go? Too damn cold for him to be stuck outside on my account. I'm not intruding, am I? You expecting someone?"

Conor walked to the door. "No. I mean, just my girl. You sure? I can't promise he'll behave."

Phil nodded, took another drink of his beer. Conor shut the door. Benji's demeanor was no longer aggressive. He stood at Conor's side, staring at Phil. When Conor came back to the couch, he followed. Then, when Conor took his seat, he jumped up, positioning himself between the two men. Conor looked like he wanted to say something, or even kick the dog off of the couch, but instead he turned his attention back to Phil.

"Anyway—you were asking about—"

"Yes, Sir. I sure was, wasn't I?" Benji didn't take his eyes off of Phil, just sat between them and stared. Phil wasn't just able to see him how he truly looked, but also what the dog projected—what Conor saw. He breathed heavily, his tongue out, his expression now harmless and indifferent. "Why don't we just take it from the top? Tell me everything that happened the way you *do* remember it."

Conor hesitated. Phil knew why.

"Don't worry about sounding crazy, Mitchell. I already got the story from Sims. It's not our job to worry about your mental health. I just need to determine if a crime was committed."

Conor shifted uncomfortably.

"Not by you," Harris went on. "By that fucking rat-basket, Valentine."

"Well the truth is," Conor said, his voice as unsure as any Phil had ever heard. "I don't think he actually shot anybody, and I don't wanna get anyone in trouble for something they didn't do."

"So you lied? On your original statement?"

"No. I think I saw it all wrong. Because of the crash. Or the stress or whatever."

"The stress, huh? Mitchell, you like boats?"

"Excuse me?"

"Boats, man. You know, floating vessels? Wood? Metal? Fibreglass?"

"I don't know. I mean —"

"'Cause it sounds to me like you don't got both oars in the water, man. You sure you're not bat-shit fucking bananas?" Before he could answer, Phil broke out laughing. "I'm just messing with you, compadre. Nah, you're all right. The stress. That's it. Happens all the time. People's memories get all foggy in accidents. Thousands a people swear they saw Jesus' face in the dust clouds on nine-eleven. Even more said they saw the devil. Hell, I black out every time I get into a brawl. But either way, if that spook's running around town with a piece, scaring the shit outta decent people, then you can bet I got something a my own for his ass. Why don't we take it from the top? Go ahead'n tell me everything, starting with the girl."

Conor just stared ahead at the black screen of his TV set. He seemed to be somewhere in his memory, and not liking what he saw. Benji didn't move, just sat between them, crouched down on his muscular legs, his seemingly endless razor sharp teeth wrapped around his head in a predatorial smile that only Phil saw. For the first time, he averted his huge black eyes from the cop and looked at Conor. A thin tongue shot out and ran over the man's cheek.

"Fuck. Benji, down." Conor shoved him off the couch. He moved quickly away and began sniffing around the house. Then Conor took a deep breath and told Harris everything that had happened that morning. He kept reiterating that he didn't know how much of it had really happened.

"Maybe I'm crazy," he said at one point, trying to laugh it off.

He wasn't crazy, though, and Harris knew it. He didn't take any notes. Not with paper and pen, at least. When Mitchell was done, he asked Harris if he wanted to see the car.

"No need," Harris responded.

He flashed a confused look. "Sure? It's no problem. It's parked right out front."

Phil took a drink from his bottle. "Aaahhhh. Positive. I believe you."

At some point, Benji had stopped sniffing. He now stood in the corner watching. Phil stood up. "Guess that'll be it, then. If you think of anything else, be sure to let me know, got it?"

"Uh, yeah. Sure thing. There a number I can reach you at?"

"Sims gave you her card, right?"

"Uh, yeah."

"Just call her phone."

A phone vibrated next to Conor on the couch. Conor picked it up and looked at the screen, trying to hide his expression. That would have been next to impossible though. Since waking up this morning, Phillip Harris had found himself so efficient at reading body language, that he was damn near psychic. Written across Mitchell's face was a strange combination of frustration and fear. Phil glanced down at the screen.

Incoming call from: Jeremy.

"Suppose I'll let myself out, then." He extended his hand to Conor, who dropped the phone, stood up, and accepted it. "Thanks again for your help."

"Yeah," Conor said absently. "No problem."

When Harris reached the door, he turned back and said, "Oh yeah. One more thing. I noticed you got three cars out there. All yours?"

"No. Just two. The Mazda's my girl's."

Phil looked around. "She here? Thought you said she's on her way."

"She went for a walk. I think."

Everything suddenly came into focus. Phil didn't know how he knew. He hadn't been changed a whole day. It was all so simple though. Benji's agenda, the reason he hadn't killed Mitchell—or changed him yet. He smiled and nodded to Conor. Then the dog. Then he let himself out and drove to his momma's house out on Cherry Lane.

* * *

The whole encounter was wrong. Conor couldn't pinpoint what it was. The way Harris talked? The way he moved? The way he smiled? He tried to remember everything he had known about him from school. There wasn't much though. Phillip Harris had always been into sports. Conor never followed the games, but he was pretty sure he had been captain of the football team. He had always been obnoxious in class. None of his crude comments had come as a surprise, nor the fact that he had been driving around, drinking in his patrol car.

But had he? Conor hadn't seen the beer before he came inside. In fact, he specifically remembered him using both hands to light his cigarette. Maybe the bottle had been in his pocket? But there was more. He was sure he didn't see it anywhere as Harris left. The cop's hands were both empty, and there were no noticeable bumps in his clothing. And no beer bottle anywhere in Conor's house.

It was just one more piece of evidence to add to the case for his newly discovered insanity. Shelby's phone buzzed again, and the screen announced a text from Jeremy.

*Who the fuck is Jeremy?*

Conor had never stooped into the ugly pool of jealousy, and still didn't intend to. He had never heard her talk about a Jeremy, though, and whoever he was, he never called while Conor was around. He considered reading the text, not snooping, but checking for any clue as to where the hell she was and if she was okay.

She wouldn't be mad if he did. He had talked to her that morning, told her about the accident. She knew he might be coming home. And wherever she was, she had left the phone anyway. There were obviously no secrets on the thing.

Still, it seemed somehow wrong to breech her privacy. Especially since she hadn't been gone long enough for him to be justifiably worried. Instead he called John and told him that he wouldn't be in after all. Then he sprawled out on his bed and stared up at the ceiling. Until Benji began to whine. Lifting his head, he saw the dog at the door. Benji paced once, then looked expectantly at Conor.

"Again?" Conor rolled out of bed, let him out, and closed the door. He had already shown that he wasn't a runner, and he was smart enough to bark when he was finished.

But Benji never did bark. It was close to a half hour later when Conor finally checked the yard and saw that the dog was gone. Just like Shelby.

# Chapter Four

All the houses on Garden of Eden Road were old. They were surrounded by pastures, which were still yellow from summer, but frozen over this time of year. They were mostly located at the end of long driveways. About a quarter of a mile ahead, was the bottom of Duke's Hill, where less than a year ago Billy Swanson had been paralyzed in a skateboarding accident. Harris took a right onto Cherry Lane.

Cherry wasn't a paved street like Garden of Eden, but the houses were all only a few years old. There were nine in all, and one of them belonged to his mother. He parked the cruiser, stepped out in a pair of Levis, and a tan T-shirt, and lit a self-rolled cigarette that he hadn't even reached for. When he was done, the red lighter vanished from his hand.

He didn't knock, just walked into the three-bedroom home. No lights or electronics were on. It was just as cold inside as it had been outside, but Phil didn't notice, just knew. In the living room was a couch, a coffee table, a Lazy boy recliner, and an entertainment center with a medium sized TV set.

His Momma sat naked—save for a pair of large, hoop earrings—in the chair crocheting what looked like a green beanie cap. Her wavy dishwater hair hung loosely over her pale shoulders. The chair rocked back and forth as she worked. Phil shut the door behind him. She looked up briefly, smiled, then returned to what she had been doing.

Phil wasn't no sicko, and he never looked at her sideways. But he would had to have been a fucking retard to not know that she was an attractive woman, and he wasn't no fucking retard neither. He returned her smile, sucked on his cigarette, and took a seat on the couch.

"You didn't say anything about dogs."

At first, she didn't respond. She finished the loop that she was working on, and slowly and dramatically set the project and hook down on one of her smooth legs. Then looking up at her son with a forced smile, she said. "Okay. What about dogs?"

"There's dogs, too."

"Well, didn't I just give birth to an honor student?"

"Fuck. Not dogs. I mean, like us. People are making them."

Celia Harris seemed to consider this for a fraction of a second before responding. "Nope."

"What do you mean, 'nope'?"

"You're wrong. Or lying."

"I ain't lying, Momma."

"Then you're wrong."

"I ain't wrong neither. I know what the fuck I saw."

Phil's Momma picked up her project and resumed crocheting.

"There's a dog," he repeated.

She just pressed her lips together in a tight smile, and rocked in her chair. Phil saw her both as she truly was, and as she projected. The projection was only the way she remembered herself. It was that way with all of them. Phil knew because she had told him. After he woke up and came out of the dirt, after he ate Esther Murdock's internal organs, after he walked the rest of the way to her, she told him why. Because she was his maker.

Not because she made him twenty-two years ago with his Dad, but because she had put her eggs in him days ago and buried him in Walter Murphy's woods. She told him everything she knew about what they now were, which wasn't much. She hadn't mentioned dogs, though.

"You think I'm stupid?"

"Sweetheart, I'm your mother."

"I saw a fucking dog. And it's changing its owners. Already changed the girl."

"Then you saw a dog. What do you want me to do about it?" She pulled the hook, and her project—which he now knew was, in fact, a beanie that she had made for his brother when he was a child—in opposite directions, causing her breasts to thrust forward.

"Nothing, I reckon. Just thought I'd tell you."

"Jesus, you sound like your Father."

"When's he coming?"

"Soon."

Phil's father, whose name also happened to be Phillip Harris, was buried shortly after he was. Celia informed him that morning he would come to them, and they would put their family back together.

"What about Janet?" he had asked of his father's wife of thirteen years.

His momma had informed him that she wouldn't be a problem anymore.

"I'm hungry," he said from where he now sat on her

living room couch.

"Then eat."

Phil didn't excuse himself as he stood up and walked into the hallway, which was even darker than the living room. He could see perfectly. The walls were covered in pictures of him and his brother. Mostly from when they were kids. One was from Daniel's wedding, though, and one was a military photo of Phil in his formal Navy clothing. There were none of his parents.

He passed the restroom on his right and stopped in front of the very next door to his left. Opening it, he stepped inside the room that had been his as a child, but now served as a guest bedroom. It was bare, with nothing but a bed with no sheets or blankets, and a nightstand with a digital clock.

Phil looked down into the bed and smiled. "Morning, Janet."

Laying spread-eagle in the dark room, her wrists and ankles handcuffed to the four bedposts, was Phillip's stepmother. She wore blue jeans and a salmon colored blouse. Multiple layers of grey duct tape were wrapped around her head, and over her mouth. It pinned her brown hair to her neck preventing her from screaming. Her eyes went wide at the sight of him and her stomach heaved up and down.

Phil had always liked Janet. Even when she stole his dad away from his momma and split what he always thought was a happy family. She still treated him and Daniel good. She let them spend as much time as they wanted over, even let them drink beer.

He wouldn't need to bite her. All that did was paralyse them so they couldn't run, and Jan wasn't going anywhere. He left the door open as he walked over and sat down on the bed. Jan pulled on the cuffs, made a noise through her nose. He guessed that she saw him how he actually looked.

He didn't waste any time as he reached down, hooking two claws into the collar of her shirt. Grasping the thin fabric, he pulled downward. It didn't tear smoothly down the middle, but ripped by her left shoulder. He took it in his other hand as well, and continued to rip until it was a shredded pink mess that he tossed to the side of the bed, leaving Janet in nothing but her jeans and a white bra. Phillip Harris wasn't no sicko, but his dad knew how to pick them.

Janet pulled harder on the cuffs, tossing her body to one side, then the other, humming louder through her nose.

"Ssshhhh." Phil began to stroke her hair. "Relax. Relax now." He intended his voice to be a whisper, but he reckoned she heard him in his new voice anyway. It had scared the living shit out of him when his momma had spoken to him in hers before she did the deed with him.

Janet stopped struggling, and her eyes met his. They were huge and terrified. Her hair was soaked in sweat. Her forehead wrinkled, and tears began to pour down her face. Phil continued to stroke her hair lightly, then ran a clawed finger down her cheek, smearing the tears.

She tried to speak, to form words in her throat, through her nose. Phil smiled wider, and she did the closest thing she could to screaming. She started to fight again as he moved the back of his hand down her face, then turned it, taking her throat gently in his three claws. She thrust her body as far away from him as the cuffs would allow.

He moved his hand slowly down the middle of her chest, then snatched her bra, ripping it off in a single pull. He had seen her tits before. Once, in the sixth grade as he passed by the bedroom and caught her changing with the door open. They had never discussed it, or how she had caught him whacking off later that same day. Some things were better left alone.

They were small, but her nipples were perky and pink. She breathed in and out deeply, an animalistic groan escaping with every exhale. Her eyes were flooded over, but she didn't try to blink the tears away, just stared up at him wide eyed. Then he went to work on her pants, unbuttoning them quickly. He didn't use the zipper, but took one side of the 'v' in each of his clawed hands, ripping them open, and exposing a pair of red lingerie panties.

Janet thrust her pelvis up, making a bridge of her body, then let it fall back onto the bed. Pulling on the cuffs, she screamed through her nose. She attempted to twist, to turn, but she wasn't going anywhere.

Phil adjusted his own body so he was directly over her. He grabbed her by the hips, pinning her down hard. His claws poked at her pale skin, but didn't penetrate the surface. "Janet, I'm gonna need you to chill the fuck out."

Her groans turned to jerking cries. The way a young child might cry when she doesn't get her way. Suddenly, she stopped struggling, just cried harder and harder. There were so many tears, she must have drank a gallon of water before his momma had taken her.

"Ssshhhh, darling." He ran the back of his hand up her belly, between her tits. "Ssshhhh. Don't be afraid. Relax for me now. Can you do that?" When she didn't answer, he said, "Jan, if you don't relax, I'm gonna have to bite you. Now my momma bit you and I don't think you liked it much, did you?"

She looked up into his eyes, and he knew that she was begging him not to exist. To kill himself, or starve to death and leave her alone.

"Her bite froze you, and you couldn't move for a long time, right? You wanna be froze again, Jan? Do you?"

Her cries grew weaker, quieter, and she shook her head vigorously, her body continuing to jerk. Puddles of tears soaked the mattress on either side of her head.

"Good, 'cause I don't wanna bite you. So you can just cool your jets, okay? Stop all that kicking and screaming. Are you gonna do that?"

Jan closed her eyes for the first time since he entered the room. She held them tight, her chest thumping up and down a few times, then she opened them again and nodded reluctantly. Phil's eyes moved down her body, watching her midsection heave with every breath. He looked at the smooth skin just below her abdomen, and above her pelvis. Then he dragged the tips of all three claws lightly down her body, starting at her clavicle, and watching tiny geese stand up over the surface of her torso.

When he reached the soft portion only inches away from her womanly part, which he hadn't seen as a boy, he stopped and slipped one claw between the panties and her skin. Her stomach sank inward, and her back arched. The sound that came from her nose was choked by wet mucus, but she almost seemed to say his name, forming the word in her throat.

Phillip.

She said it again and again as he slid the red lace down just an inch. Then he buried the razor sharp claw knuckle deep inside of her belly.

Janet's body bridged again, pressing his claw deeper into her. She screamed so loud through her nose that the high pitched noise seemed as if it came from her mouth. Her back crashed back down onto the bed, and she began to writhe back and forth. He pulled his claw out and thrust it back in, hitting the mark in spite of her moving. This time he sliced her open, dragging his claw sideways along her body, and a pool of dark blood flooded out and poured over her stomach in every direction.

Phil reached inside of her, and for a moment they looked like puppet and puppet-master— her, fighting and screaming, him, elbow-deep in her gut. When his hand re-emerged it held a ball of red mesh, some organ that he couldn't name, but looked delicious nonetheless. He stuffed the whole thing in his mouth and chewed, chewed, chewed.

Next, he pulled out a long, fleshy tube of intestine. It still connected inside of her at both ends. After swallowing what was in his mouth, he went to work on it.

His stepmother didn't die before he had finished eating. She stopped fighting, though, seeming to accept what was happening and staring up at the ceiling finally dry of tears. When he was done and her entire torso lay open—her insides completely destroyed—he cut her throat with his sharpest claw, jamming it in behind her windpipe and sawing his way out. She choked and gargled, then extinguished.

Looking back over his shoulder, he saw his momma standing in the doorway, still completely nude, a smile on her face. She entered, sat down next to him on the blood soaked bed, and put an arm around him, laying her head on his shoulder.

"Thought we were saving that for your Dad."

"I was hungry," he responded.

"I see that."

"We can get him something else."

She stroked his back lightly. "I don't see why not." For a moment there was silence, then she spoke again. "You'd better hurry then. He'll be here soon."

* * *

The hours might as well have been days. Conor waited and he waited, and Shelby didn't come back. To his relief, neither did Benji. He told himself that maybe the dog had gone to find her. It was ridiculous, but not as ridiculous as the alternative, which his mind wouldn't stop pushing on him.

*Find her? Why would he find her? He's the one who hid her.*

He considered, and reconsidered just getting into her damn phone. But what good would that do? What could he possibly find that would tell him where she was? It was close to six in the evening when he finally pulled Sims's card out of his wallet and dialed the number. The call was answered after one ring.

"Mitchell!"

"Uh, yeah. Phillip?"

"Call me Phil. What's up, man?"

Conor grew queasy. Why the hell was Harris answering her phone? His mind, which only seemed to speak with a devious smile lately, told him to hang up. What did it matter anyway? Today wasn't even real. It was just a dream, just another to add to the strange ones he had been having lately.

But his mind was a liar. He knew because that's what all crazy people had in common. Their minds lied to them. Hanging up would just cause Harris to show up at his door again, smoking, drinking—smiling.

"Yeah," he said. "I think I need to file a missing person's report."

There was the unmistakable sound of a lighter flicking on the other end of the line, then, a second later, "'Kay. Shoot."

"Excuse me?"

"You said you got a missing person, right? Let's hear it then. Who you lose, buddy?"

*Wake up you son-of-a-bitch. Wake up. Wake up. Wake up already.*

"My uh—Yeah, my girlfriend. She never showed up."

Harris let out a shrieking laugh. "Never? Dog eat her or something?"

"What?"

"You know, 'dog ate my homework.' 'Dog ate my girlfriend.'?"

"Jesus. Are you—?"

"Tsh. Never mind," Harris went on. "How long she been gone?" Conor heard a long exhalation, and imagined a thin cloud of grey smoke coming out of the sheriff.

"Since this morning."

"This morning," he said in the tone of a man who was jotting down notes. "M'kay, what time?"

Thinking a second, Conor said. "Um, I wanna say sometime around eight or—nine. But I guess it could've been—"

"You wanna say sometime?"

"I don't know," Conor replied. "Around the time you showed up, I guess. A little before that."

There was silence for a long moment, then when Harris spoke again, Conor could almost hear the smile around the words as they came out. "Mitchell, that's net even twenty-four hours. How the shit you expect me to file a report that early?"

"What? I don't know. How long do you have to wait?"

"Well, there's a minimum time before we can consider her totally missing, you understand? Damn good reason for it, too. If we just entertain every yahoo who calls in 'cause his girlfriend stands him up, you can imagine how much time our officers waste running around town with our thumbs up our asses. Have you considered the obvious answer to where she is?"

Conor didn't like this cop. Not just in the way he hadn't cared for him in high school, either. He didn't like him like he didn't like Benji. "What would that be?" he asked.

"Come on, Mitchell. You're a smart guy. Don't tell me science club's all for show. Use your damn head, man."

"Okay. How long do I have to wait?"

"Before you can file a report?"

"Yeah."

"Twenty-four hours. And that's the minimum."

"Twenty-four hours," he repeated. Great. Just long enough for somebody to be strangled, buried—God knows what else. Conor's mind flashed to the missing man and the boy on the news.

"Very good. So you figure out what time the chica left, then you go ahead and gimme a call at that time, tomorrow. If she don't come back, that is."

"Okay." He didn't know what else to say. This was wrong. He had never dealt with a missing person before, but he didn't have to, to know that this wasn't how this was supposed to go. There was more that he had thought he would tell him. That she had left her car and phone at his house. That she had school in the morning. But it was clear at this point that it would all just be filed under, 'the obvious answer to where she is.' Conor knew what Harris's answer was, but he found himself asking anyway.

"You really don't get it?" Harris responded. "Or you're fucking with me. Come on, Mitchell, don't fuck with me, man. This is serious shit. Calling in a missing person and all."

"I guess I really don't get it then." Conor heard the defeat in his own voice.

"Okay. Lemme ask you a question. She hot?"

"What? I don't see how—"

"Damn it. Don't be a fucking retard, dude. Just answer the question. Is she fine, or what?"

What was happening?

"Yeah," Conor answered because there was nothing else to do at this point. "She's a good looking girl."

"Haaaah! Not bad, Mitchell. Not bad at all. But here's the problem with fine bitches—And trust me, if anyone knows, it's me—They disappear. All the time, my man. You gotta keep 'em on a short-ass-leash."

Conor didn't speak, didn't even know what to say.

Finally, Harris went on. "Seriously, though. Come on, Conor. She's probably out giving up the kitty to some stud in a pair a shit-kickers. Why else would she leave her phone and her car at your place? She don't wanna be reached, bud."

Harris knew. Of course he knew. He had asked Conor about the car. He had even seen the phone. And he didn't seem to think there was any cause to worry. But how could he not? Conor knew then, beyond a shadow of a doubt, that he was wasting not only his breath, but his time. To try any harder with this cop would only further prove his insanity. So instead, he said goodbye and assured that he would call in the morning if Shelby didn't show up.

"Good," Harris said. "And, Mitchell?"

"Yeah?"

"Don't call no one else. I'm the best friend you have right now, understand?"

"Yeah," Conor said. He didn't understand.

"All right then. You know what? On second thought, you call either way. I wanna know when she *does* show up. If you don't call, I'll just go ahead and stop by tomorrow. How's that sound?"

"Sounds good," Conor lied.

"Good. I gotta get off the line, Mitchell. Having dinner with my folks tonight, and my Dad just showed up." Harris hung up without saying goodbye.

As the evening went on, her phone rang two more

times. Both calls were from Jeremy. There were texts too. He eventually turned it over so the screen was facing down, and set it to silent.

That night, he lay in bed with his eyes closed. Shelby had left his house key on the nightstand, so he left the door unlocked for her. He longed for sleep. It only made sense that falling asleep in a bizarre dream would wake him to reality. But his thoughts were loud. It was impossible to silence his lying, smiling mind, which didn't seem to have anything productive to say. Then, sometime after two, it finally did.

*Jeremy, genius. It's her.*

And that was it. It had to be.

Conor's heart sped up as he rolled out of bed and walked in nothing but his black boxer briefs to the couch, where her phone still sat. How the hell hadn't he figured it out before? But why? Why would she be calling from another phone instead of just coming over? Maybe something had happened to a family member. Maybe somebody had picked her up and taken her to the hospital, and she didn't have Conor's number committed to heart. She was calling her phone, hoping that he would get the hint and answer.

He picked it up realizing that somewhere in an irrational part of his mind, he almost hoped that that was the case. That somebody close to her had been hurt, hospitalized, because that meant that she was okay. His thumb was just over the button which would have brought the screen to life, when he heard scratching. His head snapped in the direction of the noise—the front door.

*Benji.*

The dog had come back.

*No,* he thought. *Not now. Go away.*

He couldn't deal with anymore impossibilities. He needed to get a hold of his girlfriend, and in turn, get a hold of his sanity. How could it be that Benji just so happened to show up right now?

*Because, genius, it's been outside watching this whole time and it knows what you're doing.*

He had to ignore it. It didn't make any sense, but neither did anything else that had happened since Benji had come into his life. If he didn't ignore it, it would find a way to stop him from contacting her. He, and the dog who walked upside down on ceilings, were engaged in a sick game that he didn't yet understand.

He pressed the button, and the phone lit up. Squinting into the light, he read the screen. Twelve texts, and five missed calls.

More scratching. Barking.

He selected to view the missed calls. There were four from Jeremy, and one from him. Benji's frantic fit grew in intensity, and the noise echoed through every dark corner in Conor's mind.

*Ignore it,* he told himself. *Don't you fucking let it in.*

But it wasn't the bark of a dog who wanted to be let inside. It was the panicked warning of a dog who sensed danger, or heard an approaching intruder.

He pulled up Jeremy's number. The area code was local. It had to be her. There was no other option.

*Except for the obvious answer.*

*"Woofwoofwoofwoofwoofwoofwoof!*

*Woof! Woowooooo!"*

Conor had never been so grateful to not have neighbors. Had he lived anywhere else, somebody would have called the cops already on the noise. Somehow, he knew who would show up if that happened. It was like Harris worked every shift and answered every call.

Benji just kept barking. He kept scratching, and Conor knew that he needed to do something.

"OKAY, DAMN IT! Fuck. Just shut the fuck up!"

Tossing the phone onto the couch, he turned toward the door. That's as far as he made it. The barking and scratching stopped immediately and something dark and dirty poured over him like water. How was this happening?

*Because, genius, it's a dream. That's how dreams work.*

He couldn't open the door. But he couldn't pick the phone back up either, couldn't make the call, because Benji knew. The dog knew what he was doing, and if he tried to call Shelby, it would bark again. It would scratch at the door and it would stop him somehow.

Conor Mitchell stood on the cold, wooden floor and it occurred to him that he wasn't going insane. He wasn't dreaming either. His mind may have been a liar, but whatever was happening was real, and he was in real trouble.

Before he had time to process anything else, the knob twisted and the door swung open, letting in the sound of a light rain. For a brief moment he entertained the idea that he would see Shelby standing on the porch. That the dog had actually fetched her and brought her back to him like she was a stick.

But Shelby wasn't there. Benji was. And though it wasn't Benji, he knew that it was. What stood on his front porch, water dripping from its lumpy body, was something that only should have existed in nightmares. It walked in on two muscular legs, looking right at him. It was the same size as Benji, and it was smiling. Its movements weren't right. Somehow they weren't right in the same way that Harris's words and mannerisms hadn't been right. They were unnatural in a way that he couldn't even begin to conceptualize. Its legs curved sharply and it took big steps that brought to mind thoughts of a tiny T-Rex. Then his next thought overshadowed everything else.

*It's gonna kill you.*

"No," Conor said, because he didn't know what else to do. He backed up until the backs of his knees met the couch, then he fell, landing softly on the cushion.

It opened its mouth and released a bark that was just as wrong as its movements. It was a buzzing—like a whisper, only loud. That's not what caught his attention though. The teeth. He had never seen so many in one place. They were all pointed. They curved from one side of its head to the other like a horrible crescent moon. Suddenly he knew what it was about Benji's smile that he didn't like.

"Oh holy shit."

It turned around and shut the door and Conor saw the claws. Three of them. They clicked against the wood, scraping as the latch caught. When it turned back, he looked directly into its eyes and all he could think was, *God please help me.*

Big eyes, perfectly round, perfectly black. It was the combination of them and the smiling teeth, which wanted nothing more than to dig into his flesh that made them the worst eyes that he had ever looked into.

It didn't waste any time, just moved purposefully toward Conor, continuing to smile.

There was no nose. The arms were lined with lean, stringy muscle that sat beneath a thin layer of dark, bumpy skin. Conor was looking at something that appeared to be some cross between an insect and a reptile.

*Get up. Get up. Get up.*

But his body didn't want to obey. All he found himself capable of, was backing further into the couch and hyperventilating. Benji didn't stop or slow down. Within seconds he was only feet away. Only then did Conor jump to his feet and stumble over the backrest, landing on his back on the hard floor in time to see the horrible thing coming up and over. After him.

He rolled, stood up. Benji landed next to him and he heard clicking as the claw hit the wood. Its mouth opened wider than it should have been able to and came at his leg.

"No!" Conor yelled, leaping back over the couch. He landed on his side on the cushion, rolling onto the floor. Then he scrambled to his feet and backed away simultaneously, tripping on the coffee table and knocking various items onto the floor. Recovering quickly, he broke for the door.

There was clicking and scratching and he saw Benji on the wall. It crawled on all fours, somehow sticking to the wood. It scurried quickly, making it to the door first. Then it stuck there, and its head bent around impossibly. It smiled at Conor, seeming to invite him to reach for the knob.

*A grasshopper,* he thought. *The face looks like a grasshopper.*

There were sharp ridges running up its spine and all four limbs, like little spikes.

"Fuck you!" Conor yelled.

Continuing to smile, it opened its mouth again and he knew it was going to attack. Conor turned and ran for the kitchen.

*A knife. I need a fucking knife.*

Behind him, Benji's claws scratched on the floor so fast that he knew he had no chance of outrunning it. The sound conjured memories of a vacation he had taken as a boy with his family. Of turning on the light in the hotel bathroom and watching cockroaches scurry quickly into the fleeing darkness.

"Abash!" He flew forward, catching the floor with the palms of his hands just in time to keep from smashing his face into the wood. *The fucking battery.* Why hadn't he just put it in the goat? Ignoring the throbbing pain in his foot, he rolled onto his back and saw Benji coming at him on all fours, its mouth open.

He had just enough time to notice the thin black tongue in its mouth, before cocking his foot back and planting it in the thing's face. The teeth were as sharp as they looked. They cut into the bottom of his bare foot as Benji let out what should have been a high pitched whine, but instead was a clicking, buzzing noise from hell. It flew back a few feet, landing on its side, then kicking wildly as it turned over onto all fours.

Conor stood up, reached down with both hands, hoisting the heavy battery over his head. Benji charged again, and he stepped back, bringing it down as hard as he could on the ugly fucker's smiling face.

This time as it cried out, it did sound like a dog for just a second. Then it let out a long hiss. Its legs collapsed under it, and splayed out to the sides. Conor picked the battery back up, brought it down harder this time. He felt the head give underneath the weight, and dark blood splattered out in every direction.

He brought it up one more time, only it didn't make it far. The battery grew instantly heavy. His fingers released involuntarily and it dropped, landing on Benji, who now lay motionless aside from one leg, which twitched wildly.

Conor's arms fell to his sides. A new panic overtook him. Then the floor came at him rapidly, as his whole body went limp and the side of his face collided with the wood. His first thought was, *I'm paralyzed.*

But his higher senses took over and he knew there was no way. No reason that he would be paralyzed. Then he tried to stand, to move—just to wiggle a finger—and he knew. It was the bite. When he cut his foot on the thing's mouth. There was something in its saliva. Some kind of poison. And now he would die.

He wondered what position his body had landed in,

wanted to look and see. To at least be able to laugh if he had landed funny. But all he could do was breathe and stare at the wall a few feet in front of his face. Benji was somewhere behind him. Dead, he hoped.

The studio was silent. Not even the sound of a car passing on the highway made its way in, and Conor became cognizant of his heart thumping against his ribcage. He tried to control his breathing. To exhale hard. Maybe he could muster a moan.

But nothing happened. His involuntary functions were on autopilot. All there was to do now was lay and stare at the wall and wait to die.

* * *

"You hear about that chick in California?" Dale had asked him one morning from the passenger seat of his car. It hadn't been the Buick, or the goat. It was an old, beat up Impala station wagon, and it was a miracle it still ran. He had driven his best friend, who only lived one house over across the field, to school every morning since he was the only one with a car.

"Don't think so," Conor had responded.

"Some sick shit. It came up on my feed last night."

Conor smirked, not meaning to. His friend had taken to believing every fake news feed that he came across. Conor had found it all pretty amusing, and hadn't yet corrected him on any of them.

"Some old chick owned monitor lizards. You ever seen them things?" He was overweight, poorly dressed in dirty blue jeans and a generic T-shirt, with a nasally voice.

"Big fuckers," Conor said, though he hadn't ever actually seen one, and had no clue what they even looked like.

"You think? Well apparently this old bag used to walk

the fucking things on leashes. Two of 'em. And let 'em eat people's cats and dogs and shit."

"What?" Conor had asked. "What the hell does that even mean?"

"No bullshit. If she was walking 'em and they ran into a small dog, she'd just feed the thing to her lizards. Anyway, ready for some sweet irony?"

"Sure. Why not?"

"Well, last week she gets bit by one of 'em. She don't think nothing of it, and she don't get mad either. Just mosies about the house, straightening up and whatnot. Well, all the while, the lizards are following her, standing around watching her. Can you guess why?"

"They got a taste and wanted more?"

"Not quite. Turns out, the little fuckers got some kind a poison in their saliva that paralyzes their victims. Puts 'em to sleep or something. That's how they hunt in the wild. So they're following her around the house, watching and waiting for her to fall asleep. She just thinks they're being affectionate. Like they're fucking dogs or something. Like, 'Oh, poor babies. Mommy forgives you.' Sheah. So she passes out and the fuckers turn her into a buffet. They found this chick's intestines strewn all over the damn house."

Conor had just laughed, rather than point out that there would have been no way for anybody to know the story in so much detail if she had been home alone with the lizards. Wasn't it true, though, that some reptiles had some kind of a sedative in their saliva? He had decided, rather than engage in a discussion about the likelihood of the story, to inform Dale of the difference between irony and coincidence.

Now as he lay on his side, unable to even control his own breathing, he tried to remember everything he had ever read or heard about animals that were capable of inducing paralysis in their victims. But there was close to nothing. Only stories like Dale's. There weren't many of them, either. And why not? Why hadn't he been taught in school about dangerous animals?

But what bit him wasn't an animal. It was some kind of a monster that belonged in a bad horror film. Whatever it was, it had the ability to alter its appearance. This morning it had looked like a dog. Now it was...what? A reptile? A giant, smiling insect? And the claws? The closest comparison he could think of was a bird's. There had been three on each of its four limbs.

It shouldn't have been able to stick to the wall, should have been too heavy. But it had done it and last night hadn't been a dream, either. The dog, who hadn't really been a dog, had actually walked up the wall, and stood upside down in the corner watching him like a fucking spider.

As the hours went by, he knew that the bite wasn't going to kill him. He knew when a bead of sweat rolled down his face and into his eye. The eye blinked automatically. He had no control over the function. It was hot, though. Normally he would have gotten up at some point and turned the heater off, depending on what time he had turned it on. Now it was cooking inside of the studio and he didn't feel a thing.

No, he wouldn't die. But would the paralysis wear off? What if it didn't? Harris had said he would show up in the morning if Conor didn't call. And Shelby? He tried not to even think about her and what the dog may or may not have done with her.

The wall was a stained wood design. Conor had never paid much attention to it before. Now he lay on his side, unable to look at anything else, or even close his eyes. A swirl of different shades of brown stood in front of him, and at some point in the night, it began to morph. To swirl and move, and eventually form shapes. Soon the shapes made sense.

First, they were faces. Not living faces, but skulls, with wide open mouths who seemed to be crying out in agony. Then they were insectile faces with hundreds of pointed, smiling teeth, and huge, bulging eyes.

Then a train. The old steam engine from the town center drove right through it all, distorting the image like a hand, dragged through water. Steam floated out of the engine, mixing with the swirls of brown stain as the locomotive passed. He saw it all in 3-D.

Then the train let out a loud whistle and disappeared. Conor's eyes opened. He had fallen asleep. So his eyes could close if he slept. It made sense. They were able to blink. Not by his command, but they blinked nonetheless. How long had he been out?

With some effort, he moved his eyeballs upward, which was sideways for him. Was there light? He couldn't tell. The blankets over the windows kept it out too well. Plus, the days had been dark and cloudy anyway. He must have been laying there for hours before he fell out.

HONK! HONK! The train whistled. Only it wasn't the train.

HONK!HONK!HONK!HONK!
HOOOONNNKKKK!

A car horn. Somebody was outside. Somebody? He knew who it was. And he knew now that he had been out even longer than he had thought.

A noise escaped his mouth. He hadn't meant for it to happen. It just came out. A low moan. He tried to inhale—to do it again—and found to his delight that he was able. Not just to inhale, but to moan. Not loud, but it was there. So the paralysis would wear off. The horn didn't go off again. Instead, he heard the sheriff's door open, and close a moment later.

*No,* he thought. *Go away. I'll help myself.*

Then there were footsteps on the porch. With the side of his head against the floor, he heard them resonate through the wood. They weren't the heavy footsteps of a cop's boots either. Claws scraped with each step.

Conor waited for the smiling voice of his subconscious to tell him that there was another monster outside, and that it was Harris. But the voice never spoke. There was no need, he guessed, because he already knew. Harris wouldn't be calling an ambulance, or rushing him to the hospital. He would finish the job that Benji had started.

Knocking appeared. There was nothing strange or unnatural about it, but it terrified him anyway. With every thump, Conor's heart beat harder. Then he remembered that the studio was unlocked.

Knock. Knock. Knock. Knock.

"Mitchell." The voice was muffled by the door, but he heard it well enough. It radiated out of the wood like the scratching footsteps had. And it wasn't human. It was the clicking, buzzing, loud whispering voice that Benji had barked at him in, only hours ago. It was identical, only it was forming words. "Mitchell. You in there?"

Every hair on Conor's body seemed to stand up in a wave, starting at his head and working its way down.

Knock. Knock. Knock. Knock.

"Mitchell. Conor. You awake, man?"

Conor could moan. Maybe it wouldn't be loud enough to be heard, but then again, maybe it would. He didn't though. Instead, he lay quietly praying that whatever was outside his house would go away.

Claws clicked against the metal doorknob, the knob twisted, and Conor knew that he had less than minutes left to live. His own intestines would be found strewn about the house. Or maybe not. He hadn't found Shelby's.

Whatever the dog had done to her, he had hidden her afterward.

*It buried her,* he thought. And somehow he knew that it was true. The dog had killed her and buried her like a bone. Then, when Conor had been close to finding out that she was really gone, it had tried to do the same to him.

The doorknob didn't move any more. It was released, and twisted back into place automatically. For a while, there was nothing. Then movement once again on the steps. A moment later the car door opened and closed. The car came to life, crunching gravel as it pulled out.

Only now did Conor moan. Then again. He tested it to see how loud he could project his voice. Not loud, and there was no way he would have been able to move his lips or his tongue to form words, but it was a start. His phone buzzed on the nightstand and he knew that it was Harris. He lay there for what may have been an hour, and groaned until finally a word came out.

"Hell." That was it. Hell. He tried again. This time only managing, "How." Then again. "Hewb. Hewb. Hell. Helllp. Helllp."

He knew nobody could hear him, and he was glad. He didn't actually want help. Not from anybody who might show up at least. He wanted to help himself. To come out of the paralysis and get the fuck out of here.

"Helllp. Help. Help. Help. Help—"

Time seemed to go on forever before he finally felt how hot it was. That's around the time his left arm moved. Not far, it rolled off of his side, landed on the floor with a "thump." He let out an in voluntary laugh. He couldn't help it. It just came out.

Then he jerked, and was able to roll, causing his body to go stomach-down. His neck was still bent, with his face toward the wall. Pushing the floor with his hands, he made it a few inches up, and crashed back onto the floor.

It was his right arm. It still wasn't moving. Conor moaned loudly, and brought his knees under him, pushing off with the left hand. His body was heavy, and it wasn't easy. He felt like he had drank a bottle of NyQuil. With great effort, though, he got to his feet.

He began to panic when he tried again to move his right arm. It just hung loosely at his side. Everything else was functioning. Maybe not at its full capacity, but it was at least moving. Had some kind of nerve damage been done to the arm? Would it be permanent? There was a familiar pain as blood flowed into the limb, and relief fell over him. It had just been asleep from the weight of his body resting on it—for how long?

Looking toward the window, he saw a hint of light coming in through the tiny space between the blanket and the edge. Then his eyes fell on Benji.

"Oh, Jesus." He took a step back. The thing somehow looked worse, lying dead in what must have been blood. It was black, though, and not red. Its head was completely destroyed, and its legs still stuck out to the sides. The battery sat next to it. It was like looking at a dead spider, which was rarely easier than looking at a live one.

He needed to go. Needed to get the fuck away from the thing. But where? This was his home. Where else was there to go? Without another thought, he went to the bed and pulled his clothes on. It was difficult with one arm, but by the time he walked out the door, keys in hand, he had full function of both.

It was cloudy, but the sun looked like it wanted to come up. His phone told him that it was almost eight. Six hours he had lay, unable to move. He had no idea how many of them had been spent sleeping, and how many he had been conscious. The experience already felt like a distant nightmare.

He started the car and didn't wait for it to warm up.

Pulling out, he headed for the junction, which connected Highway Twenty with Highway Nine.

* * *

When Conor looked in his rear-view, he didn't recognize what he saw. The man looking back seemed to have aged ten years since he last saw him. Sweat pasted his hair to his forehead, and huge dark circles lined the bottom of bloodshot eyes. He looked like the living dead. His right foot ached where he had kicked Benji's tooth.

He focused his attention back to the road. In front of him, the back of an old, green pickup approached. Glancing down at the dash, he saw that he was going ten miles over the limit. He eased his foot off the gas and kept pace with the growling vehicle.

A nineties model Honda passed on the other side, carrying a couple of teenagers. Conor thought about the girl he had hit around this time yesterday. It had been real. Oh yeah, it had been real, and the police had covered it up. He needed to get his family and get the hell out of town. What if they wouldn't come with, though? Why would they? How did he expect them to believe a crazy story like the one he intended to feed them? But all he would need to do was take them to the house. Show them Benji. Then they would have no choice but to believe.

He considered going back and loading the thing's body into his car, then deciding there was no way he was touching it, reconsidered. He would drive his dad there and show him. His mom would be at work. It didn't matter. He and Brett would go to the Food Outlet and get her.

His thoughts were disrupted when something up ahead caught his eye. There were two of them, walking hand-in-hand on the sidewalk. One was large, the other only a little bigger than Benji. They were horrible in the light of the morning. He clearly saw the color now. Some shade of greyish green, so dark it was almost black. They walked slightly hunched and T-Rex like, the way Benji had.

Somehow, Conor knew that they were mother and son. Though his eyes took in the monstrosities that they were, in his mind, he saw another scene perfectly. A thin, attractive woman with dark hair, and a boy in jeans and a yellow shirt. He only saw their backs and didn't care to see any more than that. He averted his eyes as the Buick came close.

The intersection was just up ahead. The green truck's blinker came on, indicating a right turn. Conor pulled into the middle lane to take a left. Driving the truck, was another one.

*Ignore it,* he thought. *Just ignore it before it notices you.*

He looked away, seeing a man in another pickup waiting at the light across the street. Without lifting his hand from the wheel, the guy smiled, waving his fingers at the green truck. In his peripheral, Conor saw the thing in the truck wave back and he knew that he was seeing something that others weren't. Something that, just last night, he hadn't been able to see either. The light turned green and he took the left, glancing without meaning to, just in time to see the mother lift her clawed foot and plant it in the boy's smiling insect face. The boy fell to the ground and disappeared as the Buick traveled further away.

What the hell was happening? And why could he see it when others couldn't? Was it because he was aware of it now that he had been attacked? Or maybe it was the bite? A small church passed on the right, and he saw a man holding hands with one of the things, walking toward a car in the parking lot. He didn't stop. Just kept driving until he reached Highway Nine, then turned right.

It was all farmland. Most of the houses were located down long driveways, and surrounded by fields, which served as home to countless cows and horses. During the summer, it always smelled like manure. This time of year, however, a trained nose could recognize the scent of wet grass. It was the smell of autumn, and it always made Conor feel at home. Now he needed to get his family and get as far away from it as possible.

But then what? If the police were involved in whatever was happening, wouldn't they just track him down? Find him wherever he went?

Within a few minutes, Dale's house appeared on the left. It sat on a hill that overlooked his giant yard. Unlike Conor, he still lived with his parents. Conor slowed down, flipped on his blinker, then as an afterthought, hit the gas and kept driving past the driveway.

*Family. Get your family. You can call Dale later. Tell him what the hell's happening. He won't believe you, but tell him at least.*

The Mitchell residence was the next one up. Conor took the left and began down the quarter mile long driveway. Halfway, he had to stop at the closed gate. He laid his hand down on the horn, pressing for a long moment. A few seconds later, the electronic gate swung open. He hit the gas and it closed again behind him. The side of the house passed on his left, and he pulled up next to his Dad's big black truck, between the front door and the garage, which he had lived in as a teenager.

The property was big, with a gravel road that circled around the garage and passed sheds and the barn, then led back to the driveway. As a child, Conor had ridden his bike for miles around and around that small road, and even jogged it during his high school years. He killed the engine, unlatched his seatbelt. Then opening the door, he stepped out to the sound of barking and his blood ran cold.

*No. No. No. No*

It was the same buzzing voice that Benji had barked with. And it was close. He stumbled back into the car, slamming the door just as one of them ran around the side of the house, smiling and barking at him. It was a little bigger than Benji, though.

"Toby," he said.

His dad's Airedale. He knew the same way he had known about the little boy and the woman. With his eyes, he saw a monster, but with his mind he saw the dog. It slammed into the Buick, and scratched at the door. Its head was just level with the bottom of the window, allowing it to look in at Conor. It stopped barking. Conor stared back into its black eyes, fighting the urge to scream. To jump. To piss himself.

Toby's eyes told him more than he wanted to know. Everything the Airedale remembered of him. Memories of going for drives in Conor's station wagon when he still lived at home. Of running, playing, and wrestling with the boy. The warm feelings of affection that the dog had always had for him. Only now they were nothing more than residue, left over. It thought it still felt, but it didn't.

There was only awareness of affections, which didn't exist anymore. And he knew that this thing wasn't really Toby. Whatever it was, it had Toby's memories, and that was it. It thought it was Toby, but Toby was dead.

The worst part, though, was the hunger. Conor saw the hunger in this creature so vividly that he almost felt it too. He saw what it wanted to do with him. To rip him open like a Christmas present and eat his insides. Then it would bury what was left of him out behind the barn. There was no ill intention either. It still thought that it was his dog and that it loved him. But it wasn't, and it had a nature to attend to.

After what felt like forever, Conor seemed to come out of a trance and he was able to finally look away. He turned the key and the Buick came to life. Then his door opened and Toby came around the side. Conor put it in drive and slammed his foot on the gas, taking off before the thing could touch him. He pulled the door shut, locking it as he drove. The car flew around the garage at close to forty, but had to slow down where the road connected with the driveway. His phone vibrated in his pocket as he took the corner. He dug it out, looking at the screen.

Incoming call from: Dad.

He accepted it.

"Conor." The buzzing, monstrous voice didn't surprise him. He had known the second he saw Toby. "You leaving, son? You just got here."

They didn't know he could see them. How could they?

"Yeah." He tried to keep his voice steady. "I just remembered something, Dad. I'll be back."

"What? Well at least stop and say 'hi,' ya goomba."

"No. I can't. I gotta go." He stopped the car halfway up the driveway. "You wanna open the gate?"

"No." The voice was almost too much to handle. Every word sent a new kind of chill through Conor's body. "What I want, is to spend some time with my boy. Come on back to the house and come in. What could be so important you can't stop for a minute?"

"It's my oven, Dad. I left my oven on."

"Yeah? Well good job, genius. Wanna burn your whole house down?"

"No. No. I don't know what I was thinking. Could you open the gate please? I really need to hurry."

"The gate?"

"The gate, Dad." Conor looked in his rear-view and saw Toby running after the Buick. "Please." He tried to keep the panic out of his voice.

"Suppose I could do that. But it's a shame. Haven't seen you in about forever. How you been holding up lately?"

If there had been any doubt that this wasn't his Dad, it was gone. "I've been okay, Dad." A feeling came over him that was almost as alien as the creatures that seemed to be taking over his town. A tingling in his chest. Water building up behind his eyes.

In the mirror, Toby was now on all fours, growing in size as it ran surprisingly fast and surprisingly insect like. Its body hunched low, and its legs moved individually and quickly. It was a scurry. Its feet threw gravel as they moved and it was getting close. Another one came around the house, walking upright and talking on a cell phone. It was much bigger. The size of a large man.

"Dad, the gate's electronic. You can open it from the house."

"Oh, it's no problem," the thing buzzed. "I'll be right there. Stay where you are. I tell you I grew some nice looking tomatoes this year?"

*Fuck this.*

He didn't take the time to tell him tomatoes were out of season. He threw the phone onto the passenger seat and stomped his foot, pinning the pedal to the floor. The Buick picked up speed, slowly at first. It slammed into the gate at just over thirty miles per hour, sending the phone flying to the floor. The gate bent outward, but didn't open as Conor was thrust forward and the car struggled against it. The wheels spun in the gravel, it moved a few inches, then back. Then again. And again.

There was scraping on the back of the car. He turned to see Toby climbing up the back window. Conor put it in reverse, stepped on it again. The car flew backward toward the thing that thought it was his Dad, which just continued to walk toward him.

Conor slammed on the brakes and heard claws scratch above his head like nails on a chalkboard as Toby was launched back and rolled down the window onto the driveway. He put the car in drive and took off again. This time the gate came off of its hinges on the left side, swinging open, scraping the car as he left it behind. When he made it to the end of the driveway he turned right and gunned it.

He had seen it all in the dog's eyes. Somehow he had been able to read its thoughts. They weren't logical, organized thoughts either. They weren't much more than desire, intention, hunger, with memories that it used to assist it in getting what it wanted. Memories that somehow directly affected those desires.

He pulled his seatbelt on, looking at the dash to make sure he was doing the speed limit. The last thing he wanted was a run-in with the police.

"Conor? You there, son?" The phone lay on the passenger side floor. He considered ignoring it, then unlatched his seatbelt, reached down, and picked it up, putting his seatbelt back on. "Conor? Can you hear me?" It was the voice of death, trying to lure him to the party that everybody else seemed to be attending.

"I hear you," he responded.

"Now why you wanna go and ruin the damn gate, boy?"

"Sorry. Sorry, Dad. I'll fix it when I come back."

"Damn straight you will. You were rude to Toby, too. You know how he gets when he sees you. Maybe if you came around more often he wouldn't act like such a retard every time you show up. You know your Mom wouldn't mind seeing you once in a while either."

This wasn't his Dad. *No fucking way.* And whatever it was, he couldn't let it know that he knew. But no matter how hard he tried to fight them, tears had somehow managed to escape his eyes for the first time since he was a young boy. He did his best to keep his voice from betraying them.

"Yeah. Yeah, I know, Dad. I've been thinking about that lately. I think I'll start coming over on my days off, and helping more with the animals."

A car passed, going the opposite direction. A giant bug sat in the passenger seat, while an elderly lady drove. A young boy, who couldn't have been much older than six or seven sat in the middle backseat.

"Yeah," the thing replied. "Sure could use the help. You know my back's not what it used to be."

"I know, Dad." Wet mucus teased the rims of his nostrils as he refrained from sniffing.

"Oh hell. We just wanna spend some time with you, Conor. You know we had this crazy idea that once you and your sisters moved out it would be some kind of a paradise around here? Your mom and I would have the place all to ourselves—be able to do whatever we want. Wherever we want. Turns out the place is more of a fucking madhouse without you than it was with you. You've always been a good boy, Conor. I ever told you that?"

Conor took a deep breath. "No. I don't think you have."

"Well you have, son. I've always loved you. I know I wasn't always the best at showing it. You gotta understand, though, I'm just a mean son-of-a-bitch. It's who I am, Conor, and if Cindy and Catey had been boys, they would've gotten it all just the same as you. It never had anything to do with our—well you know. Our—"

"Dynamic."

"Yeah. Our dynamic. It never had anything to do with that. You know that, right?"

"Yeah. Yeah, Dad. I guess I do." He couldn't do it. Couldn't keep his voice from shaking, no matter how hard he tried. "Why now though?"

"What? Why am I telling you all this?"

"Yeah."

"Seems like as good a time as any, doesn't it?"

"Sure. I guess." He reached his turn and took it without stopping or using the blinker, forgetting momentarily about avoiding the police.

"Listen, Conor, I'm gonna jump in the truck and come on over. Just in case you lit the damn place on fire."

"No, Dad." Panic spread out from his chest. "It'll be okay. I'm sure there's no fire. I'll just turn off the oven and come right back."

"No. No. No. It's no problem, damn it. Let me come over and make sure. I'll feel a whole hell of a lot better that way."

"No. You stay home. Please. I've got it. I know there's no fire. I just need to get the damn oven off."

After a pause, the creature hissed, "Sure?"

"I'm sure, Dad."

"Well shit. Okay. Why don't you bring your dog back with you?"

"What?"

"Your Mom says you got a new mutt. Bring him over and let him play with Toby, at least."

"Okay. Yeah. Sounds good. Listen, I'm gonna get off the phone before I get a ticket, Dad."

"'Kay. Hurry back though."

"I will."

"Hey, Conor?"

"Yeah, Dad?"

"You know it's better."

Conor felt the world collapse under him.

Brett went on. "Everything. Everything is so much

better like this. If you would've told me, well, I guess I wouldn't have believed you. Shit, I would've ran like hell. I've never felt so alive though, son. Your mother too. I've never seen her so happy. All we're missing now is you and your sisters. Have I ever led you wrong, son?"

"Dad, I'm hanging up."

"Answer me, Conor. Now I may have been a mean son-of-a-bitch, but have I ever led you wrong? You'll be better, son. You'll be better and you'll love it. Then, when Cindy and Catey come home for Turkey-Day, we'll have them back too. We'll all be together. Like before. Don't you want that?"

Conor hung up and tossed the phone back onto the passenger seat. At some point the tears had stopped. There had been so many, though, and in such a small amount of time. He had forgotten what it was like to let them out. Somehow, in spite of everything, it felt good.

# Chapter Five

Conor got into his contacts and selected John's number. He put the phone on speaker.

"Conman!" The answer came swiftly. No crackling. No clicking.

*Thank God.*

"Yeah," he said.

"Bud? You there?"

"Yeah."

"I can't hear you too good, Conman. I think ya got bad reception, where yer at."

"John," he raised his voice. "Can you hear me now?"

"Better. What's up, bud?"

"Are you at home?"

"Yep. Unfortunately. Everything cool?"

"Can I come over?"

After a brief pause, John said, "Course you can Conman. Know where the house is?"

"No."

"Want me ta text you the address?"

"Uh, yeah. That would be great."

He made sure to follow the speed limit, even though if the police wanted to pull him over they would do it no matter how fast he drove.

"No problem, man. Yer driving right now?"

"Yeah."

"You in trouble, man?"

"I don't know how to answer that."

"What? Jesus. Where are you?"

"I'm in Sedrow."

"At yer house? Of course not. Yer driving. Fuck, man. Is this about yesterday, or—?"

"I don't know, John. How soon can you text me the address?"

"Soon as we hang up. Unless ya need me to stay on the line."

"No."

"Fucking great, Conman. What the fuck you get yerself into, bud?"

Up ahead was the junction that would take him back to Highway Twenty. He turned without coming to a complete stop.

"Could you just text me the address?"

"Uh, sure. How soon should I be expecting you?"

"Soon," Conor replied. "Hey, John?"

"Yeah, man?"

"Don't tell anyone I'm coming, okay?"

"Yeah. Whatever man. You already know. Just hurry up."

Conor hung up, and set the phone again on the passenger seat. When he reached the highway, he saw one of them walking by itself. He knew it was a woman in a business skirt and heels.

*How long,* he thought. *How long has this been going on, and how far does it reach?*

He turned onto the highway, looking into the small parking lot of the twenty-four hour gas station, where nothing seemed to be out of the ordinary aside from the monster standing outside of a Cavalier, pumping gas and smiling. He ignored it.

A couple minutes later, he pulled into his driveway, and parked next to the goat. Shelby's car was still there. Leaving the motor running, he jogged up the porch steps, and in the front door. The heat hit him instantly. Then the smell. He turned the heater off and walked over to the kitchen area, tearing open the garbage bag that sat on his counter.

*All right. You can do this. Just don't look at it.*

He shook the bloody comforter loose, and flipped the light on. Then he made the mistake of looking. The thing's corpse was hideous, rotten already. Flies buzzed around it hungrily. It was still juicy, but large patches of its skin had decomposed and withered away, where exposed bone could be seen. The eyes were gone, and thick black liquid oozed out of the sockets.

How though? It had only been a few hours.

He quickly threw the blanket over it, then kicked it and scooped it up, trying not to touch the lump underneath. He held the blanket by its four corners, carrying it like a sack to his car. He tossed it in the trunk and pulled back onto the highway.

He passed the round-a-bout. Then K.C.'s Auto Glass. When he passed the spot where he had hit the girl yesterday, he thought of Percly Valentine. How was Percly tied to all this?

A red light up ahead had traffic stalled in front of the Buick. He brought it to a stop behind a grey sedan, careful not to look at anything but the road.

Was Percly one of them? No. That wasn't it. Not because he hadn't seen. He hadn't been able to see them at the time anyway. It was the gun. The transient had shot the girl by his car. He doubted the ugly sons-of-bitches used guns.

The light turned green and traffic picked up.

If Percly wasn't one, then what did that mean? Was the girl one? Of course she was. That's why he had shot her. He had known. Then the police had covered it up.

Conor hit his blinker, took the next right into the parking lot of the Food Outlet.

* * *

Harris followed the old Buick at a safe distance. He tapped his fingers on the steering wheel with the twangy music coming from the speakers in his cruiser. He sang along to the verses he knew.

"Should a been a cowboy—Should a learned to rope and ride—Na, na, na, na, na, na, na, na. Cattle drive—"

The highway was busy with people on their way out of town, headed to their jobs. It had been much less active this morning when he had stopped by Mitchell's house. He no longer had any intention of eating, or even changing the man. That was for the dog, or his girlfriend to do. The same way that it had been for Harris's own momma to change him and his dad. Somebody needed to keep an eye on Mitchell, though, until it happened, and he couldn't very well expect a fucking dog to do the job.

Mitchell knew something. He didn't know everything. How could he? He knew something, though, and that made him a liability. His chica had disappeared yesterday morning. That meant she would be coming back tomorrow, around the same time. Lovely, how that worked. It didn't seem to matter the size of the body. Two days was the time it took to change. Forty-eight hours. Longer than Phil had even been out of the dirt.

Tomorrow, Lori would come out and she would belong to him. The same way he and his dad belonged to his momma, she belonged to her therapist, and her therapist belonged to another.

Mitchell was only three cars up. Any more distance and he might lose him. He had been so close to just going inside his house this morning and doing the damn deed himself. Even had his hand on the doorknob. It was tempting. Oh, it was like a cold beer on a hot fucking day. But somehow he knew better. Not just because of what Momma had told him either. Something inside told him to mind his own territory.

Then he saw the kid driving, and read his body language. He was so good at reading body language lately that he could practically read minds. Conor Mitchell was freaking out. So he followed him.

Traffic stopped in front of the cruiser, at a red light. The Buick switched lanes, and the right blinker came on. He could pull him over for failing to signal on time, but that would only increase his panic. He might even try to flee, depending on how much he knew, and the last thing Harris wanted was to cause a scene.

"Stealin' a young girl's heart—," he sang. "Just like Jean and Roy—Na, na, na, na. Campfire songs—Oh, I should a been a cowboy."

Harris stayed in his lane. As soon as Conor turned, he could flash his lights and flip a bitch. On second thought, he brought his small walkie talkie to his mouth.

"All units on patrol. Over."

"Yeah." The response came through almost instantly. "I hear ya, boy."

"Yeah, Dad, we got a fee'er, I think. You wanna get all the boys and watch every exit? Probly shouldn't let this one leave town. Over."

"For the love of—turn down the fuckin music, boy. I can't make out a thing yer sayin'."

Phil killed the music. "Yo. Over."

"Harris?" another voice came through.

"Yeah," Phil responded. "All units on patrol. We got a green sixty-seven Buick Skylark, license plate—"

As he gave the description of the car, the light turned green. Instead of taking the turn, Mitchell drove across the street, then took the first right into the Food Outlet.

"Copy that," his dad said over the radio. "Location?"

"Highway Twenty." Harris took the left, looking for somewhere to turn around. "Vehicle just pulled into the Food Outlet. Suspect's name is Conor Mitchell. I'll continue to tail him, but we better not let this one leave Woolley. Over."

"Conley?" Phil Senior said.

"Sir? Over."

"You take Francis Road. I'll watch the freeway. I'll get one a'the city boys to stand by at the end a'the highway."

"Hey, Dad? Over."

"Yeah?"

"Don't change him. Just detain the son-of-a-bitch if he tries to leave. Over."

"Copy that."

Harris hit his lights, flipped a U-turn, then killed them, pulling back up to the intersection as the logistics were worked out over the radio. Every cop in Sedrow had been changed now, and they weren't using their police radios anyway. Phil, his dad, Conley, and every other Sheriff in the Lyman precinct had taken to carrying two transmitters in their car. One was kept on the station that Sheriff's dispatch used, the other was a small, store bought walkie talkie for communicating amongst each other.

Phil scanned the parking lot across the street. It was mostly empty, allowing him to catch sight of the Buick instantly. Conor parked close to the entrance. The light turned green. Phil took a right, then another. He pulled up behind the town center, where the old steam engine sat amidst statues of Indians and random animals. Killing the engine, he stepped out and a beer bottle appeared in his hand. After taking a long swig, he let out a cloud of smoke as if it had been a cigarette. Then he climbed into the locomotive.

An empty wine bottle sat next to a black sleeping bag and an old backpack, which was stuffed full of what he assumed was Percly Valentine's clothes. That was another liability that would need to be dealt with once they could find the dirty rat-basket.

Phil kicked the items aside and stood watching out the window. He had a perfect view of the parking lot from here. The Buick sat for a long moment before the door finally opened and Mitchell stepped out.

* * *

The world seemed to sink under Conor's feet a little with every step. He didn't want to go into the store, wanted to just drive the hell out of town. He couldn't though. Not until he saw his mom. He already knew what he would see, but he still needed to see it. His heart wouldn't accept it until it was registered through his eyes.

The automatic doors slid open in both directions as he stepped under the motion sensor. Taking a deep breath, he let it out slowly, trying to maintain a neutral pace. It was warm inside the market. The row of checkout lanes came instantly into view. Only one of them was attended to, by a girl who Conor went to school with. He felt a thin ray of hope at the sight of her. She wasn't one of them. She smiled as he approached.

"Mandy." He tried to keep his voice as calm as possible. "Is my mom here?"

When he was close, her smile faded as she eyed him up and down. "Jesus, Conor. Are you okay?" Mandy Kinsley was an attractive girl. She had been on the cheer squad, and hadn't spoken two words to Conor until his mom hired her at the outlet.

"Yeah. Yeah, I'm fine. Is she in yet?"

She watched him close as she spoke. "Your mom? Well yeah. I mean she's in the back. Conor, are you sure you're all right?"

"Could you just page her for me?"

Behind him, the doors squeaked open. He looked back and saw one of the insectile monsters step in. It stared at him hungrily with its bulging, black eyes, and Conor's head filled with an image of a middle aged, heavyset woman in a pair of plaid pajamas. Then another. It was early morning in the woods. The sun was just beginning to come up, and birds chirped in the trees. He saw it all with perfect clarity as if through her eyes as she looked down at the plot of dirt she sat in. She had been buried, and she had just dug her way out.

"Conor?" Mandy's voice played over the image, but he couldn't break away from the thing's thoughts. He saw it all, from its birth that morning, to what it wanted to do to the girl working the counter. To bite her. To drag her limp, paralyzed body out into the woods and slice her belly open. To lower its ugly face into the cut and vomit its eggs inside of her. Then it would bury her while she was still breathing, and she would change. She would become one of them.

It wanted the girl, because it had been in the store before, when it had been human. It had wanted her then, too, only for other reasons. It had wanted to plant its face between her legs, and fall asleep next to her. To love her. And if it got what it now wanted with her, it would own her. If not Mandy, though, somebody else in the store would have to do. The thing needed release. It was almost overwhelming.

"Conor? Conor, I'm gonna call for help."

The thing looked away and the store came back into focus. It walked smiling into the aisle, and disappeared around a corner.

"No," Conor said between heavy breaths. He became aware that he had backed up into the checkout counter and was clutching it with both hands. He turned to once again face Mandy. Their eyes met and she shrieked. "Don't call anybody. Please. Just page my mom."

Her eyes slowly widened. She opened her mouth to speak, but her lips just quivered.

"Mandy—"

"Okay." She began to tear up as she reached for the phone. "I'll page her. Jesus, Conor, you're scaring me."

"You should be scared." He kept his voice low.

"Why?" Hers was weak.

When Conor didn't respond, she just looked at him as if trying to read his face. Then, with shaking hands, she dialed a number and spoke into the receiver.

"Alice, please come to the front of the store...Please." She didn't break eye contact as she set the phone back down, and a single tear finally rolled down the side of her nose.

"Everything okay?" A voice came from one of the aisles. Conor looked to see a tall, thin man—about his age—wearing a Food Outlet apron. He stood near the middle of the aisle, looking at them suspiciously. Mandy glanced at him, then back at Conor but didn't answer. "Mandy?"

Finally Conor offered a subtle nod. She nodded back,

speaking slowly. "Yeah, Gil. Everything's cool."

There was silence for a moment, then Gil said, "You sure?"

"Yeah. I'm sure. This is Conor. Alice's son."

At the mention of his boss, Gil stared for another second, said, "Oh, hey," then turned reluctantly and went back to what he was doing. When he was out of earshot, Mandy whispered, "Conor, what the hell's going on?"

"I don't know. You need to leave though."

*"What?* Leave? What do you mean 'leave'?"

"Jesus. I don't know. I just know that— "

"Conor!" The crackling, buzzing voice came from the aisle where the guy had been. Conor looked and saw something that thought it was his Mom, approaching quickly. Before he could stop himself, he made the mistake of locking eyes with it.

"No!" He took a step back. The thing stopped twenty feet away, smiling at him. He saw its mind and knew that it was making a face which should have shown concern.

"Conor?"

"No, Mom."

She wanted to do it to him. Everything the other one wanted to do to Mandy, and she would, if he didn't get out of here. Now.

"What is it, son?" The thing resumed walking.

"Come on," Conor looked at Mandy. "For the love of God, come with me. We need to get the fuck out of here."

"What?" She shrieked, but her voice was unsure. "What are you saying, Conor? What are you—I can't just—I can't—"

He didn't stay and listen. Just turned and ran for the door. It opened when he was close and he bolted to his car. Jumping in, he peeled out of the parking space. When he made it to the exit, he looked in his rear-view and saw Mandy run out of the store, her hair flying behind her. He hit the brakes, put the car in reverse.

Then the monster, who thought it was a fat woman in pajamas, scurried out and wrapped its claws around her neck. Her mouth opened wide and she was dragged back inside.

Conor put the Buick in drive and slammed his foot down on the gas. He flew out of the parking lot, and onto Cook Road at twenty miles per hour, the Buick quickly picking up speed. Cook Road was surrounded by fields with houses spaced apart by multiple acres. It led to the only freeway entrance in town, and was usually empty at this stretch.

Up ahead, a huge tractor drove along the road. He caught up to it in seconds, swerving around it at just over sixty-five, almost colliding head on with a station wagon. The wagon's horn blared behind him, but he didn't slow down, or even look back.

He passed a few vehicles along the way, and within minutes a line of traffic came into view, stopping at the intersection that led to I-5. His breath was rapid as he pulled into the turn lane. He would be safe once he made it onto the corridor. There was now no doubt. He had seen it in his mother's horrible eyes. She wouldn't leave Sedrow Woolley. None of them would. This was their nest, and she hadn't wanted him to leave either.

The light turned green, and cars began to deposit onto the freeway. Conor slapped the steering wheel. *Move. Move. Come on, you sons-a-bitches. Move faster.* He was three cars away from the ramp when it turned red again.

One left turn. That's all that stood between him and safety. One left turn in which he would drive around a small shopping center with a teriyaki restaurant and a liquor store in the corner of the intersection. The only bikini barista coffee stand in town, sat in the parking lot, and he could see one of the creatures that thought it was a young girl in a G-string working the window where a row of cars waited to be served.

There was a gas station on another corner. People went about their business as usual, pumping gas, shopping, coming in and out of the restaurant. But only half of them were people. That had been a consistency all morning. Half monsters, half people. How long, he wondered, had it taken to change half the town? How long until the rest turned?

Tap. Tap. Tap.

Conor's head snapped in the direction of the noise.

"Conor Mitchell?"

Just outside the passenger door, a tall one stood smiling. He looked into its eyes, knowing it was once an older man—who bore a striking resemblance to Phillip Harris—in a sheriff's uniform. He didn't respond, just stared at the thing. It tapped the glass again with one of its long, pointed claws.

"Could you pull into the parking lot please? I'd like ta have a word with ya." The sheriff's cruiser was parked on the shoulder.

"No," Conor finally responded loud enough to be heard through the glass.

"Don't be a fool, son." the thing buzzed. "Pull over and step outta the car, now. I need ta talk ta ya."

"No. I'm not doing that."

The creature put its hand on its waistline, as if reaching for an invisible gun. "I'm not gonna ask again, boy. Pull the fucking car over. I don't wanna hurt ya, now."

The light turned green, but the car in front of the Buick didn't move. The driver, sat staring in his rear-view mirror. Conor felt something well up inside of him. His lips peeled back and he bared his teeth at the ugly fucker. He screamed as loud as he could. It didn't even flinch, though, just stood and stared, smiling. It wasn't happy. It wasn't *not* happy, either. It just smiled.

Every time he looked into their eyes, he knew more than he had before. More than he wanted to know about them. More, he knew, than they even knew about themselves. He looked at the car in front of him, where a man with a receding hairline was now twisted around in his seat.

He yelled again. "Go! Go! Go! Damn it! Go!" He motioned for him to move. The guy didn't, though. Neither did the cars in the lanes on either side of him. He laid on the horn, but still nothing.

"Conor Mitchell?" The insect sheriff projected its voice. "I'm gonna go ahead an give you one last chance ta comply. If you don't pull off'a this fucking road on the count a three, I'll be compelled ta use force. Do you understand?"

"FUCK YOU!" Conor gripped the wheel as tight as he could.

"One!"

Conor laid on the horn again, and multiple other cars honked back.

"Two!"

*Fuck this.* He hit the gas. The Buick lurched forward, slamming into the sedan in front of it. The driver, who was still looking back, jerked and began to scream something he couldn't hear. Conor backed up into the car behind him, pushing it a couple feet, then moved forward again into the other car.

He moved the shifter back into reverse as the Buick's passenger window exploded inward, causing glass to fly everywhere. He looked and saw the sheriff sliding into the car. Its mouth was wide open, coming right at his face.

"Oh God!" He reached over, planting his palm between its eyes, pushing, feeling the bubbles on either side of his hand. They were dry, but the skin between them was bumpy and slimy. It was all terrible and backward. The thing came at him with so much force that he knew he wouldn't be able to resist it. All he could do was try to avoid the teeth. The poisonous teeth that would send him back into paralysis if just one of them broke his skin.

He laid his foot back down to the floor and the car jerked hard as it slammed into the one behind it. A symphony of horns rang out from all directions. Then the teeth were so close that they appeared huge in front of his face.

He braced himself for what came next, wishing he would have known sooner. Maybe he couldn't have saved the people he loved, but if he were going to die anyway, he could have died trying. Now, he would join them, and a monstrosity posing as him would wander the town, spreading whatever evil this was until everybody was gone. And then what? How far would it reach?

A thin black tongue shot out, touched his face, then the monster retreated, slipping back out the window. The world seemed to fall silent as Conor realized he hadn't been bitten. He glanced to the right and saw the thing outside of the car, smiling, holding onto the window ledge. Then he saw why.

Percly Valentine had it by its legs, one under each arm. He pulled and he pulled in short, jerking motions, wrenching it away from the Buick. It wouldn't release its grip though. Finally he dropped the legs and reached into his trench coat. The sheriff began to pull itself back into the car as Percly brought out his revolver and put it to the back of its head.

BOOM!

Every other sound came back into focus with the gunshot. The sheriff let out a loud hiss as cold, black blood sprayed Conor's face and the inside of the windshield. Horns continued to honk everywhere. Somewhere, a car alarm screamed. The monster stopped hissing and fell limp over the edge of the window.

Percly pulled it out, letting it drop onto the road. The man in the sedan in front of Conor jumped out and ran at the transient, but Percly raised his gun and pointed it between his eyes. They went wide as he took a step back, getting into his car. Percly unlocked the Buick's door and jumped in.

"Go, motherfucker! Go!"

The sedan peeled out and flew onto the freeway. Conor just sat frozen, until Percly yelled again.

"Come on, nigga! Drive!"

Outside, another sheriff's car pulled up behind the one parked on the shoulder. Conor put the car back in drive and hit the gas in time to see Phillip Harris step out and watch him drive away.

* * *

The freeway was packed with morning rush hour traffic. The Cook Road entrance wasn't too bad, but Conor knew in a few minutes everything would slow down. By that time he would be in Burlington and away from immediate danger.

Percly smelled. Even with the passenger window gone, Conor could smell stale body odor. He sat in the passenger seat with his gun on his lap and his eye patch over his forehead, staring into the mirror on his door. It was impossible to read his expression through his thick beard. Once they were a distance away from the off-ramp, he said, "Shit. We got a friend back there." His voice was strangely nasally and low at the same time.

"What do you mean?"

"I mean us being followed. Two cars back. Blue Honda."

Looking in the rear-view mirror, he saw the car with the damaged front bumper that he had backed into.

"See the driver talking on the phone?" Percly asked.

"Yeah." Conor looked back at the road.

"Tellin' the cops were we're at. I take it you know by now, I'm not one of 'em?"

"Neither am I."

"I know."

"So what do we do?" Conor asked.

"I look like I know? We better figure it out though."

"Let me think." Conor looked again in the rear-view. The guy had probably already given a description of the Buick and their location to the police. "What's this guy's problem, man?"

"Shit. What you think?" Percly continued to stare into the mirror. "You think that man saw us kill a giant cockroach back there, or murder a police officer?"

"Cockroach?"

"Yeah, cockroach. You hard a hearing?"

"No—I just—"

"Look, can we focus on the issue at hand for now? We'll have plenty of time to talk about the bugs later—if we live 'til then."

"We need to get off the freeway," Conor said.

"Ya think?"

Conor hit the blinker, veered right. Up ahead was an exit. Behind him the beat up Honda switched lanes.

"Maybe he wants to collect your insurance information," Percly snickered.

Conor pulled onto the off-ramp, and into the line of vehicles waiting at the intersection. The Honda pulled up behind them, and the man squinted at the Buick's back bumper.

Percly said, "Take a right."

Looking right, Conor saw nothing but fields and houses. Without asking questions, he hit the blinker again.

"Don't look back," Percly went on. "Try not to let him know we see his ass."

Conor nodded. Then it occurred to him that he knew close to nothing about the man in his passenger seat. He opened his mouth, not sure of what would come out and heard himself say, "We can't kill anybody."

"Just drive."

Conor looked down, automatically, at the gun in Percly's lap. He gripped it tightly, his finger resting over the trigger. Conor felt something dirty stir in the bottom of his stomach. *I can't do this*, he thought. But when the light turned, he took the right. The Honda followed, then slowed down, keeping a distance. Once they were far enough from the intersection, and there were no other cars in sight, Percly told him to flip a U-turn and Conor felt an irrational sense of relief rush through him.

"Jesus," he said as he turned the car around in the middle of the road. "I thought you were trying to lure him out here to—"

"Block the road."

"What?"

The Honda came at them from the other direction. The driver wore a baffled look, staring into the Buick's windshield, which was still splattered with black blood. He steered with one hand, held the phone to his ear with the other.

"Block him! Block him! Come on now! Block him in!"

"How?" Conor shrieked.

Percly reached over and took the wheel. He turned the Buick until it was in the left lane, driving straight at the other vehicle.

"Shit!" Conor slammed on the brakes. The Honda swerved, attempting to drive around them.

"Come on, nigga! Block his ass!" Percly raised his gun, nudged the side of Conor's head.

"Okay!" Conor put the car in reverse and turned the wheel blocking the road. The Honda came to an abrupt stop, only feet away. Percly jumped out, running around the front of the Hick, pointing his revolver at the driver.

"OUTTA THE CAR! RIGHT NOW! COME ON!" The guy didn't move, just stared at the homeless man wide eyed. Percly pointed the gun straight up and fired a shot that echoed through the sky. "OUT MOTHERFUCKER OR I'LL KILL YOU! DO YOU HEAR ME?"

The man cried something that Conor couldn't make out, his phone pressed tightly to his ear. Hunching down, he stared into Percly's face as he stepped out. "Yes...yeah. He told me to get out...Out of the...I already did. No. No. No...I..."

"Drop the phone!" Percly walked up and slapped it out of his hand before he had time to comply. He stomped on it three times, crushing it thoroughly.

"Listen man," the guy threw his hands up, "You don't have to—"

"Shut up! Conor! Pop the trunk."

Conor jumped at the sound of his name. He considered putting the car in drive and getting the hell out of there. But then what? Percly Valentine was the only proof that he wasn't insane. The only other person who seemed to know what was happening in Sedrow Woolley. There was nothing more to think about. Reaching under the hood, he pulled the lever that opened the trunk. The car jerked as it popped. Percly took the man by his shirt collar, leading him to the back of the car.

"Nononono! Please, man. I'm claustrophobic! You

can't put me in there. I'll fucking freak."

"Shut the fuck up and move!" Percly shoved his gun against the back of his head. The car jerked again, as the trunk slammed. There was banging and yelling as he struggled to get out. Then Conor remembered what else was in there.

"Percly!"

"What?" He was already running toward the Honda.

Realizing what the plan was, Conor stepped out. "We're stealing his car?"

"'Less you feel like gettin' pulled over and hauled back into Sedrow."

"There's a body in the trunk."

Percly stopped just outside the driver's side door, looked at him, and tilted his head. "What?"

"A body. One of the—things. I killed it and put it in my trunk. It's back there with that guy."

Considering this for a moment, he said, "Well let's get the motherfucker. We'll bring it with."

Conor popped the truck again. The door flew open and the claustrophobic man sprung out and took off, full sprint through the field before they even reached the back of the car. Conor watched him, then turned his attention to the item in the truck. It smelled worse than Percly, and he imagined that it was already further decayed from when he retrieved it this morning. Taking the blue blanket by its four corners, he heaved it out. The middle sank heavily, dripping black blood.

"Sweet mother of Christ," Percly said.

"Where should I put it?"

"In the Honda—in the trunk." Percly just stared at the bundle. "You sure it's dead?"

"I'm not really sure of anything. You wanna get the trunk open for me so I can set this thing down?"

Percly stared a little longer, swallowed a lump in his

throat. "Yeah." He walked to the other car. "We need to get the fuck outta here. Now."

After loading the dead monster into the car, Conor fetched his cell from the Buick and both men jumped into the Honda, Percly driving. They were in motion before Conor even had his door shut.

Conor asked, "You know how to drive?"

"Why?" Percly looked at him. "Cause I'm a nigga? Or cause I'm a bum?"

"I didn't mean to—I was just thinking—I mean you don't have a car, do you? Or—"

"Where we goin'?"

The Honda pulled back up to the intersection. Percly took a right onto the main road. Behind them, three Burlington Police cars sped toward the Buick.

"My friend's place in Mount Vernon, I guess. That's where I was headed before."

"Works for me—for now at least. We can sit down and figure out what the hell we gonna do next. You sure he's cool?"

"Ah—yeah. I mean—"

"I mean," Percly spoke slowly. "Is he gonna turn us in?"

*Turn us in?* The weight of the words fell over Conor like a building crumbed in an earthquake. He wasn't just running from whatever evil was spreading through his town. He was likely a fugitive of the law already. "No. I don't think so."

"Guess that's the best we can do at short notice. Shit, we can't stay long anyway. Can't stay long anywhere if you ain't noticed. I bet them motherfuckers got us pinned as cop killers already. They'll have every cop in the state lookin' to bring us back to their department for questioning. How do I get to your friend's house?"

"Hold on." Conor pulled up the text. "Let me punch

the address into the GPS."

They were just crossing the bridge that went over the Skagit River, into Mount Vernon. Percly looked over at Conor's phone, then back at the road. "Uh-uh. Throw that motherfucker out the window."

"My phone?"

"Naw, your purse."

"What?"

"Yeah, fool. Your phone! Don't you think they can track you that way? Especially if you type in where we goin'. Might as well just call and tell 'em to meet us there."

"Well excuse me. I've never ran from the police before."

"What? And I have?"

"I don't know. I don't know. Fuck! Can we just focus on our problem right now? I don't know how to get to John's house because I've never been there. He texted me his address this morning. I was gonna use the GPS."

"Throw the phone, Conor. Before we get over this bridge. Can you do that for me?"

Conor looked down at the phone which contained every bit of contact information he had for everybody he knew. Then he rolled down the window and tossed it over the side of the bridge. "Well what now?"

"I don't know," Percly responded. "We can't go to your friend's place if he texted you the address. Shit, they might be there already. Let's hope they don't get the Mount Vernon cops to take him out to Sedrow for questioning. Have you seen what these things do?"

Conor hesitated, then said, "I've seen."

Percly gave him a curious look. "What's that mean?"

"I don't know. It's hard to explain. I've been seeing their thoughts all morning, though." There was silence between the two men as Percly seemed to be deciding whether or not to believe this bit of information. Conor, not comfortable with it, said, "I mean, not really. I'm not sure if they think. There's memories, but everything else is more like—intentions, I guess."

"Intentions?" Percly turned off the main road, into a residential neighborhood.

"I mean it's not the type of thoughts that you and I have. They don't reason. They just know what they want and how to get it."

"Instincts."

"Yeah. But it's a little more complex, I think. They can plan. I guess they reason in that way, but everything they plan has to do with getting what they're after."

Nodding, Percly asked, "And what exactly is that?"

"To spread. That's all I know. Some of them are hungry, others want to lay eggs. They want it so bad it's like an itch. Like a bad one, though. It's how they spread. They eat, and then they lay eggs inside of somebody. They're some kind of fucking asexual."

"Asexual? You mean they don't have sex?"

"I don't know if they do or not, but they don't reproduce through sex."

"The other night, I saw one burying a dog alive. It sliced the motherfucker's gut right open and buried it next to the train in the town center."

"It was an incubator," Conor said, thinking of Benji.

"That's what it's called?"

"I don't know." He shook his head. "I just meant that's what the dog was being used for. They lay eggs inside of their abdomen and use them like incubators. They're still alive when they bury them for some reason. Then the eggs hatch with the person—or the dog's— memories and they crawl out of the dirt thinking that's who they are."

"But they're not?"

"No. No, those people are dead."

Percly paused a moment, then said, "What about the victim?"

"Victim?"

"I mean the first one. The one they ate to get—pregnant, or whatever. What happens to them?"

At first Conor didn't answer. Then when the silence grew once again more uncomfortable than the question, he told the homeless man that they're dead too, only no giant insect is walking around with their memories.

"And you got all this just by seein' their thoughts somehow?"

"I was bit this morning. The bite paralyzed me, but right before it kicked in, I killed the son-of-a-bitch. When the paralysis wore off, I could see everything, though. I can see what the fuckers are, and what they think they are. I don't really understand it, either, to tell you the truth."

It was unclear whether or not Percly believed him. He just stared ahead at the road. "Well, what now?" he asked.

"How do you know my name?"

"What?"

"You keep saying my name. How do you know it?"

Percly looked at him again, and for a second Conor thought he might put the gun back to his head. "How you know mine?"

"Well, we've met. I've given you—ah, change. I just kind of assumed you've had the same interaction with so many people—you know what? Never mind. I don't know what's next. I think we need to warn my friend that they might be coming."

"How?"

"I don't know. I should've got his number before I threw my phone. I suppose I could call the shop and get it."

"Then I guess we need to get to a phone."

"Hold on." Conor reached in his pocket, brought out Shelby's.

Percly's head snapped in his direction. "Where the hell you get that?"

"It's my girlfriend's." He dialed the number to Skagit Brake and Muffler.

Percly looked back to the road, sitting tense in his seat. A minute later, Conor had John's number.

* * *

Each of the children were asked the same questions. Who lives in the house with you? Where's Mommy right now? Where's Daddy? How about big brother and sister? Everything else that needed to be known was on file.

One-by-one their families were rounded up with the help of the SWPD. The officers were well fed. They didn't get to change the children, though. That was for the teachers. It was a special morning at First Step Preschool.

"Single file," Ms. B. said lovingly, as the four and five-year-olds boarded the yellow bus. "And no cheating. Cory, that means you."

Cory scrunched up his face, flashing his best angry lion look. He made a claw and scratched at the air in her direction. She scrunched up her own face, swatting right back.

The boys and girls were all excited. The field trip was not only a surprise, but the first one ever. Today they would see how ChapStick was made.

"Ms. B.?" A boy with messy brown hair asked from near the back of the line. He thrust his hand in the air, waving it back and forth. "Ms. B.? Ohh! Ohh! Ms. B.?"

"Yes, Tyler?"

"I gotta take a piss!"

"Can it wait?"

"No. It's a 'mergency."

Ms. B.'s smile widened. "Well hurry back. And it's pee, not piss."

Without another word, Tyler ran for the school's entrance. Little ones chit-chatted amongst one another about the latest episode of Paw Patrol and recent birthday parties. Near the middle of the line, which was moving quickly into the bus, Trista stood silently, indifferent as always to the fact that none of the other kids liked her.

She was a head taller than any of the boys in her class, and much heavier. She wore the same dress that she had worn Friday. It was too small for her wide frame, and Ms. B. suspected that it hadn't been washed since its last use. There was no doubt that her tattered jacket hadn't.

Trista often wore the same clothes to school for days on end. She was not only fat, but she smelled. Ms. B. had never much cared for her, herself. Sure, there was a touch of sympathy for the girl that she would had to have been a monster not to feel. But how hard would it be to put on some clean clothes, or go outside to play once in a while—maybe burn some calories?

After today, Trista wouldn't have to worry. She and her classmates would be stored in the ChapStick factory until Ms. B. had changed every one of them. Then they would belong to her. They would be one big family. Both of the teachers at First Step would change her own class. Then Trista would have friends. She wouldn't be picked on anymore.

In the parking lot, a police patty wagon sat with the children's families in the back. There was no reason to lock the doors. Every one of them were paralyzed, stacked neatly atop one another. They would be used as food.

Tyler re-emerged off to the side, running out of the school and retaking his place in line.

"Hey!" Steven Cranston cried. "No cuts!"

"But I was here!"

"Ms. B.!"

"Steven," Ms. B. said, "don't you want to sit by your friend on the bus?"

"Yeah, but he took cuts."

"Well, he just left for a minute to use the potty."

"So?"

"So why don't you give him his place back?"

Trista was just heaving her heavy body up the steps, onto the bus.

"Oh-kay," Steven said reluctantly, bashfully. Ms. B. knew the boy had a crush on her. It happened all the time. It was cute, really.

Once both classes were boarded, she climbed the steps, sitting down next to Mrs. Metcalf, who was twice her age and had worked at First Step most of Ms. B.'s life. Neither woman spoke. A high-pitched symphony of children's conversations rang out as the bus came to life and exited the parking lot. The patty wagon followed.

* * *

"We need to stop at a bank," Percly said from the passenger seat. They had pulled over and switched places since Conor knew his way around better.

"Why?" he asked.

"We need money."

Conor hesitated before saying, "I have some put away."

"Good. We need to stop and get it out before they freeze your account."

Conor thought about this. He was probably right. It wasn't a good idea to use the debit card anywhere either. That was just another way that he could be tracked. When he made the call to John, he had tried his best to stress the urgency of the situation, telling him to meet up at

Walmart. John said he could be there in ten minutes. Conor was a minute away. The Mount Vernon branch of his bank was right up the street.

"We better do it now." He turned toward the bank.

"You know, normally I wouldn't care two fucks about your finances," Percly said. "But in light of our current predicament, I have to ask. How much you got put away?"

"Just under seven."

"Seven hundred?"

"Seven thousand."

"Well I highly recommend you take out every penny."

Though he would have preferred to stick to back roads, there was no way to get to the bank without using Mount Vernon's busiest strip. Conor thought about the gun in Percly's lap as they approached.

As if he could read his mind, Percly said, "I ain't gonna rob you, just so you know. Don't even think that. Shit, we can part ways if that's what you're thinkin'. I don't think that's our best plan of action, but I don't need you feelin' like some kind a hostage either. Listen, I'm sorry 'bout pointin' the gun at you back there. You understand that I had to get your attention, though, right? Our lives depended on it. And our lives depend on us makin' wise decisions now. I, personally, think we're better off together, but the choice is yours."

The thought of splitting up hadn't even crossed Conor's mind. "No," he agreed. "We should probably stick together. At least until we figure out what the hell we're gonna do." He pulled into the bank's parking lot.

"We gotta get rid of that phone," Percly said.

"I know." Conor killed the engine. He pulled the key out of the ignition, then, hesitating a moment, pushed it back in before stepping out and walking into the building.

Inside, it was mostly empty. A woman stood in front of the counter, being helped. A young attractive girl smiled at Conor from behind another. In his peripheral, he saw the security guard next to the door. The girl's smile faded when he was close, and he remembered how he had looked in the mirror. He did his best to keep his composure, but his heart beat like a bass drum as he emptied his savings. With a shaking hand, he stuffed the bills into his pocket.

He made a quick exit, feeling the security guard's eyes burning into his flesh as he passed. Climbing back into the car, he became once again aware of Percly's stench. He ignored it as he pulled back out onto the main road.

Less than four minutes later, the Honda pulled into the Walmart parking lot. Conor was relieved to find it more packed than he expected. He parked between two cars and pulled the phone out of his pocket, glancing down to see if he had missed any calls from John. There were none. He scrolled through the missed calls from last night, selecting, "Jeremy." Percly watched as he put the phone to his ear. The call was answered after the second ring.

"Shelby?" It was a woman's voice.

"Hello," Conor said. "Can I speak to Jeremy please?"

"Who is this?"

"This is Conor. I'm calling for Jeremy."

"I beg your pardon? Who?"

"Yeah, my name is Conor—"

"I know who you are," the woman snapped. "Put my daughter on the phone."

Conor tried to process what he was hearing.

"Hello? Can you hear me? I want to speak to my daughter right now."

"I'm sorry," he finally managed. "Is this Shelby's mom?

"Is this supposed to be some kind of a joke?"

"No. I just—" The phone beeped in his ear. Pulling it away from his face, he looked at the screen and saw a number which wasn't assigned a contact, but he recognized. It was John's. He put the phone back to his ear. "I'm sorry. I have to go."

"What? Excuse me? You wait one minute. Where the hell is my—"

Conor accepted the call. "John?"

"Yeah, bud. You here?"

"I'm here. Where you parked?"

"Not. I'm driving around the parking lot. I don't see yer car."

"That's because it's not here. Pull up in front of the store and I'll find you. Cool?"

"Cool."

Without another word, Conor hung up and started the car. When he made it to the entrance, John's car was parked out front. He pulled up next to it and honked. John looked over, examining the car. His eyes landed briefly on Percly before flashing Conor a questioning look. Ignoring it, Conor waved for him to follow and drove to the back of the lot, where no other cars were parked. John pulled up next to him.

"Sure he cool?" Percly didn't look at Conor or the other car as he spoke.

"We're about to find out, aren't we?" Conor popped the trunk before stepping out into the cold. Afternoon was quickly approaching and the day was as bright as it was going to get, though the sky was lined with a thick layer of clouds that looked like grey cotton candy.

John was already out, waiting at the back of his own car, smoking a cigarette. "Jesus," he said when he saw Conor. "You look like shit."

"Thanks." Conor stepped up next to him and leaned against the car.

"Friend a yours?" He blew out a cloud of smoke, motioning with his eyes toward Percly, who still sat staring forward in the passenger seat.

"Kind of. Listen man, thanks for coming."

"Yeah, no problem, bud. Not like Denise was givin' out blowjobs at home, anyway." He chuckled.

"Look, John, I don't have a lot of time, but I need to tell you something and I'm not really sure how."

"Just shoot from the hip, Conman." He spoke conspiratorially out the side of his mouth, revealing his missing tooth. "Ain't much can surprise me these days. I think I pretty much seen it all."

"Yeah, somehow I doubt you've seen anything like this before."

John smirked, squinting at a white van as it passed in front of them. Taking a long drag of his cigarette, turning the red tip to ash, he said, "Listen, Conman," then exhaled a grey stream. "Don't worry about it. I already know the deal."

Conor didn't respond, just listened, feeling his heart rate pick up again.

"We all been there, bud. I just don't wanna see you throw yer whole life away. Yer a good kid, man. Know what I mean?"

"No," he muttered. "I don't think I do."

"Well I'm not gonna stand here an preach ta ya, man. It's not my job, and frankly, I just don't want to. Fuck, look at me. They don't call me John the Baptist. I'm no sculpture a perfection. But shit, man, lemme know what I can do ta help and I'm here. S'all I'm saying."

"John, I don't know what you think is going on."

"Come on, Conman. John ain't blind. Hell, I had you figured out the other day at the shop. You ain't slept in days, kid. I see it. How long you been using?"

"You think I'm on drugs?"

"Come on, man. Why else would you've called me of all people?" He flicked ashes onto the pavement, taking another puff.

"Why? Are *you* on drugs?"

"Shit. Course not. I don't make my history secret, though. Everyone knows where I come from."

"Sorry to hear that," Conor replied. "I'm not on drugs, though."

John peered at him skeptically.

"I'm not using anything, John. I wish it were that simple. Unfortunately, I needed to see you because I think I may have put you and your family in a lot of danger."

"Conman—"

"Just hear me out, man."

John's mouth hung open momentarily, as he seemed to be trying to figure out what to say. Then he shoved the butt of his half smoked cigarette between his lips and looked away.

"What I'm about to tell you is fucking crazy and I know it. So I'm gonna just go ahead and show you first. Why don't you take a look in my trunk. It's open."

"The rice burner's yours?" John cracked a smile.

"No. Just check the trunk, John. We need to hurry."

The smile disappeared as John looked at Conor, trying to read his face. Finally he dropped the cigarette, grinding it into the pavement with his shoe. "Okay, man. Sure." He walked to the Honda. "Let's have a look." He pried the trunk open and his face instantly scrunched up. Leaning back and fanning the air with his hand, he said, "Jesus. What you got in here? A dead body?"

"In the blanket," Conor said.

John's expression grew serious. His jaw hung slightly as he looked at Conor.

"Come on, John. We don't have a lot of time. Just check it out."

"Look, Conor—"

"You're gonna have to trust me, man."

198

After another pause, John leaned back in and once again made a disgusted face. Coughing a couple times, he reached into the trunk and uncovered the dead bug.

* * *

The ChapStick factory wasn't operating today. The children were still let in. Once inside, they were led through the rows of assembly equipment, then the two classes split up. Trista's face said that she suspected something was wrong before hers was escorted into the dark storage room. She didn't say anything, though, just followed.

Ms. B. selected two of them—a boy and a girl—then locked the door behind the others. The two children didn't begin to panic until they heard the cries of their classmates as it slammed shut. She smiled down at them, (reassuringly, she thought) and they both screamed so loud that it echoed through the warehouse.

They turned to run at the same time, but she caught them both easily around their necks. Picking them up off of their feet, she bit Adam lightly on his chest and set him down. Then Kate. The children stumbled to their feet, ran a few steps before falling limp on the cement floor.

She dragged them outside by their hair, and loaded them into the back of the patty wagon on top of their parents and siblings. Mrs. Metcalf was stuck to the wall, high up in the corner where it met the ceiling. She stared down, smiling at two children from her own class, who lay still atop the pile of motionless, breathing bodies. Ms. B. crawled up the wall, seemingly oblivious to all of the horrified eyes staring up.

They were driven out to Walter Murphy's woods, which now consisted of mostly empty holes in the dirt. Mrs. Metcalf took her children somewhere out of sight.

First, Ms. B. sliced little Kate open, vomited her eggs into her, and buried her alive. Then, she opened up one of the parents and ate his insides, impregnating herself again. In under an hour, she was ready to go to work on Adam.

Long before she was done, Officer Brady had the paralyzed bodies out of the wagon and arranged neatly on the forest floor. He was just finishing the tubular flesh of a teenage girl's intestines while she stared up at the tree canopy, barely breathing. Ms. B. chose Steven's father, who like his son, had always had lingering eyes.

When she was done, she moseyed out of the woods and climbed into the passenger seat of the patty wagon. Mrs. Metcalf sat in the back by herself. Brady was in the driver's seat waiting. Without a word, he started the monster of a vehicle and they were off, headed back to the ChapStick factory to fetch more children.

* * *

The dead thing in the trunk was even further decayed, just as Conor suspected. It had begun to turn to some kind of black gelatine in certain places. Somehow, even the bones were rotting. The effect was even more horrifying than when it had been solid. Its broken skull, with all of its terrible, smiling teeth was still mostly visible. What remained of the body was even more insect-like than before.

John gasped, took a step back. Then he heaved, as rotten air filled his lungs. When the fit passed, he looked again in the trunk, and instantly looked away, squinting silently into the distance.

Conor moved to put a hand on his shoulder, catching himself at the last second. He would let his friend's thoughts run their course. Shutting the lid, he invited him to sit in the Honda. John turned and looked at him as if he had just told him the world was about to end. All Conor could do was look back as if it were. Finally, some unspoken understanding seemed to pass between the two men and they both stepped inside, Conor in the driver's seat, John in the back.

Conor was relieved to see that Percly's gun was still concealed. He didn't look back at John or introduce himself, though. Starting the engine, Conor backed out of the parking space.

"Where we goin'?" John's voice was flat.

"I don't know," Conor replied. "I don't think we should just sit here, though."

"Jeez. Why?"

"I'll get to that. For now just try and trust me, okay?"

"Conman, yer not givin' me a shit ton ta work with here. Trust you? What is this, a fuckin' movie? You sound like a damn mental case, bud. What the hell did I just see, and where did you get it?"

"It was my dog." Conor pulled the car out of the lot, driving toward the back road.

"No shit? Sure didn't look like no fuckin' dog ta me."

"That's because it's not. Not now, at least. It was when my girlfriend brought it home the other day—well it looked like one. But it changed. It attacked me last night and I killed it. Smashed the fucker's head with a car battery."

Finally Percly glanced over at him, but didn't speak.

John said, "So you crushed your dog's head with a battery?"

"It was gonna kill me. I think it already killed Shelby."

"Who?"

"My girlfriend. She disappeared yesterday. So did the dog. When I came home, her car and cell were at my place but her and Benji were gone. Then last night the dog came back, but it wasn't a dog. It was that thing in the trunk.

Look, I know how this shit sounds, but you saw it, John."

"Okay," he consented. "I saw it. So what exactly did I see? Cause it sure as hell wasn't no dog."

"I don't know," Conor replied. He pulled into a residential neighborhood.

"Conman, why don't we go to my place?"

"No. I think they might go there looking for us."

"For fuck's sake. Who?"

Conor took a deep breath. Then he told him everything, starting with the accident yesterday morning. When he was done, the first one to speak was Percly.

"I saw the motherfucker too."

Conor looked at him, then back at the street. He had driven around the block twice already.

"The dog," Percly went on. "Remember I told you I saw one burying another one outside the train the other night. I be willing to bet my nuts it was that son-of-a-bitch in your trunk. Light brown? Some kind of a Labrador?"

"Yeah," Conor said.

Percly didn't say anymore. Just nodded and went back to staring out the windshield. A lighter flicked in the backseat, and John's window slid down. Seconds later, the smell of cigarette smoke filled the car. Percly asked if he had another one, and without a word, John handed one up to him.

"Thanks." The transient produced a Bic and lit it.

"No problem."

Conor couldn't just keep driving in circles around the neighborhood. The problem was, he had no idea what else to do. He looked into the rear-view, making eye contact with John. "Well?"

John hesitated before saying, "So you guys killed a cop? And a girl on the highway—and," he tilted his head, "your girlfriend?"

"Jesus. Are you even listening?"

John didn't answer, just blew out a long stream of smoke.

"Look, man," Percly spoke up, not looking back. "You don't have to believe what he's tellin' you. Frankly, I couldn't give two fucks whether you do or don't. But Conor here, goodhearted gentleman that he is, wanted to do you the courtesy of telling you they may come to your house since you texted him your address. The one we killed was a Skagit County Sheriff. To my knowledge, them motherfuckers got jurisdiction all over Skagit County, and if they come knockin' you might not wanna answer the door."

"They won't leave Sedrow," Conor said.

Percly flashed him a questioning look.

"I saw it in their thoughts when I saw my mom this morning. She didn't want me to leave either. It's like they're nesting there or something."

"You sure?"

"Yeah—I think. Every one of them I saw still thought it was human. I mean it knew it was changed, but it had all of its old memories. They know where the town starts and ends. That's why the one by the freeway didn't follow us."

The smell of cigarette smoke was so pungent that Conor felt sick to his stomach.

"So they won't come to my house?" John asked in a tone that one might use when speaking to a small child. Conor didn't blame him. What had he been thinking, expecting him to buy any of this.

Still, he said, "They could send a real cop to take you to Sedrow for questioning."

"And I should just refuse? Take my family and go on the run?"

"I don't know."

"Then we better put on our thinking caps, boys,

because what yer selling sounds like some real-deal and a day's shit. Hell, might even befit me just ta let it play out." He laughed. "One way ta get rid a'the old lady, huh?"

Shelby's phone vibrated in Conor's pocket. He dug it out and saw a text from John.

*Talk to me alone.*

Percly didn't look, or even seem to notice. Conor didn't respond, shoved the phone back into his pocket. He rolled down his window and turned out of the neighborhood. Nobody spoke as he pulled into the Walmart parking lot, stopping between John's car and a truck which had shown up while they were gone. John climbed out, looking in at Conor. Conor didn't move. He put the car in reverse.

"Bye, John."

"Wait." John threw his half smoked cigarette to the ground. "Come an talk to me, Conor. Just you. I need ta tell ya something, man. It's private."

"No, John. I gotta go. Sorry."

"Conman, listen to me. You didn't pull the trigger right? Not on any of 'em. There's no reason for you to go to prison. Come on an get in my car, man. I can help you. We can sort this thing out before we go ta the cops."

"John, I'm leaving."

"Yer not thinking right, damn it! The cops'll understand. Yer scared. Shit, maybe yer both having some kind a fucking shared psychosis. If he shot those people, man, you gotta get away from him, Conor. Think, for Christ's sake!" He reached in and grabbed the door handle. "Come on. We'll go in together." The door opened and his hand landed on Conor's shoulder. Conor put his foot down on the gas, causing the car to lurch backward. John's fingers curled until he had a handful of Conor's T-shirt. Conor slammed on the brakes and the car stopped abruptly, rocking for a second. John threw his hands up, taking a step back. "Whoa! Chill. Chill. It's not like that, bud. I'm not the police. Just tryin' ta help."

Conor shut the door, slammed his foot back down on the gas.

"Hey!" Percly shouted. But it was too late. There was a loud crash, and the car jerked hard. Conor turned around to discover that he had collided with a red minivan. When he looked back out the front window, he saw John's hands and jaw drop simultaneously. "Fuck. Go." Percly's voice was desperate.

"Where?" Conor turned again in his seat. The van was stopped behind them, and they were boxed in by vehicles on both sides and bushes in the front. Percly reached into his coat, and Conor knew that when he saw the hand again, it would be holding a gun. What he didn't know, was what he intended to do with it.

The bushes in front of the car were thick. There was no telling if the Honda could plough through them without having room to pick up speed first. Plus, there was a curb right in front of the tires. He needed to get the van to move.

"No." He put a hand on Percly's arm. "Don't use the gun."

"Nigga—"

Conor cut him off, laying down on the horn. He stuck his hand out the window and waved frantically for the van to move. When it didn't, Percly brought out the revolver and opened his door.

*Fuck this.* Conor put the car in drive and gunned it. It jumped violently as the front wheels hit the curb. Percly bared his teeth at him, slamming his door shut. The Honda's front end pressed into the bushes and struggled to accelerate. Conor put it once again in reverse and drove back over the curb, ploughing into the van. Horns went off from every direction. He shifted back into drive. This time he heard an explosion as he jumped the curb, but the bushes gave, scratching the car as it passed over them. When they landed in the road, the loud scratching of metal on concrete confirmed that he had popped a tire.

He squeezed the steering wheel so tight that his knuckles turned white. He didn't stop, drove as fast as the Honda would go until he saw another housing development. As he turned into it, he prayed silently that nobody was out in a yard.

In his peripheral, he saw sparks fly between the front driver's side wheel and the wet road. The noise was like nails on a chalkboard. He couldn't help but think of the damage that was being done to the car as one wheel turned at a faster rate than the other. But what about the owner? What kind of damage would be done to him now that he was involved in this whole thing? And what about John and his family?

He pulled over a few hundred feet from the neighborhood's entrance and saw Percly staring into the rear-view, his gun still in his lap.

Conor said, "We need to see if there's a spare in the truck."

"I don't think so," Percly responded.

Conor looked back just in time to see John's car pull up behind them.

"What's with this guy?" Percly opened his door, but Conor barely noticed. Something was beginning to sink in. It was something that he had already known on some level since he had first understood the thoughts of the monsters in Sedrow Woolley. Something that they didn't even understand, yet it could be found with a simple glimpse into their minds. *It was that, there's no escape. No way out. Nowhere safe to run. From now on, no matter where you go, danger will always be lurking.*

The thought was overwhelming. It hit so hard that he grew lightheaded. Everything became a blur. Somewhere in the distance—in the real world—he heard Percly yelling for John to get out of the car, lie face down. Then Conor was climbing out of the Honda, stumbling into John's car, Percly was driving. Conor wanted to roll down his window, apologize to his friend, and tell him to look again in the trunk. To get his family to safety. The energy to do so just wasn't there.

"...motherfucker..." Percly's voice seemed to be coming through water. "...before they...fuckin' phone..." It was distorted, and Conor could hardly make out a word.

"Yeah." He heard his own voice as if from a distance. "Yeah. Okay." Reaching in his pocket, he handed over Shelby's phone. Percly tossed it out the window.

Some classic rock song rang out of the car's speakers, filled Conor's ears, reverberated through his head, until he could take it no more. He laid his face against the glass and lost consciousness.

# Chapter Six

Conor knew he was dreaming. It was nighttime and he was back in Sedrow. The sky was cloudy, but there wasn't any fog. He stood in the middle of the Food Outlet parking lot. Though there were no cars, the lot was packed with people, standing around, dancing, and talking merrily. It was some kind of a local event. Maybe a street fair. There was music. Where was it coming from? It sounded like a church choir, only he couldn't make out any of the words.

The parking lot was well lit by streetlamps, which stood high all over the place. There were no monsters. No insects anywhere. A group of young children ran past laughing. In the distance, Conor saw his mom standing in the crowd, talking with somebody. Who was she talking to? He started toward her, but the crowd came together, blocking his path, seemingly oblivious to him.

He opened his mouth to excuse himself, but no words would form. So he pushed, tried to shove his way through.

When he made it to the place where she had been, she was gone. He opened his mouth again, this time to call for her. Still nothing.

The music continued to play. An old couple held each other, swayed from side to side. *Mom. Mom.* No words still, only thoughts. Somewhere, Toby barked. Conor knew the dog's voice well, would recognize it anywhere.

WHAH! WHAH! A train whistle cut through the sounds in the crowd.

Then Conor found himself looking across the highway at the old steam locomotive. It sat in front of the vintage gas pump, amongst statues of animals and Indians. Only the statues weren't statues anymore. They were giant, smiling insects—all staring at the people in the lot.

The music went on, but the people no longer celebrated. A fear spread through the crowd like an electric current. It overtook Conor, and he trembled. Steam floated from the train's chimney. The bugs watched unmoving. Their smiles were the worst things he had ever seen. Something about them was so cold, so cruel. So hungry.

The huge sign, which had been carved by chainsaws long ago, was nowhere to be found. Instead, a cement tombstone stood beside the locomotive. In bold lettering, it read, "TOWN CENTER."

WHAH! WHAH!

The highway had three lanes. There was a patch of grass between the lot and the road. He shouldn't have been able to read the words. They were too small and too far away. Every detail was vivid, though. Phillip Harris stood in the window of the train, wearing an old conductor's hat. He wasn't an insect. He was himself, smiling into the parking lot. Reaching up, he pulled a cord hanging from the ceiling and the whistle cried out again, sending another surge of fear through the crowd. Then he focused his attention on Conor. He opened his mouth and Conor heard his words as if they were standing face-to-face.

"Cow catcher!"

Conor's whole body jerked so hard he thought at first it would go into convulsions. That he would break into a fit of twitching and his heart would stop, because the poison from Benji's bite was finally finishing the job. He didn't convulse though. Instead, he inhaled deeply and sat up, looking out over the dash, at the road which lay ahead. They were just pulling out of the neighborhood Conor had driven them into. He glanced over to see Percly looking at him from the driver's seat. His bad eye seemed to focus surprisingly well and the effect was unsettling.

"You cool?" he asked.

"I think I fell asleep."

"Think? You passed out." He returned his focus to the road.

"How long?"

"How long were you out? Shit, maybe a minute. You were moanin' in your sleep." He turned down another residential street. "We need to find the freeway, fast."

"Yeah. I know the way. Need me to drive?"

"Naw. You rest. You ain't doing too good. I know the way, too, but I ain't bout to take the main strips. Just point me down back roads an I'll get us there."

"Sure. When you get to the end of this street, take a left. Why the freeway?"

Percly looked at him again, like he had something alien on his face.

"I mean where are we going?" Conor peered in the mirror on his door in case they were being followed again.

"Shit, anywhere. Probably Seattle."

"What's in Seattle?"

"People. Civilization. Somewhere to blend in until we

figure out what the hell we doin'. Personally, I say we get the fuck out the country. I hear Mexico is nice this time a year."

The words "cow catcher" hadn't stopped playing in his head since he woke up from the dream. It was almost like a song, set to repeat.

"I'm not going to Seattle," he said. "Or Mexico."

After a brief pause, Percly said, "You crazy or something?"

"I don't know anymore."

Bringing the car to a complete stop, he took the left. "You not crazy. You not stupid either. Meeting that fool back there? That was stupid. You? You're not though. You just too nice for your own good. So nice, you ready to get yourself killed. Suicidal. That's what you are. But I'm not. So lemme ask you a question, Conor—where do I turn next?"

He knew if he kept directing him to the freeway, they would be there in a few short minutes. But then what? Did they split up? How, with a car, which didn't even belong to either of them? "Just keep driving," he said. "I'll let you know where the turns are."

Percly shook his head, let out a long breath, and went on. "Who you got left in that town, anyway?"

"What do you mean?"

"I mean, who you got there? You said your parents are gone, your girl, your dog. Who else you got?"

"I don't know. Nobody, I guess. Couple a friends, why?"

"They gone too, man. If they not, they ain't about to believe anything you can tell 'em bout what's goin' on out there. Just like the police ain't about to believe us. We take this shit to them, what you think gonna happen?" When Conor didn't answer, he said, "I'll tell you what's gonna happen. They gonna lock our asses up in the back of the car an take us right back to Sedrow motherfuckin' Woolley. Then we gonna be buried alive out in some redneck's backyard with bug larva in our guts. I know you think you gonna be some kinda hero—go back an save your hometown—but I'm tellin' you right now, that ain't the way it's gonna go down. This ain't no movie. You and I, we in the same boat. And if you ain't heard a word I said up until now, at least hear this. Heroes don't work in real life."

"Take another left."

"Right up here?" Percly pointed with his eyes.

"Yeah. Next turn. I never said anything about being a hero."

"Then what? You gonna wait around here to get picked up? Cause you know that's exactly what's gonna happen. You can't go on the run in the same place you wanted. Especially in a small podunk fuckin' county like Skagit."

"I didn't say that either. Take this right up here."

Percly hit the blinker as a black SUV passed, going the opposite direction. "You sure about what you said back there? That they won't leave Sedrow?"

"I don't know. I mean, yeah. I'm not sure about anything at this point. I'm pretty sure, though."

"Pretty sure?" He took the turn.

"Pretty sure. That's the best I can do. I'm sure they don't wanna leave now. But when the food runs out—"

"The food?"

"Jesus. You know what I mean."

"Yeah." He shook his head. "Well, then what?"

"I don't know. I mean, think about it. They'll have to move on, right? Either that or die off. How did you know the other morning?"

"Know what?"

"When I hit that girl with my Buick. How did you

know she was one of them? Turn right onto second up here."

"Cause," Percly said without hesitation. "I can see 'em too. And that wasn't no girl you hit."

Looking over at him, Conor said, "You were bit?"

"Naw."

"Then—?"

"My eye. This one." He pointed to the baby-blue, foggy eye, which would normally have been covered by the patch that now rested over his forehead. "I only been able to see silhouettes out it since I was a kid—still only see silhouettes, really. Unless one a'those cockroaches is in front a me. I can see them babies clear as motherfuckin' day. Only see 'em with the bad one at first. The other see people and dogs, an shit. Then, they come into focus."

Conor considered this for a second. "What do you mean, 'come into focus'?"

"I mean they change. As soon as I see 'em with my bad eye, the other picks up on it too. Just takes a second. Know what I'm sayin'?"

"Yeah," Conor nodded. "I think. And you said you weren't bit?"

"You know if you gonna keep askin' me the same questions, we ain't gonna get far."

"Yeah. Sorry. Listen—up here, we're gonna have to turn onto the main road for a bit. I know it's not ideal, but it's only for a minute. Just drive a couple blocks and pull into the Safeway parking lot." When Percly grew noticeably tense in his seat, Conor said, "The freeway's right there."

"I know the freeway's right there. I ain't stopping at Safeway, though. They got stores in other cities. Ones where the entire police force ain't out lookin' for our asses."

"I'm not going in the store," Conor said. "There's

something I need in the parking lot, and I haven't seen another one in years." In spite of everything, he laughed a little. "Shit, I doubt there are more than a handful left in the entire state."

Hitting the blinker, Percly asked, "And what's that?"

"A payphone," Conor said.

* * *

Trista was scared. She was so scared that her whole body shook. It started when she got to the ChapStick factory. At first the smell of cherry flavored ChapStick had given her a warm feeling in her tummy. Then, when she saw that there were no workers—the whole place was shut off—she knew something was wrong.

Ms. B. was wrong. Something about her wasn't normal. She was nice today. She wasn't always nice to Trista. She always smiled and said nice things, (almost always, at least) but her smile wasn't nice. It was a pretend smile. A lie. She didn't like Trista, and Trista knew it.

Not today, though. Today her smile was real. It was real, and it was real scary. Today she seemed to like Trista just as much as she liked everyone else, and Trista didn't like it.

That wasn't it, though. She saw something. Something that she knew she wasn't supposed to see. Not just the way kids weren't supposed to see grownup things, but something else. When the door opened and Kate and Adam went out, she saw a monster. Not the whole thing. Just a foot. But she was sure it was a monster's foot. It had long, sharp claws and looked like it belonged to one of Aunt Julia's iguanas, if the iguanas had had dark, dark skin. The room was dark too. That had scared the other kids, and the crying all around her was giving her a headache.

When the door had opened and Kate and Adam's names were called, everybody had stopped wailing and the whole place had turned into a sniff-fest. But when the two kids ran out and it slammed shut again, the crying was even louder than before.

Trista knew that nobody else saw the foot. They just wanted out of the dark room. Not her, she knew what was out there. She tried to tell the kid closest to her, whoever that was.

"Oww, gross!" he stopped crying long enough to say. "Trista!" When he pushed her away, his hands landed right on the place that her ta-tas would someday be. She threw a kick in his direction, but missed. Trista backed up and her body found a cold wall. The other kids cried and cried, but their voices were a little further away. She tried to project her own voice over them.

"Stop crying! We need to get out of here!"

But nobody listened.

It occurred to Trista that she would die today. The monster outside would finish with Kate and Adam, then it would eat the rest of them. Or maybe not today. Maybe it was full. They would all be stored in the dark room like a giant refrigerator, then called out to be eaten, two a day.

Not Trista, though. When her time came, the thing wouldn't need another kid. Just her. She was the size of two of her classmates. Somehow, the thought of dying alone was worse than having another boy or girl with her, even if that boy or girl hated her. And every boy and girl in class did.

Trista yelled again. Still nobody listened. It seemed like she was the only kid in the room not crying. Maybe she was. She needed to do something. Her eyes had adjusted a little to the dark, but she still couldn't see anything. Only shapes that were a slightly different shade of dark in some places. Putting the palms of both hands on the wall, she shivered at how cold it was against her bare skin. Then she began to move toward the door, feeling up and down as she went. A light switch. That's what she needed.

She moved and she moved and her body bumped into what felt like empty boxes. Refusing to lose the wall, she kicked them. They tumbled down, as she continued to scale the cold surface. When she made it to the door, the crying grew louder. The kids were all waiting for it to open again, refusing to move too far away.

She felt around on one side of the door, but there was no switch. That had to mean it was on the other. Light switches were always by doors. Her hands touched the metal and she began to walk them over to the other side. But a group of crying kids who were pressed against it stopped her. Trista pushed them with her body, causing some of them to cry louder. They moved easily, though.

When she made it to the other side, she found the switch. Her heart sped up and she felt a smile touch her lips as she flipped it. But nothing happened. She took a deep breath, wanting to cry as well. She couldn't though. She knew she couldn't. What would that do, besides keep her stuck and unhelpful? She needed to think right now, nothing else.

Closing her eyes tight, she locked the tears in, but couldn't stop the snot from coming down out of her nose. She sniffed it back and opened her eyes again.

"Someone listen to me!" she screamed as loud as she could.

Somebody stopped crying long enough to yell, "Shut up, Trista!" It was a boy, and he was close to her. Really close. She reached toward the voice, her hand finding his body. Moving it up, she took a handful of his hair. He screamed like a girl, and it echoed so loud that once he stopped, the room fell silent aside from sniffing. Trista knew better than to let go.

"Listen to me," she hissed into his face.

"Let go of me, Trista! You stink!"

"Shut up! Shut up! Shut up! Listen to me, everybody. We need to get out of here. There's a monster outside. I saw it."

A girl started wailing louder than any of them had earlier. Then another. Trista needed to get the room back under control. She slammed the boy's head into the wall as hard as she could. He let out another high pitched scream, and the crying stopped once again.

"Are you even listening to me?" she cried. "Don't you believe me?"

"No! You're a stupid liar, Trista! I know! I know! I know! I know!"

"No I'm not!"

"Yes you are! There's no such thing as monsters! I hope you die, and I wanna go home!"

For no reason that she understood, she slammed the boy's face into the wall again. He screamed and struggled to get away, but she was too strong. "I saw it!" she yelled. "I saw it and I'm not lying. You're all being stupid right now and if we don't get out of here, it's gonna eat us. Do you wanna get eaten?"

A different kind of silence passed through the room as every boy and every girl considered this question. Finally, somebody said, "No." The voice was timid. She recognized it though. It was Steven.

Somebody else said, "No one's gonna get eaten and there's no monsters." But the voice had very little conviction.

"Yeah they are," Steven said, "Trista's not lying. I saw it too."

The crying started again and the boy who hadn't

stopped struggling to get away from Trista tensed up and joined in. She let him go, and he ran into the crowd.

"Steven?" she called. "Where are you? Come to the door." This was the best she could have hoped for. Everybody liked Steven. They would listen to him. When they found each other, Trista said, "Did you really see it?"

"Yeah." He was surprisingly calm.

"Talk to them, Steven. Make them shut up."

"And then what?"

"Then we can help each other. Like Ms. B. says. Teamwork."

"Ms. B.'s the monster, Trista."

Trista knew that. She didn't want to believe it, but deep down she had known. "Then we need to hurry. She's gonna eat us, Steven."

"Trista, I'm scared."

"I know," Trista said. "Me too. If we can get a light on, though, we can find a way out before she comes back."

At first Steven didn't respond. Then he said, "Okay. If they don't stop crying, though, they won't hear me."

"I can make them stop," she said.

"How?"

But Trista was already moving toward the group. She reached out, grabbing the first person she could find by the hair. This time it was a girl.

* * *

The Safeway parking lot seemed unusually busy for a Monday morning. Conor was grateful the payphone was located on the far side of the store, but still couldn't shake the feeling that everybody in the vicinity was staring at him. Even the people in the vehicles driving by on the main road. Percly waited in the car.

Conor wanted him to be right. Wanted to believe that they needed to leave. To get as far away as possible. Hadn't that been the plan this morning anyway? To get his family and go? But where? The more he thought about it, the more he became convinced that running would only prolong the inevitable. Whatever was in Sedrow Woolley wasn't leaving now, but it would. It would spread and eventually find them wherever they went. It had to be contained before it grew any bigger.

The phone wasn't in a booth, but mounted to the outer wall of the store. If a cop drove by, he would easily be able to see them. The call had to be made, though. Conor raised the receiver to his ear and fished a couple quarters out of his pocket, slipping them into the slot. A dial tone appeared instantly. He didn't have Dale's cell number committed to memory, but his friend's parents were some of the only people he knew who still had a landline. He had called that number countless times as a teenager.

The call was answered on the first ring. "Aye-low."

A chill started in his chest. He didn't know why either. He should have expected it. He did expect it, he guessed, but somewhere deep down where the chill reigned from, there had been some semblance of hope that it wouldn't be a clicking, buzzing, insectile voice on the other end of the line. A voice that sounded like the crackling of a campfire, somehow able to form words. And even though he couldn't see the thing, he knew who it thought it was.

It wasn't a cold chill, though, more like tiny hairs, standing up inside of him. It spread out and filled every limb until Conor felt his actual hairs standing up. Then, as fast as it had appeared it was gone, replaced by an anger that he hadn't taken the time to stop and feel yet. An anger that, frankly, he never even imagined existed. Baring his teeth, he squeezed the phone so tight he felt the blood rushing from his hand.

"Ay-low," the monster that believed it was Dale's Dad repeated. "Conor? That you, champ? Bout time ya called. Dale's been expecting ya all damn morning. Ay, Dale! Phone call!"

Before Conor could respond, he heard his best friend in the background. "Is it him?" And the chill returned. Not because he spoke in one of their identical voices, but because he didn't. It was him. He was alive. Unchanged. "Hello? Conor? Can you hear me, man? You there?"

"Yeah." Conor's voice shook. "Dale, I'm here."

He paused a second, then said, "Fucking hell, Conor. What did you do, man?"

"Dale, get the hell out of that house."

"The police are here, dude."

"Fuck!" Conor slammed his hand on the brick wall. "Dale, listen to me. I know how fucking crazy this all looks right now. I'll explain everything later, I promise. You need to get the fuck out of there, man. Get in your car and leave. Get out of Sedrow Woolley."

"Get out of Sedrow?" he asked a little too loud.

"Don't do that, Dale. Don't try and help them. Just listen to me."

"Jesus, bud, how long have we been friends? Are you hearin' yourself right now? This is me, Conor. I wanna help you, not them. You gotta—"

"Damn it, Dale! I'm not fucking crazy! For the love of Christ! Have I ever done or said anything to make you think I'm crazy?"

"You killed a cop, man."

"NO I DIDN'T! I DIDN'T FUCKING KILL ANYBODY! They're lying! They're lying to you right now, Dale. They're gonna fucking kill you if you don't get out of there. Please just listen to me."

"Okay. Okay. Okay. Just try and relax—"

"You want me to relax? Get out of that house." Conor

felt tears building up behind his eyes, threatening to burst out again, because even as he spoke, he knew how useless his words were. They were falling on deaf ears and there was nothing he could do to change it. But he couldn't not say it. It had to be said. "They're gonna kill you, Dale. The police, your parents, the whole town. They're gone. I know you can't see it. I couldn't either. Then this morning one of them attacked me. It tried to kill me. Man, I know how ridiculous this shit sounds, but if you don't get away from that town—"

"So that's it," the insectile voice of Phillip Harris appeared in Conor's ear. "You were attacked. Bit, huh? And now you can see. Well isn't that just how it works. That fucking dog a yours, or the chica?"

"Put him back on the phone," Conor spoke through gritted teeth.

Phillip laughed. It was possibly the worst thing Conor had ever heard. "Who? You're buddy? Naw, Mitchell. You're gonna go ahead and talk to me for a while. I knew you knew something, man. Couldn't tell how or what though, but I reckon it makes sense now. Couldn't a been the chica. She ain't been gone long enough to be back yet. That mutt finally got you? 'Bout fucking time. I sure wouldn't mind hearing how the shit you're not in the dirt under that raggedy little shack a yours, though. I mean if you got time to tell the story."

"Yeah," Conor growled. "I'll bet you would."

"Course I would," it clicked. "So why don't you take a second to enlighten me?"

The anger was back. It was overwhelming. Conor wasn't himself. Not any version of himself that he recognized, at least. Fueled by it, he spat, "Why don't you guess, motherfucker. Go ahead and reason it out, if you think you can."

"Listen, Mitchell, I'm starting to get the impression

we don't understand each other as good as I thought we did. Now I don't know anyone who likes being called stupid. So I'm gonna go ahead and just give you the benefit of the doubt and assume that's not what you're trying to say about me right now."

Suddenly another layer of reality crumbled in on itself. It became clear that he had been wrong in thinking they couldn't reason. The thing on the phone was clearly doing just that right now. As he processed this, it went on.

"How'd you get away, Mitchell? That's what I wanna know. No way you should a been able to outrun the little cocksucker. You and your little science club butt-buddy here may of spent all your time outrunning every piece of ass in Sedrow Woolley High, except each other's, but that's about the extent a'your physical abilities, isn't it?"

"Excuse me?" He heard Dale's voice in the background.

"Yeah," Conor said, "Well how about this? I killed that fucking dog. Smashed its head with a car battery. But that's nothing compared to what I'm gonna do to you, Phillip. I'm gonna fucking—"

"I know you killed him." Harris laughed. "I saw the blood on your floor. Heard about the body in your trunk too. It's on its way back into town, by the way, so it can be disposed of properly. Yeah, I just wanted to hear it from the pony's mouth, I guess. See if you really had it in ya."

He opened his mouth, not sure what he would say, then Dale cried out in pain, and Conor made an unintelligible noise in response.

Harris laughed again. "Yeah. That's right."

"What the hell?" Dale screamed. "What the hell? What the—Aahhh! Aahh! Nonononono! Aahh!" Then there was nothing.

"Stop!" Conor yelled. "Come on! Please! Just stop it!

It's me you want!"

"Not me, Mitchell. His mom's got him. 'Fraid I don't have much say in the matter one way or another. She's gonna slice him open and bury him in a hole right out in the front yard, I reckon. Come on by and we can put you next to him. It's nothing to be afraid of, Conor. You'll both be back. You'll be back and you'll be better. Don't you wanna be better-cheddar, my man?"

This was pointless. There was nothing left to talk about. All he was doing by talking any longer was putting Percly and himself at risk. Taking a deep breath, he closed his eyes, willing himself to hang up.

"Don't do it," Harris said, "Don't you hang up on me. Not yet. We still have some business to square up. You killed my old man. You and that rat-basket fucking spook. But I know you didn't pull the trigger. He's been causing a lot a trouble around town lately, Mitchell, and frankly, I just don't like him. So I'll make you a deal. You bring me Valentine, and I'll give you your friend. How's that sound?"

"You're lying," Conor said, his voice weak now. "You already told me there's nothing you can do."

"About the science dweeb? Course not. That's not who I mean, though. I'm talking about the poor son-of-a-bitch whose car you stole."

Conor felt the ground begin to sink under his feet. "John?"

"Yeah! That's the one! I'll tell you what, you bring me the nigger and I'll throw in John's family too. They'll be all yours. Shit, after you left him face down in the street, he had to call his wife for a ride. Her, the kids'n him are on their way into town right now so he can write a statement on your ass. And guess what? I already told him not to pick up any calls. Simple trade, Mitchell, them for Valentine. What do ya say?"

Conor hung up. Then he picked up the receiver and hung up again, slamming it harder into its cradle. Then again and again until he thought he might break the last payphone in Skagit County. Leaving it hanging by the cord, he climbed back into the passenger seat of John's car. Percly put it in drive and started toward the freeway.

"If we leave," Conor spoke slowly. "They'll just spread."

Shaking his head, Percly said, "What the fuck we supposed to do then?" But he didn't veer, just continued to drive toward the parking lot's exit closest to the interstate.

"I don't know, but we have to go back. We have to do something. When they run out of victims, they'll just move on. They'll spread until everyone's gone."

"That can't be right."

"I know. I know it can't, but it is. They'll spread, and they'll kill us all—not just us, but everything that eats and breathes—then they'll starve and die off. It'll be a global extinction. And it'll happen fast. We have to do something, Percly."

They made it to the exit, and Percly hit the blinker. "What, man? What the fuck we s'pose to do? Go back, guns blazin' an take on a whole fuckin' town a giant cockroaches? You really think that's gonna stop anything?"

"No," Conor said, "We should have brought the dead one from my trunk. We need another one. Then we'll have proof. It'll be enough to at least get somebody to go out there. They still might not believe us, but they'll have to check. It'll get the military involved, and at this point that's our only hope. Come on, Percly. You know I'm right. If we go back, we'll probably die. But if we don't, we'll be dead in a month anyway."

Percly didn't speak as he turned onto the main road,

and Conor couldn't read his expression under his thick beard. He pulled the car into the turn lane, bringing it to a stop in front of the red light. Just ahead, a huge green sign read, "I-5 South Seattle."

"I'm not going to Seattle," Conor said, "You can run if you want. That's your choice to make, but at least help me find another car—shit give me your gun—before we split up. Anything."

The light turned green and cars began to deposit onto the freeway. Percly followed them. "We not goin' to motherfuckin' Seattle," he finally said.

"Then what are we—?"

"We gettin' the fuck outta this town before we get himmed up. There's a hotel just up the way in Everett, don't ask for ID if you slip 'em an extra twenty."

Conor couldn't help that the thought of going the wrong way caused a sense of relief to come over him like a comfort blanket. It was still wrong though. He needed out of this car before it went any further. He had to go back to Sedrow Woolley. He started to object, but Percly interrupted him.

"Maybe I was wrong about you. Maybe you are stupid. I get it. We goin' back to Sedrow motherfuckin' Woolley. I don't want to, but we clearly don't have a choice in the matter. I'll tell you what we sure as fuck ain't doin' though. Goin' back without a plan. We gonna go to the motel, regroup, make a plan, eat a last fuckin' meal, then go on this suicide mission. Those are my terms. And if it's not too much trouble, I think I'd like to have a shower, a shave and some fresh clothes, cause I sure as hell don't wanna die no fuckin' bum."

Conor didn't have to think about it for long. A shower and a last meal sounded good to him too.

* * *

Everybody in the dark room was pressed up against the door, crowding in on one another, ready to do what they had to do. They may not have listened to Trista, but when Steven told them what he saw and what would happen if they didn't work together, they finally stopped crying. Most of them, at least.

Trista wasn't at the front of the crowd. She knew that would be the stupidest place to be when the door opened. Everybody else seemed to want to be there, though, and she didn't try to stop them. There was no light—no chance of escape any other way—and when the time came, it would be every kid for themself.

She wasn't at the back either. That would be almost as stupid as the front. Steven took the very, very front. Everybody seemed to have decided that he was the leader now, and he didn't seem to mind. Trista found herself a little sad at the thought of what might happen to him. Before today, she wouldn't have cared. He had never been mean to her, but he had never been nice either.

The breathing in the room was so heavy that it was almost loud enough to give her a headache. That's because the monster was back. They had heard the doors outside of the room and Trista imagined that if the kids around her weren't breathing so hard, she would hear the sound of monster claws scraping on the cement floor as it approached.

"Okay," Steven somehow whispered loud enough for everybody to hear over the breathing. "This is it. You all know what to do. This is our only chance. Is everyone ready?"

There were a few sniffs and a couple people said that they were. Everybody else just stood frozen.

"Listen to me," he went on. "You have to be ready right now. Be brave. If you don't, we'll all die. I know you're scared. I'm scared too, but being scared won't help us now. I need to know that everyone's ready. Don't say it too loud, or it'll hear us. Just whisper, okay? Are you ready?"

Trista knew why Steven had become the leader. He was good at it. As the whispered, "yes," began to spread through the crowd, she even found herself joining in. Found herself feeling braver and braver. Something about the way they were coming together to get out of this as a team made her feel powerful, like together they couldn't be stopped. Then the monster spoke from the other side of the door.

"Ready for what?" The voice was horrible. It crackled like the fire pit in the backyard, when Daddy threw wood in it. It was almost like a whisper too, only way louder.

A girl shrieked somewhere in the crowd. Everybody else just kept breathing hard.

"Can you hear me, children?" the monster asked. "It's me. Ms. B. Are you all okay in there?"

"We want out!" Steven called back. "Open the door!"

"Steven? Is that you?"

"Yes." Steven's voice faltered a bit.

"Well, why do you sound so angry, sweetheart?"

"I know what you are. I saw you. So did Trista."

"What in the world are you talking about, Steven?"

"You're a monster! You want to eat us!"

"Now that's just silly. Why would you say something like that? You're gonna scare everybody."

The whole room remained quiet.

Steven said, "You locked us in a dark room. You lied, Ms. B. You said we were having a field trip to see how ChapSticks're made."

"Well, you're at the ChapStick factory, aren't you?"

"YOU LOCKED US IN A ROOM!" he screamed.

"Steven, you calm down, right now! Do you hear me?

I put you in there for your own protection. I know what you saw. It wasn't a monster. There was a lizard out here. Do you know what a monitor lizard is?"

"I do!" a boy yelled.

"Ssshhh," Trista said, "Let Steven talk."

"Steven," Ms. B. continued. "Do you?"

After a moment of silence, Steven answered timidly. "No."

"Well it's a very big, very dangerous reptile. It got loose in the factory, and all the workers had to go home. We put you all in there until we could catch it. Mrs. Metcalf's class is in a room too."

"You're lying!" Steven yelled. "You're a liar, Ms. B."

"Maybe she's not," the other boy spoke up again. "My cousin has a monitor lizard. They're real."

"Then why is it dark in here?" Steven asked.

"Is it?" Ms. B. responded. "I must have been in such a hurry that I forgot to turn the light on."

Trista couldn't take it anymore. She had had more than enough. "Her voice!" she yelled. "Listen to her voice! She's a monster, damn it!"

That's when the door opened. Just a little, and everybody took a step back.

*No,* Trista thought. *This isn't right.* They weren't sticking to the plan.

The monster said, "Where is that fat little shitbag? Trista? Come on over here and talk to me."

A tiny bit of light came through the slit in the door and the kids up front all screamed at the same time. Trista refused to let any of it affect her. She needed to continue to use her head, not her feelings. Even though Ms. B. had always told them to use their feelings. Ms. B. was wrong and she wanted to eat them all.

Pushing the kids in front of her, she screamed, "RUUUUUN!" Her throat burned as the word forced itself out, but before she knew it she was in motion, along with everybody else. Then there was more light, and she knew the door was wide open. She didn't take the time to look, just pushed and ran, and within seconds she was out of the dark room and in the big open ChapStick warehouse. It was still dark, but not as dark as where she had been.

Somebody screamed. Somebody else choked. Trista just ran. Soon the crowd thinned out and she was running full sprint. She didn't think, just moved. A sharp pain shot through her body, starting at her chest. Stopping dead in her tracks, she realized that she had run into something. Some kind of a long metal counter. Only then did she turn and see what was happening around her.

There were two monsters. They moved so fast that she could barely see them, but she could tell that they were ugly. They ran around on four legs like lizards, only their faces looked like bugs. Trista heard their claws as they scurried around, this way and that, biting kids so fast that they didn't even stand a chance.

Everybody who was bit took a couple more steps, then fell motionless. Trista had expected something like this. There was no way they could all make it, but at least this way some of them would.

One of the monsters stood up on two legs, grabbing a girl with a braided ponytail around the neck. She choked as the thing picked her up. It flung her across the factory, and she slammed hard into a big metal piece of equipment. The other monster scurried toward her.

The first one grabbed a boy by his feet and he fell down, banging his face on the pavement. There were bodies everywhere, and only a few children left running toward the door, screaming. Trista didn't follow them. There weren't enough to keep the things occupied. Instead, she ran for the room she had seen Mrs. Metcalf take her class to. She opened the door, and the crowd inside almost ran her over as they poured out crying.

So they knew too.

The two monsters pounced on them, and only then did Trista break for the door that led outside. Halfway there her foot caught something and she went down hard, barely breaking her fall with her hands. She looked at what she had tripped on. It was Steven. He lay motionless, staring over at her. He was still breathing and his eyes told her that he was terrified.

Trista stood back up and ran. She collided with the door, pushing it open with all of her strength and weight. The fresh air hit her lungs and she took the deepest breath she had ever taken.

*Don't stop. Don't stop. Don't stop.*

She didn't check to see who else made it out, looking instead at the police wagon in the parking lot. Officer Brady had to be one too. She cut left and ran through the grass until she made it to the small gravel road on the side of the building.

She ran and she ran, until she couldn't run anymore. Then she slowed down and tried to breathe. The breaths came in choking gasps, and she wondered if she would die after all. Her chest burned and her heart beat like an angry gorilla inside of her ribs.

Leaning down, she put her hands on her legs, only now seeing that there was blood on her dress. Was it hers, or someone else's? Who cared? When she could finally breathe again, she stood up and started walking fast away from the factory. She needed to find somewhere that she recognized so she could find her way home. Or maybe she could find a police officer. A real one.

A few minutes later she got her wish as a Sedrow Woolley Police car pulled up next to her. The window rolled down and a man smiled out at her.

"Hiya. How ya doing today?"

Trista opened her mouth to respond, but the words caught in her throat. Instead her stomach began to jerk, and for the first time today, tears poured down her face.

"There. There." The cop opened the door, stepped out of his car. "Don't cry now. It'll be all right. What's your name, sweetheart?" He walked over, kneeling in front of her.

"Tr—Tr—Trista," she finally managed.

"Oh, well that's a pretty name, Trista. How come you're not at home, darling?"

"I was—I was at school." She sniffed. "We went to the ChapStick factory to see how ChapSticks are made. Then—Then—" She couldn't say it. How could she? The officer wouldn't believe her anyway. Now that she was so far away, she wasn't sure she even believed it anymore.

"Come on." His voice was soothing. It reminded her of Grandpa, before he died of a bad heart. "Come here, sweetie." He put his arms around her and held her tight. That's when she lost it. She exploded into tears so violently that her body trembled.

The whole thing had been so unfair. She hadn't done anything wrong, just gone to school like she had every Monday since the year started. And she had been so excited when she found out that they were having a field trip.

She threw her own arms around the officer and hugged him as tight as she could, not wanting to ever let go. Not until she felt the bite. It wasn't hard, just enough to break the skin as he sank his teeth into her shoulder.

At first it hurt. Then she didn't feel anything. She let go, pushed away from him, looking into the face of another smiling monster. She gasped and her mouth hung open until she collapsed onto the sidewalk.

"There. There, baby." The voice sounded exactly like Ms. B.'s now. He scooped her up into his arms and carried her to his car, opening the back door and setting her inside. "Don't be afraid, little one. I have a surprise for you."

Trista tried to move her head, to look around, but she couldn't. She could only move her eyes. She looked up into the face of another one. And a smaller one next to it. She was laying across their laps. They both smiled down at her and somehow she knew that they hadn't always been monsters. Neither had Ms. B. They had been changed into them.

Trista could see inside of her head what they had looked like before. She saw both of them on the news the other night with Mom and Daddy. It was the man who disappeared and the boy who had been with him.

The man raised a sharp claw, and she knew that he thought it was a knife. A big knife, with a thick blade. Hooking it on the bottom of her dress, he began to slowly lift it upward. Trista had never been so afraid in her life. She wanted to scream, to kick, to cry. But nothing happened. Not until the boy reached over and grabbed the man's face with his own three claws. He slammed the man's head into the back of the hard plastic seat and hissed loud.

"No! She's mine!"

The man stopped pulling the dress up, but didn't push it back down either. He just smiled at the boy, then looked forward. Trista heard the driver's door open, and close again. Then the car moved.

* * *

The room wasn't worth what the kid had to pay for it, but Percly got the impression he didn't care. Money was the last thing on his mind. It only had one bed, a bathroom, and a table with an ashtray where Percly sat chain smoking from the pack of Marlboros he got Conor to buy him. Next to the ashtray, sat a half drank bottle of orange Cisco. He probably would have got him something pricier, but what was the point? He'd been drinking cheap wine for years, and had grown a little accustomed to it, he guessed. Next to the bottle, was the shiny blue 44. magnum he'd taken from a house days ago.

The shower didn't get rid of the stench of homelessness that still clung to his body like a woman not ready to accept that it was over. It wasn't as prevalent as before the shower, but he knew it was still there. Not because he could smell it—no, Percly was used to the odor—but because the kid was easy to read. His face was like a book with large print. The relationship between Percly Valentine and homelessness was over, though.

Why? Because by the time this was over, he would be dead. They both would. What choice did they have though? The kid was right. Percly knew he was. If they didn't try and fix this shit—impossible as that would be— they'd be dead within weeks anyway. The cockroaches weren't about to stop anytime soon, and at the rate they seemed to be able to spread, they could infest the whole world before Christmas.

So Percly let him buy him a change of clothes too. Nothing fancy. No need. It was just something to be buried in anyway. Not in a casket either, but in the dirt, somewhere in the woods of hoity-toity Sedrow fucking Woolley. They wanted Conor to be one of them, though. He'd be buried as well, but then he'd come back.

Percly hardly recognized the man in the mirror after shaving. Then, when he did his head as well, he couldn't help that he almost teared up, remembering the person he once was. It was tempting to forget that that person had long ago been replaced by a transient now into his fifties.

Conor sat on the edge of the bed, and neither of them

had spoken since Percly came out of the bathroom. Putting a cigarette out and lighting another, he finally said, "Thanks."

Conor looked over, faked a half grin. "For what?"

"Everything. I dunno. The clothes, the smokes, I guess."

"You sure that's what you wanted?" He nodded toward the wine bottle.

"Yeah. It's fine."

"Any good?"

"Wanna try?"

Conor shook his head.

"Listen," Percly said, "You know there's nothing you could've done about your friend? That fool made his own bed, not listenin' to you this morning."

Conor looked away, didn't respond, so Percly went on.

"Think about it, man. I'm serious. Think long and hard and you tell me if there's anything you could've done short a kidnappin' his ass and locking him in a trunk that would've helped."

"Then maybe that's what I should've done," he finally said.

"Yeah? And what about his family? You gonna find his house and tie all them up too? Then what, Conor? Use your fuckin' head, kid." Percly took a long drink from the bottle, setting it back down a little too hard next to the gun.

Conor's eyes fell on the revolver momentarily, then the bottle again. "What's that shit taste like."

"Like warm piss and cool aid," Percly replied.

Conor extended his hand, and he hoped the kid didn't drink too much so he could still catch a buzz. It was one of many moments he'd experienced as of late in which it was impossible not to hate himself on just about every level there was to hate somebody. Somewhere along the line, something had clearly gone terribly wrong, not just with his life, but with his internal wiring. Shaking it off, he handed the bottle over. Conor tipped it back and chugged, causing Percly to tense up just a little. When Conor pulled the bottle from his face, half of what had been left was gone. He made a face that suggested it would soon be all over the floor, and said, "Ugh! Jesus. How do you drink this shit?"

"Acquired taste, I guess."

Shaking his head, he made another face. "Why'd you stay?"

"In Sedrow?"

"In town?"

"I take it you mean after I noticed the roaches."

Nodding, Conor took another, smaller drink, then made the same face and heaved a little.

Percly said, "When I saw the first one, I ran. I ran like hell toward the freeway, but it was too damn far to just keep runnin'. I had to stop, so I ran right into someone's house, hoping to God they wouldn't shoot me. That they'd just call the cops instead. Then I'd tell 'em what the hell I saw.

"At the time I was cursin' myself for not having a phone. You know, one a them fuckin' Obama phones from the welfare office. Turns out not having one's exactly what saved my life. That, and the fact that the house was empty."

"Abandoned?" Conor asked.

"Naw. It was lived in for sure. Furniture. Appliances. Even a car out front. Just a dingy little two bedroom joint, too. The front door was unlocked, but I didn't imagine that was too uncommon out in the sticks. Soon as I was in, I was hollerin', 'Don't shoot! I ain't here to hurt no one. I just need a phone!' I wasn't 'bout to turn no light on neither with that fuckin' thing outside.

"Soon as I figured out the spot was empty, I knew something was wrong. Not just because of that, but because of the type a place it was. One of the rooms was for a kid. Other was obviously a single woman. I know people work and shit, but it was too damn early in the morning to be taking kids to day-care. I mean if they was up gettin' ready, I could've bought it. And if you saw this place, you'd know who ever lived there wasn't paying to go on no vacation."

Conor took another drink from the Cisco, killing off the rest of it. "Maybe they slept somewhere else."

A disappointment that was more in himself than the fact that the booze was gone flooded through Percly's body as he said, "You mean like she stayed over at her man's place or something?"

He nodded.

"I dunno. I can't really explain the feelin'. I know it could've all been just a combo of what I just saw, and the empty house making my head act funny, but that shit was eerie. I ain't never known something like I knew it wasn't right that morning."

Percly couldn't read Conor's face and he didn't know if the kid believed a word of what he was saying, but he nodded in consent, and asked what he did.

"Shit. Made myself a sandwich. Posted up a while, then, when I thought that ugly motherfucker was gone, I left. Problem was, I started seein' 'em all over the fucking place. I had already figured out it was my bad eye I saw the first one with, so obviously I didn't cover it up. To answer your question, I was gonna leave. Busses don't run on the weekends, but I was on my way to the freeway to stick my thumb out when I heard a scream, peeked over a fence and saw one a'the cockroaches face deep in a teenage girl's stomach in some backyard. Was a hole already dug, too?

"The thing turned and looked at me and I ran again, hid in another house, empty as the last one. That's where I got this bitch right here." He put his hand over the gun. "Turns out a lot a fuckin' houses in Sedrow empty these days. Mostly old folks houses though. They don't seem to be changing them, just killing 'em off."

"Eating them," Conor said.

"Yeah."

"So when I ran into you this morning," Conor said, "You were on your way out again? Hitchhiking?"

"Naw. You better believe I got me a motherfuckin' car. Took it right out some fool's garage. Then I saw you in trouble again—Lord knows why I keep running into your ass—and I got out the car to render assistance." He tilted his head. "Again."

"Thanks."

"Don't mention it."

After that there was silence. It only lasted a moment, but it felt like longer. Percly didn't want to know why, but the truth was, he did know. They both did. Everything was out in the open now. Everything Conor knew. Everything Percly knew. And it was time to figure out their next move. But neither of them really wanted to do that, because they both knew they were about to plan a suicide mission.

They could have talked more. Percly could have told him that he hadn't always been a smelly, dirty bum who lived in a vintage train in his town center. That he wasn't even from Washington, let alone Sedrow Woolley, and that everybody he ever had back in Louisiana was dead, and he had a drinking problem that wouldn't allow him to stand on his two feet and get off the streets, where he'd lived for the past—how many years? Fifteen? More?

And Conor could have told him all about his own

family and his girlfriend who were all dead as of late. About growing up in po-dunk Sedrow fucking Woolley, roping goats and chickens, and driving big trucks though the mud.

They didn't talk about any of that though, because none of it would have changed a thing. Instead, Percly looked down at his watch. It was just past four. He took a breath, opened his mouth to ask how the hell Conor intended to catch one of the things when they did go back. But Conor spoke first.

"Why cockroaches?"

"What do you mean?" Percly asked.

"You keep calling those things cockroaches. Why?"

"I dunno. I guess it's easier than callin' 'em locusts. In fact, I ain't called 'em that once 'til now. Not out loud at least. You bet your ass that's what they are though."

"Locusts?"

Conor stuttered, "Locusts."

"Like some hybrid breed?"

"Try some Biblical breed. Ain't you ever read the scriptures?"

Conor chuckled. "The Bible?"

"What else would I mean?"

"I don't know. I ah—"

"Seem like there's a church on just about every corner in that town. You tellin' me you don't go to none of 'em?"

"No. I mean, yeah. I've never really been a church guy."

"Shit," Percly said, "Neither have I. That don't mean I never read. Book a Revelation talks about this shit, plain as day. Says in the end times, giant locusts'll plague the earth."

Conor considered this a second. "No shit? You think that's what this is?"

"'Less you got a better theory." When he didn't

respond, Percly said, "Should be a Bible in the drawer over there if you wanna read, but unfortunately ain't nobody wrote shit about how to stop the motherfuckers." He took another deep breath. "It's getting late, Conor, and I imagine we better get to figuring out how we plan on catching one if we gonna do this."

Conor hesitated a moment, looked down at the empty bottle in his hand, then said, "Yeah. Listen, I saw a bar up the street. Let's talk about it over a drink. Something better than this shit, at least. My treat. Then we'll have that meal, and hope it's not really our last. How's that sound?"

Percly didn't have to think about it. "Yeah," he said, "Sounds about right to me."

# Chapter Seven

Nothing in downtown Sedrow Woolley would have looked out of the ordinary to the unsuspecting eye. It was mid-afternoon, and Highway Twenty wasn't crowded with rush hour traffic yet. Just the normal thin stream of vehicles passing through on their way to and from the upriver towns or the Upper Skagit Indian Reservation. It looked like any other cloudy Autumn day.

Then a buzzing insectile voice rang out of every monster at the same time. "FIND HIM!" Some were in houses; others were just coming out of the earth. Others, still, were in vehicles or walking the sidewalks. It was so loud the entire town heard. Even those who were still left unchanged.

Not even a second later, rustling came from every direction. Then the streets were covered in people, hunched down, scurrying on their hands and feet like some kind of ridiculous four legged insects. They weren't really people, though, and their claws scraped the pavement as they ran. They almost appeared to be crawling on top of each other like maggots on a rotting corpse.

They moved so fast it was impossible to make sense of the scene until one jumped, flying through the passenger window of a passing car. The horn went off, then the vehicle ploughed through the crowd, onto the sidewalk, collided with the post office, smashing a few of them and coming to a stop against the wall. Another jumped into a different vehicle. Then another. Others scurried into businesses and houses. There was screaming and crashing and car alarms and Conor stood up so fast that his barstool slid back and his drink fell to the floor where the glass shattered and the blue liquid stained his white shoes.

The bar in Everett was a dimly lit hole in the wall that was likely infested with cockroaches like their hotel room and his hometown. It was a dirty rectangular structure. Percly sat next to him, babying his own drink, looking at him wide eyed.

"Hey!" a tall, lean man with a beard, standing behind the bar snapped. "You two need to leave! Get the fuck outta here! Now!"

Ignoring him, Percly asked Conor if he was okay.

"No. No. Jesus, no. We need to go."

"Didn't you hear me?" The bartender made his way toward them, an empty glass in his hand. "I said get your friend and—"

Percly brought out his gun and pointed at the guy's face. He threw his hands up, took two big steps back. "Okay, man. Okay. You're okay. Just chill."

The place was mostly empty, aside from a few washed up looking alcoholics sitting alone in different places. They all just watched amused as Percly finished his drink, put an arm around Conor's shoulders and led him out.

It was dark, but Everett was a mid-sized city. People at

a bus stop eyed them as they walked.

"Put that fucking thing away," Conor muttered.

Percly tucked the huge revolver into his waistband, covering it with his shirt. "What is it, man? Tell me what's the matter."

Conor stopped walking. "I saw. I saw what's happening in Sedrow right now. I don't get it, but I saw it. And I heard it too. We need to get back now, Percly. No meal. No more drinks." Conor wasn't a drinker anyway. He had begun to feel the effects of the alcohol back at the hotel when he finished the Cisco. What was he thinking? How was this supposed to help?

"What the hell are you talking about?" Percly asked. "You saw it? You saw what?"

"I don't know. I had a dream earlier, in the car, but I don't think it was really a dream anymore. Or maybe it was, but this is different. I was just sitting there and we were drinking and we were and talking about—what were we saying?" He shook his head. "Who cares? We were talking and then I was back in Sedrow. I don't know how, but I was just there. They all spoke at the same time. Every one of the cock suckers, and it was so loud the whole town heard it."

"Okay." Percly shook his head. "Fine. You heard a voice. What did they say?"

Sirens wailed in the distance. Conor had heard them countless times since arriving in Everett. The first time he had tensed at the noise. Then it occurred to him that it was probably as normal of an occurrence in this city as a dog shitting in the park.

"'Find him.' They said, 'Find him.' Then they attacked on the whole town. There were hundreds of them. Maybe thousands. I don't know, man. They were everywhere, though. All attacking at the same time. And they were looking for me. I don't know how I know. I just do."

"What? Why you? This shit don't make sense, Conor. How could you even see something like that?"

"I told you! I don't fucking know! Obviously they share some kind of collective consciousness. It makes sense, right? They're obviously telepathic. They can distort people's perception of them. Except me, I see what they really are. I must be sharing that consciousness."

"It still ain't addin' up, though. I see 'em too, and I ain't seen nothing like that."

"You don't see their thoughts, though. Just their true appearance. The only thing that doesn't make sense is—" He went into deep thought.

"What?" Percly snapped.

"It was afternoon. In the vision. It was mid or late afternoon. It's night now. Unless I saw something that happened—"

He fell silent as the Sirens grew louder. Closer. Percly looked in their direction. So did Conor, seeing the people at the bus stop, also gazing toward the noise. They were at the top of a steep hill, however and Conor couldn't see if it was a cop car, an ambulance, or a fire truck approaching. Then he heard the 'woop, woop, woop,' of a helicopter, and looked up to see not one, but two flying overhead, lights shinning down in the same direction.

Relief flooded through his veins like it had been injected with an IV. He didn't want to feel it, couldn't help it. They were caught. That meant rest. Even if it also meant the end of humanity. He would be snug in a jail cell waiting to die, rather than playing hero just to die anyway.

The Sirens and helicopter blades were so loud that he almost didn't hear the scurrying that accompanied them. Claws on pavement. So many that it sounded like an army of tap dancers, growing closer and closer. Only then did it make sense why it was still daylight in his vision. It had all happened much earlier. Hours ago, while Conor had been shopping, showering, drinking in a dirty little bar in Everett. And they hadn't been looking for him, either. Why would they? His mind was connected to theirs. They knew where he was. No, they had been finishing off the town of Sedrow Woolley before they came to him because that's just what they do, and they wanted him and there would be no escape.

The unmistakable sound of a gunshot rang out, then a car horn. There was a crash and another horn, which gave way to a symphony of them. More gunshots. Then nothing but clicking, scraping, growing closer.

Conor had another vision. A family of three, in a small house out on Cook road. A young couple and their toddler, screaming as Conor burst through their door. The man and the slightly overweight woman were on the couch, watching a medium sized flat screen television mounted on the opposite wall. The boy sat at their feet, playing with a small dog. A dachshund.

The dog yapped as Conor picked it up first, taking it in both claws and ripping it in half. Both adults had already jumped to their feet, but he paid them no mind. Not yet, at least. He snatched the boy by his shirt, lifting him up off the floor and looking into his crying face.

"You hear me?" Percly's voice brought him back to the present. "Hey! Hey! Come on, man! Get it together!" Breaks squealed loudly in the distance.

"What?" Conor asked as the group waiting for the bus began to scream and run in his direction. Three cars flew up over the hill, one in reverse, retreating from wherever it had been going. The lights beaming down from the two helicopters moved the same way.

"Still think you seein' 'em in Sedrow Woolley?" Percly yelled. "Come on, man! Move!"

The shadows appeared first, stretching up over the hill,

and if he hadn't known any better, he would have actually thought they were human. The car moving in reverse veered, coming right at Conor and Percly just as the insect monsters emerged, crawling on all four limbs. There was nothing human about them anymore, and though Conor saw into their minds—knew who they thought they were—he knew nobody else did. There were so many of them it was impossible to count. A small army.

Percly tugged on Conor's arm and the next thing he knew they were both sprinting away from them. In his peripheral, Conor saw the backwards moving car just miss him. He felt the wind as it passed, slamming into the building. A man screamed—then, less than a second later, fell silent. Looking back, Conor saw the bartender, smashed between the wall and the car. A shotgun rested in one of his lifeless hands, on the hood.

Then the fleeing group from the bus stop disappeared into the crowd of monsters as it seemed to pass over them. The creatures dove though car windows and bit the drivers. Vehicles collided with telephone poles, mailboxes, buildings, and people. When Conor looked forward, Percly was at least ten feet ahead of him, turning into an alley. When Conor caught up, he reached out, pulling him in just as the stampede of monsters passed, seeming not to notice them.

A siren rang out around the corner, coming from the direction they were all headed. Car alarms went off. Soon there was so much noise, the sound of the helicopters disappeared. They were still there, though, flying overhead, watching everything.

"Come on!" Percly pulled again on Conor's arm.

The alley was a dead end. There was a brick wall at the end, if the creatures started to pour in, there would be nothing they could do. The alternative, however, would be to step back out with the crowd, which was so gigantic it hadn't finished passing yet. Percly jogged around a green dumpster. When Conor caught up, he saw why.

*A door.*

A green one, the same color as the dumpster. Percly punched it so hard he left a small dent in the metal. Conor scanned it, realizing why immediately.

"Where's the handle?" He asked, even though the answer was clear. Where it should have been, was nothing but a circular portion of metal, indicating that it was meant to be opened from the inside only. "Percly, where's the fucking handle? How are we supposed to—?"

Before he could finish, Percly brought out the revolver, pointed it at the metal disc and fired three times. Conor backed up as sparks flew from the door, and a hole almost as big as the disc appeared. Percly reached his fingers into it, but immediately jerked his hand back.

"Fuck!" He shook it.

"What! What is it?"

"Aaahhh!" Percly fired three more shots into the door, then stuck his gun into the hole, using it like a crowbar to wrench it open just as the last of the crowd passed at the end of the alley.

"They're gone," Conor said, "They're gone. We can go back—"

"Come on!" Percly yelled. "Get inside, man!"

Before he finished speaking, two of the things came around the corner from where they had all run. Conor felt every hair on his body raise as they stopped in the entrance of the alley, stood on two legs and looked at him, tilting their heads.

Then he was in the woods. Somehow he knew he was back in Sedrow Woolley, looking down at the dirt, which still wrapped around his waist where he sat. There were other graves nearby, but he was the only one awake.

Metal clinked against the pavement like a wind chime,

and Conor glanced over to see Percly slipping gigantic bullets into the cylinder of his gun, one at a time. The monsters walked purposefully toward them, huge smiles on their ugly faces, and then Conor knew why they left Sedrow Woolley. They knew, too, but they didn't understand it. Not like he did.

Percly clicked the revolver shut, then fired two shots so close to Conor that this time his ears rang. One of the things went down hissing and twitching, but the other scurried over, climbed onto the wall and moved sideways along its brick surface. It came at them so fast it might have been a dog, running in a field if its movements weren't so unnatural and disobedient to the laws of gravity. Percly fired again, hitting it, causing it to fall from the wall. It shook itself off and charged them once more on four legs.

POP!

Finally it hissed, collapsing onto the pavement and curling up like a dead spider.

"Come on," Percly said, "Get inside, and tell me what's going on in that fuckin' head a yours."

Percly went in first, then Conor stepped into a small entrance, no more than four by four feet, that gave way to the bottom of a staircase. The door slammed shut behind him.

"Can we lock it somehow?" Conor asked.

"How do you intend to do that?"

"I don't know. I mean, shouldn't we find something to prop it with or something?"

Ignoring the question, Percly said, "What the hell's going on, Conor?"

"I keep having visions. I can see their memories. I ah, I mean things that happened before they left Sedrow Woolley."

Percly paused a moment, seeming to silently talk

himself into going along with this reasoning. He pursed his lips, then relaxed. "And you sure it ain't all just in your head?"

"Oh it's in my head. It's still real, though."

"You mentioned a collective consciousness."

"Yeah. That means—?"

"I know what the fuck it means. I just don't know how to make sense out of it. Why now? Why all of a sudden these visions?"

"Because they're close. That's all I can think of. The closer they are, the stronger the bond is."

"Were you having 'em before you left Sedrow today?"

"No." Conor shook his head. "I don't know. I don't think so. I mean, I had the dream. And when I was in the outlet, I saw into one of their minds. A woman. I saw her memories. And my dad's dog. But I don't think it was like this."

More sirens appeared, and something exploded outside. Then machine gun fire rang out. Both men looked toward the closed door briefly, then back at each other.

"And you think they came here looking for you?" Percly asked.

"I know they did. Well, maybe not looking for me, but they came because I'm here. I brought them, Percly. I did this."

After a short pause, Percly said, "Don't get sentimental on me, now. Ain't no time for that shit. At least we ain't gotta worry 'bout catchin' one a the roaches now to give to the military. Sound like they out there dealin' with 'em already."

"I don't know if they'll be able to," Conor replied. "There's too many. They'd have to just nuke the whole fucking city."

Neither man spoke for a long moment, then Percly finally turned and began to make his way up the stairs.

"Where are we going?" Conor called after him.

"This way." Percly didn't look back. "Less you wanna just stand at the bottom a'these steps all night like a worm on a hook."

Without another word, Conor followed.

* * *

People seemed to come out of every dark crevice like cockroaches, wide eyed and panicked. At first, none of them seemed to know what to do. Then, when their minds finally allowed them to believe that thousands of giant insects were really moving up Broadway in a horrifying stampede, most of them just froze until they were consumed by the creatures.

Though the sky was black and grey and neither the moon, nor the stars could be seen through the thick clouds, the night was illuminated surprisingly well by street lamps and businesses that hadn't yet closed. A twenty-something-year-old man was dragged motionless into the grass surrounding a fast food restaurant, where his abdomen was sliced open while a crowd of people inside pressed against the window watching in horror. Eggs were laid inside of him, and a hole the same size as his body was dug in under a minute. Before he was done being buried alive, the restaurant was surrounded by creatures, which began to jump like a small army of flees crashing through the windows and pouncing on everybody inside.

They hopped into cars, and seconds later the vehicles crashed. Screams came from every direction, but they were mostly cut short. Insectile monsters crawled quickly up the side of a four story apartment building, slipping into every window. Then the entrance on the bottom floor flew open and they poured out like a stream of water, each smiling and dragging paralyzed victims along. Some weren't utilized as food or incubators, but merely killed and buried.

As the crowd moved, countless shallow graves were left behind in plots of grass by the sidewalks. Sirens cried out from everywhere, but all the nearby police cars were empty, their drivers having been pulled out and put in the dirt. Up above, there were now four helicopters. Two appeared to belong to news stations, one possibly the police. The other, Daryle Colombo knew, was a military chopper. They were unmistakable for anything but vehicles of war. Especially to eyes that could see as sharp as his now could.

And if that weren't enough to be sure, the machine gun fire that began to spit from the thing as it lit up on both sides confirmed it. Some of Daryle's companions went down hissing, while sparks flew on the pavement in a zig-zag line that passed only feet from him. Paying it little mind, he just kept walking. He was hungry again.

He had eaten, laid eggs, eaten, laid eggs, and eaten again so many times since coming out of the earth and finding Andy. Each time was the same. After coughing his spawn into somebody's stomach and burying the victim alive, the hunger returned. Instantly. Then he would find another to eat, and soon the itch was back. The need for release. It was worse than going a day without jerking off. So he would lay his eggs. It was an endless cycle in which he had no control over his urges, nor did he care to. It was the cycle of life.

Andy was somewhere in the mess of it all. He knew, because he belonged to the boy. He couldn't stray too far, because his nature wouldn't allow it. Not that he wanted to anyway. Until the Humvees arrived, full of uniformed soldiers clutching M-16s, and looking terrified and little, Andy was one of the first to be killed. The vehicles came from behind, four of them, and the soldiers stood shooting at the back of the crowd, which quickly turned and scurried over them, overtaking them before they knew what was happening. The soldiers were buried and the crowd was back in motion in under a minute.

And just like that, there was no more Andy to stick close to. They were all connected, Daryle knew, and he wouldn't stray far from the rest, (not because he couldn't, but because he didn't want to) but where he wanted to go wasn't far. He took a right, broke away from the crowd, which continued on the way they were going.

Within minutes, he was on a residential street, where people stood on lawns—mostly with phones to their ears—and peered out of open doors as if they would catch a glimpse of what was happening out on the main road. An old green SUV sped around a corner, brakes squealing, and barely missed Daryle. It didn't stop, he knew, because the driver saw Daryle, rather than a colossal insect.

Daryle looked down at the knife in his hand—his favorite knife—and became aware that the song was playing again in his head.

*I'm on a highway to hell—*

Closing the blade, he slipped the weapon into his pocket, straightened his FAIRFAX hat, and approached a man standing in his lawn with two young boys. "Excuse me."

The guy eyed him skeptically, his hands on his sons' shoulders. Then he said, "Jesus. Were you out there?"

"Out where?" Daryle tilted his head.

An explosion that shook the ground erupted and people began speaking loudly across yards to their neighbors.

The guy looked again at Daryle as if something was wrong with him. The boys both cowered against his legs. "Out there," he said. "The news—It's—what in the world's going on? Did you see those things?"

"Oh," Daryle laughed. "Yeah. Those. No. No, I wouldn't worry about that. Listen man, you wouldn't happen to know the way to the ninety-nine, would you?"

"The highway?" The guy looked past him briefly, then back into his eyes. "What? I mean, yeah. It's just," he nodded back the way Daryle had come. "For the love of God. What the hell is happening out there?"

Daryle said, "I wanna say I read online that that's known as—the track?—in this town?"

"What?" The guy made a face like he smelled something foul. "The what?"

"The track—" Daryle waved a hand thoughtfully. "You know, where a gentleman might find a— well, a date? I'm from out of town, you know, but whenever I travel, I read up on where I'm going. I'm Daryle, by the way." He extended his hand.

The guy took a step back, pulling his boys with him. His mouth opened, but at first, no words came out. Then he said, "Boys. Inside." He stared at Daryle's hand as the children ran in their front door.

Daryle looked down, finding his fingers wrapped around the handle of his knife, the blade pointing at the man. Shutting it once again, he dropped it into his pocket. "Anyway, I had a job in this shitty little town called Sedrow Woolley. Ever been there? Well, if you haven't, let me save you a waste of a day that could be put to better use humping or dumping. Shit," he laughed, "Even both if that's what you're into. Don't go. Nothing there."

More machine gun fire came from further away, and more people poured out into their yards looking toward Broadway. There was another explosion. This time the sky lit up and a woman screamed. Others gasped and pointed. Daryle looked back just in time to see two flaming helicopters drop like shooting stars. They disappeared over houses and buildings as they crashed to the earth. One exploded, lighting up the sky again, and drowning out the sounds the other made as it impacted. The police and military copters still hovered over them, shining spotlights down where they had landed. A small sedan, which had been headed toward the main road came to a screeching halt, and began to move in reverse.

"Oh shit!" Somebody yelled. "Holy—!"

"Fuck!" Somebody else called out. "What the fuck? What the fuck? You see that? It's the news! The fucking news choppers just collided with each other."

"No! What? No!"

Daryle redirected his attention to the man in front of him. "Cows."

"Excuse me?" he shrieked.

"All they got in that town. Can you believe that shit? I mean, I'm from Colorado. I know about farming towns. Personally, I live in Denver now, but I grew up just outside of South Park. Yeah, that's where the show's supposed to be based. I'm an engineer, by the way. Industrial automation. So my company sends me—"

"Can I help you with something?" The guy looked around at his neighbors, a fair amount of them who were alternating between staring at him and in the direction of the fallen helicopters.

"Oh, shit!" Daryle laughed again. "Right! The ninety-nine. Would you say that's where the prostitutes tend to be in this city?"

"I don't—I—You need to get off my lawn. Now." He tried to be assertive, but there was little-to-no conviction in his voice.

"Hey, listen, man. No reason to be a dick. I'm just looking for a good time. I told you, I'm from out of town."

"Leo?" a man from across the street called. "You

okay?"

Daryle didn't look back. He had already seen the guy on his way in. Leo looked over his shoulder, then back into Daryle's eyes. He seemed to be considering what the right answer was, searching for it somewhere in his face. Finally he said, "Yeah. Yeah, Dean. I'm good."

"Sure?"

"Yeah. I'm sure." He paused, lowering his voice so only Daryle could hear. "Listen, man, if you can't see, the world's being invaded by some kind of aliens. It's all over the news. There's obviously something wrong with your head, and I sympathize with you. But I have two little boys in that house that I need to worry about. I'm sorry for your luck, but please go somewhere else."

Daryle smiled, and a second later Leo's eyes grew wide with panic.

"So," Daryle said, "That a 'yea' on the ninety-nine? You know, I'm pretty sure that's right anyway. I googled it, of course. You know if you type in, 'Prostitution, Everett,' there's enough forums about that fucking highway to keep you busy all night? Think you could just point me in the right direction?" He looked around. "I'm guessing this neighborhood leads to a dead end? Only way out's the way I came?"

Leo's jaw hung slightly, but he didn't speak, just nodded a little too fast.

"I imagine the highway runs parallel with the freeway," Daryle went on. "So if I just go out and take a left, I should run into it?"

"Yeah," Leo finally managed, clearing his throat. "Yeah. Just—ah, go out and take a left. You'll find it that way." His whole body shook as he turned toward the house.

"Wait," Daryle snapped, causing him to jump and spin back around, noticeably tense. Daryle looked down at his pants, seeing a lumpy bulge in the right pocket.

A long string of gunfire crackled, followed by another explosion. As Leo looked toward the noise, Daryle thrust the camouflage knife into his neck, just behind his windpipe. His mouth opened wider than it should have been able to as Daryle retracted his hand, severing through the man's throat. Air hissed from his lungs, mixing with blood and creating a gargling noise.

Leo's hands came up, clutched at his throat. He looked pleadingly into Daryle's eyes, and Daryle knew he saw him how he really looked. And that as his eyes fell on the weapon that had killed him, they perceived a long, razor-sharp claw, rather than a knife. Daryle dropped to the grass and began digging before Leo had even fallen. He heard neighbors scream and doors slam shut, but didn't look.

Before burying the man, he removed the keys from his pocket. Then he climbed into the red minivan parked in front of the house, started it, and headed toward the ninety-nine.

* * *

The huge revolver hung at Percly's side as he and Conor made their way up the stairs, which quickly gave way to a long hall with doors lined along the dirty walls on each side. The place wasn't very well lit, and smelled of cigarette smoke. Conor had already figured out that it was an apartment complex. They didn't stop on that floor, but continued up three more storeys before Percly started knocking on doors and attempting to turn knobs.

"What are you doing?" Conor asked.

"What's it look like?" He pounded on a door marked, '21.' "Hey! Open up! Come on, man!" Then moved to another.

"We're breaking into somebody's house?" Conor

wondered what good it would do to be inside one of the rooms, as opposed to out in the hall. If the things outside wanted in, it wouldn't matter where they were in the building. In fact, it was a miracle they hadn't come in on their way by to clean the place out.

Ignoring the question, Percly moved along, knocking on every door, and trying every knob on one side of the hall. "Get the other side," he barked. "Less you'd rather we stand around with our thumbs in our asses."

"Doesn't anyone live in this building?"

Percly stopped and looked at him. "What? Course they do. What exactly are you asking?"

"Where is everybody? Why's it so empty?"

"You think they live in the hall?"

"No—I just, I don't know."

"Come on, Conor. Knock on doors, big man. We can discuss how people in low income neighborhoods live later. If the human race survives that long, at least. We need to get into these rooms and start warning folks. See who's got weapons or other resources, cause I'm willin' to bet, ain't many niggas in here got cable. Ain't seen the news, and just looked out the window to see some giant cockroaches eatin' motherfuckers. Probably in there shittin' themselves right about now."

Outside, something exploded, followed by a sequence of crashes and scraping, then another explosion that shook the building.

"Jesus," Conor said, "Was that a fucking helicopter?"

Percly looked toward the stairs for a moment, then back at Conor. "Come on, man. Doors." He turned and went back to knocking and turning knobs.

"What if they don't want us in their apartment?" Conor called after him. But before Percly could answer, Conor was back in Sedrow Woolley. There was no indication that that was where he was, he just knew. It was dark. Dirty. But there was light in the distance. He was just coming out of the earth, crawling toward it. He was under some kind of a structure. A small animal scurried by. A possum. Conor reached one claw out, snatching it before it knew what was happening. It kicked and fought, cried and bit at him. But there was no use. Conor brought the animal to his face, biting it back.

"Conor! Conor, come on! You hear me?"

Conor looked over to see Percly inside one of the apartments, his head sticking out the door. "Yeah." He jogged over. Before he made it though, another explosion rang out inside the building and Percly collapsed onto the floor. It only took Conor a second to realize that the gun had gone off in his hand. It now lay on the floor in front of him. Conor stopped running and watched as Percly climbed onto his hands and knees, looking back over his shoulder.

His eyes went wide as the end of a silver aluminium baseball bat moved so fast that Conor almost didn't recognize it, in a downward arch and slammed into the top of his head, making a hollow "thong." Percly's expression went blank. He collapsed face down on top of the weapon. Then his body moved, slid back into the room just an inch. Then another. He was being dragged inside. Conor heard the gun scrape against the floor under him.

His first thought was, *they're inside the building*. But he knew better. Whoever was dragging Percly Valentine into that room was struggling, only managing an inch at a time. And if it were one of them, it wouldn't have used a bat. Without another thought, he started running again. He needed to get the gun.

One last heave and Percly disappeared around the door, leaving the weapon exposed. Conor was only feet from it when a black man who was taller than him, and bigger around than Percly stepped out, clutching the bat in both hands, ready to swing. His skin was much lighter than Percly's, and his curly hair was tied back into a ponytail. He wore wire glasses and a devious smile.

"Y'all motha fuckas thought you was 'bout ta come up, huh?"

"What?" Conor stopped running, threw his hands up.

"Oh, you picked da wrong nigga." He continued to smile as he advanced on Conor.

"No! No! No! No!" Conor backed up, cowering. "Please. Don't hit me. I didn't mean to—"

The guy swung the bat, and though he wasn't yet close enough to be hit, Conor ducked anyway.

"Yeah, mutha fucka. Yo ass betta run. I catch you, it's game on." He swung again, this time closer.

Conor ducked, covering his head. *Run,* he told himself. *Turn around and run back the way you came. He's far enough back. You can still get away.* He couldn't though, and he knew it. He couldn't just leave Percly.

"Come on, man," he pleaded between breaths. "Relax. Please, just relax. Don't you see what's going on outside? Don't do this."

Behind him, Conor saw a heavyset redheaded woman in a sundress step out of the apartment, assess the situation, and pick up the gun. She examined it like it were some kind of artefact, then let it hang at her side, her finger on the trigger.

The bat-wielding man's smile morphed into an angry baring of teeth. He said, "Come on, nigga, fight me! Don't start coppin' pleas now. You had the nuts ta come up in my pad'n try ta rob me. Put yo hands up! Let's go mutha fucka. Put 'em up!" He made like he was going to swing again, but didn't.

"I WASN'T GONNA ROB YOU!" Conor yelled. "NOBODY WAS GONNA ROB YOU!"

"Mutha fuckin' right you wasn't." He cocked the bat.

"Wait! Wait! Wait! Wait!" Conor held both hands out, palms facing him. "We just needed somewhere safe! Those fucking things outside! Jesus. Please, man."

Another door opened, and a younger, black man stuck his head out. "Tone? You cool?"

"Shit," the man whose name was apparently 'Tone,' said, "I cool as the north pole. Riot break out'n niggas get ta lootin'. You know how it go. These ones here just picked da wrong crib, dats all."

Conor processed this, and said, "Riot? Jesus. This isn't a fucking riot! It's an invasion. Take a look outside, man. Those are fucking—Whoa! No!"

Before he could finish, or even try to protect himself, Tone took two more gigantic steps, swinging like a batter ready to run all the way home. This time Conor heard the, "thong," inside of his own head as the metal collided with the back of his skull. He went numb so fast that he didn't feel his head fly forward and smash into the wall—only saw red. Then Shelby's face. Then red again.

The hall came back into focus and he saw blood on the wall. A small circular stain, about the size of a compact disc. He placed both hands around it to stabilize himself, trying not to touch it. But faltering, he ran one of them through the thick liquid, smearing it and leaving behind four long fingerprints.

"Uh-lease." He tried to form the word, but couldn't. The hallway swayed, rocked back and forth like a boat in a storm. Then Tone was in front of him again, smiling wider now. He seemed to grow taller as he cocked the bat back again. Conor screamed, cried like a small child, falling to the floor and curling into the fetal position. Then the world went black.

* * *

The whole crowd stopped moving at the same time.

The ones that had been climbing up houses, buildings, and vehicles retreated, joining the rest in the middle of the street. Phillip Harris held a paralyzed girl who couldn't have been older than twenty-one in his arms, cradling her like a bride. She stared up at him, horrified, her chest heaving. Letting her drop onto the pavement, he placed his clawed foot over her mouth.

More choppers had showed up from the local Navy base. The same one he was stationed out of. They spit fully auto gunfire at the crowd, splitting Everett's main road and taking out rows of Sedrow Woolley's finest townspeople. Then, as synchronized as one of those fucking flash-mobs from the movies, everybody walked away in different directions, pouring off of Broadway, and onto back roads. Once they were a distance away, they all took on their human appearances. Soon the strip was empty aside from a few motionless, unburied victims, and wrecked military vehicles. Overhead, the helicopters quit firing, just shone spotlights at the expanding crowd, their occupants clearly confused.

* * *

The street signs told Daryle that he was almost to the ninety-nine when the urge to turn around hit him like a bag of sand. The roads were packed and chaotic, but he was almost there. He slammed on the brakes and the car behind him broke into a fit of honking. Tapping his fingers on the steering wheel, he sang, "I'm on a highway to hell—"

From the minivan's speakers, a male voice spoke frantically.

"...*not a hoax. Officials are saying to stay out of Everett. Again, if you're headed toward Everett, turn around immediately and get indoors. It's been confirmed that the city of Everett is under attack by a herd of what appears to be some kind of unidentifiable—hostile life forms.*

*"Ah—little over—ah—an hour ago? A crowd of what were believed at the time to be protesters, were seen marching along the freeway and blocking traffic in Skagit County. At some point the entire crowd broke into some kind of mass hysteria and began attacking and apparently killing people in vehicles. We're receiving different accounts, and again, each one seems more bizarre and disturbing than the last. Ah—one commonality—and I can't believe I'm saying this—is that they seemed to have somehow changed? Or taken on the appearance of some type of alien creatures. Ah—we'll keep you posted as— ah—excuse me. Jesus. We've just learned that the military has been deployed and begun to fire..."*

Daryle turned off the stereo. Fuck it. He wasn't turning around. With the tip of his razor-sharp claw, he pressed down on the gas pedal, continuing on toward the highway.

* * *

Conor opened his eyes. It was mid-to-late afternoon. Bright and sunny. The grass was a little taller than his 66 Pontiac GTO—mostly yellow, but still green in some places. Still in others, it was burnt brown. It grew on either side of the thin dirt driveway, concealing the blueish-green car from the road. His first thought was, *I'm gonna have to wash her before I put her back under the tarp.*

Then Shelby let out a moan that started strong, slowly dying in intensity and volume at the end of the breath. She inhaled deeply, wrapping her arms around his neck. Her naked body lay pressed against the leather interior of his backseat. Her hair was loose, but showed evidence of having been tied in a ponytail recently. Her legs tensed, pulling him deeper into her, and her lips pressed so hard against his that he thought they would split. There was no pain, however. No feeling at all. That's how he knew he was dreaming. That, and the fact that Shelby was dead.

"Oh fuck," she cried. "Fuck. Fu-uck. Fuck me! Fuck me! Fuck me!" Her back arched as she turned her face so she was looking at the back of the driver's seat and he knew she was going to cum. It was too much, and if she didn't stop, so would he.

"No!" he placed his palms on the seat, tried to push away, but her legs and arms tightened around him. She began to shake.

"Please, baby. Don't stop. Don't stop. Oh! Don't fucking stop! Don't stop fucking me! Oooohhhh!"

"Ooohhh!" Conor felt it coming. He couldn't let it happen though. Couldn't have a wet dream about his dead girlfriend. "Get the fuck off of me! Let me go!" He put one hand over her mouth, then the other, and pushed, pushed, pushed until he had broken the embrace. Then he pushed some more, because she wasn't supposed to be breathing. Wasn't supposed to be alive.

Her arms and legs began to flail, and her eyes went wide with a panic and fear that he felt for her because she was dead and couldn't feel anything. It was an anxiety worse than he had experienced even since being bitten by the terrible dog that she brought into his house. It fell over him like a hunter's net, and he couldn't breathe until he removed his hands to see a huge smile on her face.

"Please stop," he started to beg, but she cut him off, bursting into a fit of playful giggles.

Reaching up, she stroked his hair. "Don't be scared, handsome. This is my favorite memory. Did you know that? You and me, all alone out here, fucking in the back of this sexy car. You know I was never really jealous of it.

I was just joking whenever I acted like I was. It was fun to mess with you, you know that? You're fun to mess with. I almost came, too. It didn't even matter how uncomfortable the leather was on my bare ass. I was this close." She held up her thumb and index finger, indicating about an inch.

Conor didn't speak, just stared down into her almond-shaped eyes, sure he would cry. He felt the tears building up, filling his body, wanting out of him. It didn't have to be his own eyes either. He could have welded them shut, and they would have found another way out.

"I don't cum easy," she said. "I don't know why. I mean I've heard some girls do, but I was never one of them. It's like the first time? Okay—yeah. You know the first time with a different guy or whatever? It must be something about having something new, or not knowing what to expect, or—fuck—I don't know. It's just good. Even if *he's* not good, it can be good. Then it's not. After a while it just becomes like, blah, you know?

"I hope I don't sound like a cold bitch right now. I never meant to be. I was just—Conor, I think I was broken. But with you, I didn't wanna be anymore. I wanted to be better. I really fucking did. And I think I was getting there. I mean, I know they say you should never change for someone else, and that it has to be for you or it won't last, but I think you were fixing me. You know why? Because I knew you loved me. Even before I said it yesterday, I knew. I saw it in your face and I felt it.

"I think that's why I almost came the day we fucked right here in this field in the back of your goat. Not because you fucked me so good—I mean, you did, there's no denying that. You put it down that day—but because you didn't really fuck me at all. Does that make sense? You made love to me. And I'm stupid, Conor. I'm such a stupid bitch, because I wouldn't stop saying that we were fucking. I wouldn't just call you my boyfriend, even though I knew that's what you wanted."

"You're not real," he finally choked. "This isn't real. It's a dream."

Shelby tilted her head, offering a sympathetic smile. "Of course it's a dream, dude."

"You're dead, Shelby."

"You were always so condescending, though," she said. "That's the only thing I didn't like. I mean you never just came out and said you thought you were better than me, but you think I didn't know? You think I didn't know how you felt about my friends? My music? My choice of studies? You thought I was stupid. I mean, yeah. I was in some ways. But not the way you thought I was. You know what the worst part was, though? That you thought I was too stupid to know what you thought of me."

*Wake up,* he thought. *Wake up. Wake up. Wake up. You have to wake up now.*

But he didn't really want to wake up. He had never wanted anything less in his life. As long as Shelby Metcalf was his dreams, he could have slept forever.

"You can't wake up, Conor. It's not that simple. You were hit with a bat, dude. You have a concussion. You might even die. I won't let that happen, though. I'm gonna save you. You know why? Because I do love you. I meant it when I said it, and now I'm gonna show you.

"I'm not stupid, you know. Not really. I mean I know I act like it sometimes—fuck, all the time—but I'm not. And I'm not dead."

"Yes you are." He took a deep breath. "Everybody is. The whole fucking town, Shelby."

"Conor, you're talking to me. You just made love to me. For fuck's sake, I almost came. Could a dead bitch cum?"

The sorrow drained out of him as quickly as it had

appeared, replaced by the need to move. Not to wake up. Not to leave his girlfriend, who he would only ever see again when his mind allowed him to dream. Just to move. To do anything but lay on top of her in the back of this car. He sat all the way up and took a look around at the unmaintained field. In some places, patches were pressed to the ground from vehicles driving over them. Others were nothing more than sections of tall grass with thin game trails running through them.

To the side, was a large pit of dried mud, which he knew would have been a small swamp, had it been winter. Just around the corner, the driveway led out to Highway Nine. They were less than a mile from his childhood home. The entire scene was exactly how he remembered it.

"You didn't love me," he finally said. "You came over on the weekends and fucked me because I fed your habits." He began to crawl between the two front seats.

Shelby slapped his ass as he made his way behind the wheel. "My habits?" She laughed. "You fed my habits? What does that even mean? Weed? Alcohol? You think I couldn't get those things anywhere? You think I couldn't go to any bar in this little town and get some drunk logger to buy me drinks? Seriously, dude. That's what I mean right there. You really think I can't just get a job if I want to?

"Why do you have to be so fucking condescending? I fucked you, Conor Mitchell, because I liked you. Then— guess what? I fell in love with you. That's how these things work. It was you who wouldn't let yourself love me back. So don't lie to yourself, sweetheart. You can lie to me if you want, but don't lie to yourself. It's not healthy."

Conor squeezed the steering wheel hard, tried to pull it off. "Where are my clothes, Shelby?"

"It's your dream," she responded. "You tell me."

Looking down, he found himself fully clothed, not with what he had worn that summer afternoon when he pulled over in the field to have sex with Shelby, but what he had been wearing in Everett today. Shelby's hands touched his shoulders, then moved slowly and sensually down his chest. Her lips brushed his ear and a chill ran through his body.

"You killed our baby," she whispered. "Our cute, adorable, little doggy. You smashed his fucking head with a car battery. Who does that?" She slid easily into the front seat, then positioned herself between him and the steering wheel, straddling his lap. She too, was now fully dressed, in her black leggings and blue blouse. Putting both arms around his neck, she said, "I forgive you, though. You were scared. I know you were. Know how I know? Because so was I. When he bit me, it hurt. Only at first, though. Then it went away. I mean the pain.

"Then he changed. But not really. It was me. He changed me, and let me see how he actually looked. You know all this already, though. But there's so much you still don't know. Like the reason I could see him after he bit me. The same reason you can see now. It's because I was his. He claimed me, and that's what let me in. He let you in too, you know. And what did you do, Conor? You killed him."

"I don't wanna do this." Conor only meant to think it, but the words spilled from his mouth like water. "I need to wake up. Wake up. I need to fucking wake up. Please!"

"Not yet." She stroked his hair, cupping the back of his head. "I told you, dude. You're out cold. You couldn't wake up if you wanted. Your brain's bleeding inside of your skull like a smashed tomato. Just listen for now. I wanna help you. Will you let me do that, at least? Can I help you?"

When he didn't answer, she went on. "So I passed out

after he bit me. Then he took me by the ankle and dragged me outside, down the porch steps, and under your house. That's where he cut me," She traced a line across Conor's abdomen. "Right here. He cut me and laid eggs inside of me. It's not really eggs though. That's just what I've been calling it because it's the closest comparison I can come up with. If you saw it, you'd probably describe it as a black goo, or a tar. Fucking motor oil or something.

"He put it inside of me, then dug a cute little doggy hole and put me there before I died. That's the most important part, you know? If you die first, you don't come back."

"Get off of me, Shelby," he snapped. "Do you hear me? Get off. Get off. Get the fuck off of me, right now!"

"Ha!" She laughed. "Fat chance. This is your dream and you couldn't even get me off. What do you say we try again, handsome? Wanna go for round two?" Reaching down, she began to fidget with his pants.

"No!" He took her by the hips, hoisted her off of him. She was so light it felt like they were under water. Like she would float away if he let go, and even though he was freaked out, even terrified, he didn't want that. He set her down lightly in the passenger seat.

"Why do you think that is?" She looked at him curiously. "Why do you think you're so bad with intimacy? Is it your childhood? Your asshole stepdad? I saw it all, by the way. As soon as I came out from under the studio. You know we're connected now, right? Not like we were before—I mean. That was nothing compared to this. We're all connected. You know why? Because there is no we, Conor. Not anymore. Not for us. There's just I. And that's you. It's me, it's your mom, your dad— everybody who I've become. We're one.

"I saw your stepdad. I saw your childhood. How come you never told me? It would have helped me so much to understand you, dude. It would have only made me love you more. Can I show you something?"

He didn't look at her, just stared ahead through the windshield, which served no purpose in this dream aside from aesthetics, because there was no wind. The grass held perfectly still. Though the sun shone bright from the cloudless, blue sky, there was no heat. He didn't have to squint either. It was all real though. He knew, as she spoke, that everything she said was true. It *was* a dream. It was *his* dream—*their* dream, really—but it was also real. They were inside of his head. He was inside of theirs. And though he knew he should have been afraid, he wasn't, because they weren't afraid, and as far as they were concerned, he was one of them. One with them.

*Collective consciousness.*

He wasn't supposed to have survived the encounter with Benji. From the second the dog made its move on him, he had been a part of the mind that they all shared, because the dog had opened that mind to him under the assumption that he would soon be one of them. For some reason, this was funny. He didn't know why, only that it was. He smiled and said, "I'm in the fucking matrix."

In his peripheral, he saw her smile back. Her eyes narrowed, burning into the side of his head. "No. No. Not quite. It's not that easy, dude."

*No?* he thought. *Then why don't you explain it to me?* And of course she heard.

"I'd rather show you." She ran her hand over the smooth outer surface of the car. "Why don't you start this bitch and get us outta here? Let's take a trip down memory lane."

* * *

The ninety-nine wasn't anything special as far as highways were concerned. There was one like it in every city across the country. All with the same reputation. Daryle Colombo liked them, because he liked prostitutes. Not the kind you had to call, though. In the beginning he had liked the escorts found on local online classifieds. Then the urge to use his knife had begun to creep in every time he was with one. He wasn't a stupid man, and he knew he couldn't do that with them.

What if one of them *did* call the police? Yeah, unlikely, given their occupations, but not impossible. Or what if one time—just once—he took it further? He would be lying if he said he had never thought about it. About going all the way with one. Slashing her throat, or pounding his blade through her chest cavity. It wasn't an overwhelming urge or anything, and he had easily brushed it off every time, but what if he ever actually did it?

He couldn't have his way with call girls from the internet, because call girls required calling. His phone would be traced back to him too easily. Because of this, streets like the ninety-nine were his only reasonable option when he traveled. While researching, he had discovered that this particular highway tended to attract high crime and prostitution in just about every city it ran through. Probably due to drug trafficking, considering it ran from Mexico to Canada.

The road was cluttered and traffic moved slowly. People were clearly panicking, trying to get out of the city, and the freeway wouldn't work for anybody headed north after the mess he and the townspeople from Sedrow Woolley had left there. The minivan's speedometer told him he was going just over ten miles per hour. He slapped his hand with the beat of the song which had been playing on repeat in his head since waking up in the earth on Anderson Mountain.

Huge neon signs announced that cheap, dirty looking motels mostly had no vacancy. Ethnic restaurants with strings of lights around their roofs sat in small parking lots. A tall sign that lit up the sky advertised the Long Dragon Casino and Restaurant. Homeless people stood in groups by bus stops, smoking cigarettes, looking up and pointing at the helicopters in the distance. But where were the hookers?

Daryle knew what to look for. This wasn't his first rodeo. It was winter, and cold in the Pacific Northwest. She wouldn't be wearing something skimpy. In fact, she would likely be bundled up in a semi-expensive winter coat. There was a time when she would have been wearing jeans so tight they looked like they were painted on, just below that coat, but not in the last few years. Not since leggings had become fashionable.

This was good news for a john, as it eliminated the guess-work as to what the product would look like when taken out of the package. Everything was on full display. Sometimes you could even see a girl's beaver through the things.

A working girl would be on her phone. Well, not on it, but walking close to the road, staring down at it, pretending to send a text, the light shining up into her face so potential johns could see what she looked like. It was a prostitute's version of neon signs.

The only problem with street-walkers, was that they tended to be cheaper. Much cheaper, in fact, and as with any product, this implied lesser quality. Actually, it guaranteed it. Daryle wasn't some lowbrow schmuck. He had taste. But when one's jollies demanded the pastimes that his did, just to be pacified, one had to resign to settling for practical purposes. It was a compromise.

The urge to turn around hadn't gone away. Not even lessened. In fact, it had grown to a degree that was almost overwhelming. It was more than just an urge. It was a need. He knew why. Those hickerbillies from Woolley were going after the kid in the apartment. Daryle knew everything that they knew, and they knew everything the kid knew. The more they acquired in numbers, the stronger the connection grew, too.

He had no intention of resisting it. He would re-join them. Just as soon as he tended to the other urge which was overwhelming the one calling him toward the kid. One itch just needed scratching a little more than the other.

His thoughts didn't come the same as they once had. There was no particular succession. They were all just there at the same time. It was more like knowing, than thinking. Still, he managed to somehow become lost in them and almost miss the girl walking along the sidewalk next to the minivan's passenger door, seemingly oblivious to the chaos taking place in Everett. Her winter coat was as white as snow, with what he assumed was imitation fur around the rims of its hood and sleeves. She held her cell phone up to her chest, the light shining into her face as she stared down at the screen. And below the coat, as if in homage to the old days, she wore skin-tight jeans.

The untrained eye may not have recognized her for what she was. To his pleasant surprise, she looked nothing like a street-walker. She belonged on the internet, charging two-hundred dollars for an hour that never actually lasted an hour. Daryle guessed she was in the early stages of addiction. That whatever substance had its claws in her hadn't yet done its number on her life. Her body. Her face. Some pimp, however, had capitalized on it—used it to string her along, put her on the highway. By the time she realized she was better off self-employed, working from a computer in her own hotel room, the drugs would have taken their toll on her and it would no longer be an option. That wasn't Daryle's problem, though.

He didn't have to slow the van down much in order to match her pace. Using the button on his door, he rolled down the passenger window.

"Hey there."

She looked over at him, causing the light radiating from her screen to illuminate the side of her face, accentuating her profile. She truly was stunning—brunette, with wavy hair that hung free past her shoulders—built like a dancer. Behind the van, a vehicle's horn went off three times. Daryle ignored it.

"I'm John," he said. "Can I, ah—can I give you a ride?"

The walker smiled. "Depends."

That confirmed it. She was definitely working. The hunt was on now. This was what made the whole experience so gratifying. Building the tension, then ultimately releasing it with a climactic surprise ending.

HONK! HONK! HONK!

Finally Daryle looked back, more for show than anything. The driver of a red SUV threw his hands up like he were hoisting a giant cauldron full of shit. He mouthed the words, "Come on, asshole." The road was clearly too packed for the guy to even try and pass. Vehicles were pouring quickly into the growing gap in front of the minivan.

Though he already knew there was nowhere to pull over, Daryle went through the motions of checking. Then, flashing the driver an apologetic look, he readdressed the girl. "Okay. You have my attention."

Lowering the phone, she examined the van. "I can tell. Nice car."

"Actually, sweetie, it's a van."

"What?" She mocked utter shock. "Is that what this thing is?"

"It is." He grinned. "A minivan, in fact."

"Coming back from soccer practice?"

"You know I have to ask, have you not heard what happened over on Broadway?"

"The riot?"

"Is that what you heard?"

"I mean—look up." She pointed. "The police and military are flying around. Shit's blowing up. Machine guns are going off. It must be another protest gone bad."

Daryle nodded. "Gotcha. And you're still out—?"

"Yeah?" she tilted her head. "Out what?"

"Walking. I'm just impressed. That's all. You—"

HONK! HONK! HONK! HONK! HOOOOONK!

They both looked back at the SUV as the driver flashed his lights, then once again at each other.

"I don't think he's happy," the walker said.

"Think he might have somewhere to be?" Daryle asked. "The highway always this active, or what?"

"Not usually. Not at this time at least. Don't you think you should get outta that guy's way?"

"Ha! That's probably not the worst idea. Wouldn't wanna find myself a victim of road rage, would I?"

"No," she smiled. "Not before you finish asking me to elaborate about whether or not I need a ride."

"Very well," he said. "Care to elaborate?"

"Well actually, I would. I may just need a ride. I guess it really depends on where you're headed, doesn't it? Where *are* you headed, John?"

"Well—I was thinking one of these hotels I've been seeing might be a good place to rest my head for a while. I'm from out of town, you know."

"Yeah. I picked up on that. I think I could probably recommend a nice spot, *and* use a ride. Gas money?"

"You bet the bottom of your cute little feet. How much?"

"Well," she looked up into her eyelids. "I think I could

do a hundred."

"A hundred? Ha! That's a joke, right? How far could I get with a hundred?"

"Oh, you could get as far as you're up for with a hundred, baby."

"Yeah? You think? Let's not fool ourselves, sweetheart. I could get as far as I want for half that. This isn't LA. Shit, it's not even Seattle. Fifty."

HONK! HONK! HONK!

"Better think quick," Daryle said. "We're causing a traffic jam."

Mom always told him he could have sold ice cubes to an Eskimo. Though he wasn't fond of socializing, it seemed to come natural to him. He had sealed a million dollar contract with Vanderpool, and talked hookers below their rock bottom prices. And though closing deals at work was far from his idea of a good time, he found great pleasure in negotiating with girls who he had no intention of paying with anything but his knife.

After the briefest of pauses, in which she seemed to contemplate every place she'd rather be, her eyes lit up with an imaginary enthusiasm and she said, "Oh why not. I'm Stephanie."

John brought the van to a complete stop, causing not only the man in the SUV, but multiple vehicles behind it to honk. "Well, Stephanie, why don't you hop in?" He pressed another button and every door in the vehicle unlocked with a 'click.'

* * *

Conor pulled the goat onto Highway Nine, took a right, he shifted into second, then third gear.

"Wrong way," Shelby said. She sat with her calves pulled snugly under her ass. Neither of them wore a seatbelt. "You know there's nothing to see at your old house. Your parents aren't even there. Your friend's next door, but he's buried still. He'll be back in a couple days. I came out a little early, you know. Just a little, but it shows. You'll see what I mean. I just hope I can still make you love me."

"Where am I supposed to be going, Shelby?"

"Turn around. Drive us into town."

"Then where?"

"You don't need me to tell you, Conor. Just drive. You know the way."

The highway moved uphill and the field grew lower and lower below the goat. If he went off road, the car would flip. With the top down and no seatbelts, they would be crushed.

Shelby laughed. "No we wouldn't, silly. Unless that's what you wanted to happen. Remember, it's your dream."

Conor pushed the pedal all the way down to the floor, shifted up, and watched the speedometer climb quickly past a hundred. He took a sharp corner too easily and said, "I thought we were connected. Doesn't that make it *our* dream?"

"Yeah," she clapped. "Yeah, it does. It makes it my dream. You're getting it now. Are you gonna turn around?"

"Yeah." He moved his foot off of the gas, slamming it down on the brake and twisting the steering wheel. The tires screamed against the pavement and the car spun around, and around, and around again. Conor felt his heart rate pick up. The goat kept spinning, but didn't go off the road. Somehow he knew it wouldn't. Shelby threw her hands in the air and howled with joy. Meeting her eyes, he took note that her hair still didn't move in the wind, but held perfectly still. Finally the car came to a stop, positioned perfectly in the lane that would take them to downtown Sedrow Woolley. There was no burning fluid coming from the engine. No burnt rubber smell. Not a dent or a scratch on the car.

He looked over the hood at the clear road which lie ahead. Smiling, he let off the clutch, put his foot back down on the gas and once again accelerated faster than should have been possible, taking every corner effortlessly— shifting as necessary.

"That was ah-may-zing!" Shelby wailed. "How come you were never this much fun before? Oh, I swear I would've cum that day. I would've cum so fast. So fucking hard, all over you. You gotta get a girl excited first, Conor. That's what it is. You gotta make her want it—even beg for it—before you give it to her. Sometimes that can take all day, dude. All week. Whooo!" She leaned over, placing her hand on top of his on the stick shift, and planted a kiss on his cheek. "And wanna know a secret?" she whispered into his ear. "That's how you make a girl fall in love, Conor. Make her cum. Bitches lie. You know that though, dude. I mean who knows that better than you? A girl will always choose good sex over a good heart." She nibbled lightly on his earlobe and a chill ran through his body that he didn't want to like. Then she retreated back into her seat.

Up ahead, the junction where Highway Nine met Highway Twenty came into view. Conor tapped the brake and the goat stopped so suddenly that they both should have flown through the windshield, coming to rest at the intersection. Neither of them even moved, though. The light was green going in every direction, and the goat was the only car on the road.

The music from his other dream appeared. It was quiet—distant—but he heard it still, coming from the direction of downtown. He couldn't make out the words, and there was no instrumental accompanying it. Just singing. Voices coming together in different octaves to form notes that made him want to hear more. It was the most joyfully relaxing sound he had ever heard.

He didn't take the turn. Just sat there at the intersection knowing that he would have to do it eventually, but not ready yet.

"Why?" He asked, not looking at Shelby. "What's the purpose of all this?"

"What? Tsh. Jeez, Conor, do I need to have a reason to wanna be around my boyfriend?"

"Stop it," he growled. "Don't do that. I know you're not Shelby. I'm talking to you right now. Whoever you are—whatever you are—I'm talking to you. You wanna have a discussion with me? Don't treat me like I'm stupid. Don't try and fool me. Can you at least give me that courtesy?"

"Conor, you're making it too simple. It's not that simple, though. Look at me."

"I'm fine like this," he squeezed the wheel.

"Look at me, dude."

"No."

"Conor. You want your answer, or not?"

*No.* Not really, because whatever the answer was, it wouldn't bring anybody back. His parents, Toby, his girlfriend, they were all dead and whatever this thing was that wasn't really in the passenger seat of his car, but in his head, was a liar. He wasn't really asking, and he knew it. He was whining. Whining and somehow expecting compassion from a monster.

And the worst part, the part that made him hate himself more than he ever thought possible, was that knowing this didn't affect his actions in the least. Finally, he looked over and saw her sitting perfectly straight, her slender legs growing out the bottom of a white dress that stopped just below her knees. A netted veil rested on top of her head, brushed back so it covered her straightened hair, rather than her face.

She smiled bashfully. "As you can see, I've pictured it. More than once actually. A girl doesn't just get involved with a guy without wondering if it might go there."

*Don't fall for it*, he told himself. *Don't let it get you worked up. It's lying. It's not really her. If you let it do this to you, you let it win.*

"Who says, Conor? Who says I'm not me? Ask me a question. Anything you want. Something only I would know. Come on, dude, because I'm ready to shut this shit down right now."

"You have her memories!" he snapped. "That doesn't make you her!"

"How, Conor?" she snapped right back. "Tell me how that doesn't make me, me! How is anybody anything more than a collection of memories, smart guy?"

"Because," he lowered his voice. "It's not your memories that make you, you. It's your nature."

"Wrong again. You couldn't be more wrong. All creatures have the same nature as the rest of their kind. Humans are no exception. Take away their memories, leave them with nothing but their bare animalistic instincts, and they're all the same. It's their experiences that differentiate them, and cause them to react differently from one another to the same stimulation. See, Conor, told you I'm not stupid."

The song kept playing, beckoning him toward it. He had no particular affinity for church music, or church for that matter, but something about it was alluring.

"It's Heaven," she smiled. "Or at least the closest thing we could all agree on. We're all connected. We all know we're good people, and we all had to die to get here. I wanted it to be a surprise, but since you wanna be a dick about it, that's what's waiting downtown, Conor. Heaven. When our minds linked up, all of our unique visions of Heaven came together to form it. Your mom's there. She's been waiting for you, you know that? So has Toby. He's such a goofball. Why didn't you tell me you had an Airedale? I love those dogs."

His eyes traveled over her body, hovering momentarily at her smooth legs. She wore white heels that matched the wedding dress. He had often imagined her in heels, even considered buying her a pair because he was too shy to ask her to bring some of her own to his place and wear them in his bed. When he looked back into her face, she was smiling seductively at him. She bit her bottom lip, lowering her head in a way that accentuated her eyes as she stared up into his. He thought back to every fond memory of her that he never wanted to forget, and the sorrow returned. Taking a deep breath, he reached past her and opened the passenger door. "Get out of my car." She gasped as he shoved her into the road, revved the engine and stepped on the gas.

The goat jerked forward, screeching around the corner, and the door slammed shut on its own. Conor knew it wasn't from the momentum. The laws of gravity didn't seem to apply in this word. It shut because it wanted to shut. Or maybe because he wanted it to.

The music grew in volume as he neared downtown. Soon, he passed K.C.'s Auto Glass, and the place where he had hit the girl with his Buick. She stood by the road, smiling and waving at him. Then more people came into view. They lined the sidewalks, all going the same direction as him. His goat, however, was still the only vehicle in sight.

When he made it into town, the streets were so packed that people had to move out of his way, parting like the red sea and watching as he drove slowly through Sedrow.

Some faces, he recognized. Others, he didn't. The music was loud. It seemed to radiate through the air, transmitting in every inch of space. He still couldn't make out any tangible words, only the soft, melodic tune.

Couples held each other's hands. Some even embraced, swaying together in the street. Little children ran and played merrily. An elderly couple kissed so close to his car that he could have touched them. The parking lot of the food outlet was packed with townspeople, standing in groups and watching him with genuine looking smiles on their faces. They had all been expecting him. Waiting for him to join them. *Heaven,* Shelby's voice whispered in his head. Everybody in sight seemed to beam at this thought, as if they had all heard it.

WHAH! WHAH!

Across from the store, a young boy stood in the conductor's area of the old steam locomotive. He was so short that only his head could be seen over the edge of the window. A slender naked woman with brown hair stood below, watching him play. He reached up, pulled an imaginary cord, and the whistle blew again, sending steam from the train's chimney. Looking at Conor, he started to wave, then his expression morphed as he seemed to come to some realization. He dropped his hand, and hopped much too easily out of the train. Landing on his feet like a trained acrobat, he began to walk purposefully toward the goat.

"Phillip?" The naked woman watched after him. "Where are you going?"

"I'll be right back, Momma."

"Well don't wander too far, sweetie."

"I won't."

Conor brought the goat to a stop, and the boy opened the passenger door and climbed in. Only then was he sure he knew who it was.

"You killed my dad." Phillip Harris said.

"You're young."

"So?"

"Nothing. I was just—I mean—"

"Let it go, Mitchell. If you ain't got it yet, all those years of science club didn't really serve no purpose but to assure you never got any tail. I still think you could've played ball. Shit, God knows you're big enough. Maybe give it a try when you join me. What do you say?"

"I'm not gonna join you."

"Pretty much already have. You know, I'd just of easily cut your throat and put you in a hole somewhere, but your mom and your chica kept crying about wanting you here, so I don't figure you have a choice in the matter. Not that nigger, though. No one gives two fucks about that rat-basket, so I'm gonna go ahead and turn him into a piece of art that would make the Greeks cream their skirts. Not gonna make it fast, either, know what I mean? I was quick with your buddy—what's his name—John? Didn't change him though. Except his fine fucking daughter. She'll be back. Just cut and buried the dad, though. Sorry man."

Conor tensed up, preparing himself to shove the kid out his car like he had Shelby.

"Wait!" Young Harris exclaimed. "Stop that bullshit. Now you asked me a question, and you never let me answer."

"I didn't ask you— "

"Yes you did! Back on the other highway. You asked 'why?' Then you shoved your girl out on her ass before you got your answer. Now do you want it, or not?"

Outside, people began to press up against the goat. They were so close on all sides that had it not been a dream, the vehicle wouldn't have been able to move. They leaned in close, as if to hear his conversation with Phillip.

"You didn't recognize me, did you?" Harris asked. "I mean when you saw me like this. For fuck's sake, Mitchell. How long we been going to school together? I used to look just like this, man. Used to come here with my folks to play on the train, too. My old man was full a useless facts, you know. Used to tell me all kinds a shit about the train. Like, you know that triangle wedge on the front of it? Right there." He pointed. "The thing that looks like a fucking snow scraper or something?

"Well it was actually used for that. Scraping snow, or whatever. But it also caught cattle that found their way onto the tracks so the damn thing didn't derail. Know what they used to call it? A cow catcher. I don't know why I always thought that was so interesting as a kid, I just did. Every time we drove by the fucking train, I'd point and say, 'Look, Dad. The cow catcher!'"

"I didn't ask you any questions," Conor said. "I asked Shelby."

"For fuck's sake, Mitchell. You still don't get it? I am Shelby. I'm me. I'm you. I'm us. We're all one now, buddy. One big shared mind. What did you call it? Collective consciousness? I like that. It fits.

"But I was me, before you. Before any of you, really. So to answer your question, there really is no answer. There is no 'why,' because the way that I exist isn't the way that you do. I'm not from here. All this," he motioned with one hand toward everything around the car, "it's all—ah, shit. How do you say it?—It's just for show. I have no physical appearance, because I'm not from your world. So when you look at me and you see a giant bug, well Mitchell, that's just the closest your mind can come to comprehending what I am. What you are now."

"I'm not one of you!" Conor snapped.

"One with me," Phillip corrected. "And you sure as fuck are. Soon you will be one of us, though. You see, your chica, she's laid claim to you. She's headed to that apartment right now and she's gonna go ahead and slice you open at the belly and put her eggs inside of you. Then she'll bury you and wait for those eggs to work their magic.

"And then you know what I'm gonna do, Mitchell? And by 'I,' I mean 'you.' I'm gonna finish this fucking planet off, and move on. Because that's what I do. Been doing it a long fucking time actually."

Somewhere in the crowd, Toby barked.

"Conor? Conor?" He recognized his mom's voice right away. "Stay where you are, Conor. I'm on my way."

Ignoring her, Conor said, "You're a plague."

"That's right," a blonde girl leaned in and whispered in his ear. "At least that's the closest comparison to what I am that you could understand."

"What *you* are." Phillip pointed at him, poking his bicep lightly. "What you are now, at least."

"Conor?" his mom called. "Excuse me? Excuse me? Could you please clear a path? I'm trying to get to my son. Thank you."

Toby barked again.

"But even that doesn't get close," Phillip went on. "Not really. You'll only drive yourself crazy trying to understand what I am, or even how I am, Mitchell. You know why? Because there's nothing like me in your universe—but me now."

"You're mass extinction," Conor spoke through gritted teeth. "I get it. But what then? What do you do once you've killed everything, and there's nothing left to eat? Just go back where you came?"

"Go where?" The girl who Conor hit with his car asked from where she now stood near Harris. "I'm not from anywhere. I've always been, because outside of this existence that you would call a dimension, there is no time. My home is wherever I am, and once I'm done, I move on. We move on, Conor."

"Another fun fact," Phillip said with a smile. "The town of Sedrow Woolley used to actually be called, 'Bug.' Did you know that? Named after all the fucking mosquitoes. The people didn't like that name much, though, so they changed it to 'Sedrow.' That's Spanish for cedar, and if you don't know why cedar, then all I can say is the science really didn't serve no purpose but to—"

"I wasn't in the science club, you prick! I was in fucking shop!"

In front of the goat, the crowd parted finally and Conor's mom appeared, Toby standing next to her, his tongue out. Both of them seemed to smile. Their eyes beamed as they looked into his. Then the dream ended.

# Chapter Eight

Conor opened his eyes and looked up into the chrome light fixture. It was meant for two bulbs, but only held one. Because of this, the room was dimly lit. It reeked of cigarette smoke. It took a second to feel the throbbing in his brain, but when he did, it was almost unbearable. It came in bursts, one after another, like a subwoofer inside of his skull. He let out a weak moan, reached up and touched the back of his head.

A sharp pain hit so hard that he cried out, pulling away quickly to see thick blood on his hand. "Jesus," he groaned. "What the hell?"

"Yo, Daddy!" A raspy female voice called from somewhere in the room. "This mufucka awake!"

Conor looked over to see the heavyset redheaded woman sitting on an old, dirty looking couch. Her legs were spread, allowing a view into her sundress. He found himself momentarily grateful that they were so plump he couldn't see if she were wearing underwear or not.

Not knowing what else to do, he said, "Please. My head."

"Which one?" Tone called from somewhere in the distance.

"The white boy." She raised a glass tube to her mouth, sparked a lighter, and sucked on the end as heavy footsteps approached, shaking the wooden floor.

Conor rolled over and glanced toward the noise and his head pounded even harder. He saw Percly laying facedown next to him in a small puddle of his own blood. A heavy hand landed on Conor's arm, rolling him onto his back. He looked up into Tone's smiling face.

"Robbin' ass nigga wanna try the wrong muthafucka today. Tryin' a get a nigga his third strike. That's what the fuck ain't gone happen." He shoved the barrel of Percly's revolver in Conor's face.

"Please!" Conor brought his hands up, but didn't dare grab for the gun. "Don't shoot, man. Please don't fucking shoot."

"He right, Daddy." the redhead said. "You know you can't shoot they ass."

"Bitch?"

"You want the neighbors ta hear that shit? Put yo ass right back in the joint, and I'm tellin' you now, I ain't waitin' around this time."

"Bitch, yo fat ass didn't wait last time."

"I'm here, ain't I?"

"Dat pussy stretched out, ain't it?"

She took another pull from her pipe, and thick smoke came out of her mouth as she said, "I'm just sayin', you pull that trigger, everyone here to Bothell gone hear that shit. Blood gone get all over the crib, too. Bet yo ass ain't thought about that, did you?"

Tone appeared to go into deep thought, and Conor felt a thin ray of hope. His breathing, which had grown rapid, began to slowly calm. *Keep talking,* he thought, as if she could hear. She couldn't, though, because she wasn't one of the monster outside.

"So what?" Tone asked sarcastically. "I just let these fools go? After they ass made me swing a bat on 'em? Then what? Let 'em call the poh-leese, and a nigga get hit with assault? Get lifed the fuck out?"

"Shit," she snickered. "I ain't said that neither. Take them fools into the bathtub an get a knife."

He tilted his head. "A knife?"

"You hard a hearin', mufucka? Yeah. A knife. Unless you ain't got the nuts to cut a mufucka's throat. I know you a big man with a gun an all."

"Bitch, how bout I cut yo muthafuckin' throat? What then?"

"Shit!" She laughed. "If you can't cut they throat to save your ass from a life sentence, you sure ain't about to touch mine."

Conor began to panic again. "Listen, man—" He tried to sit up, but Tone shoved him back down.

"Lay yo fuckin' punk ass down, bitch."

"Don't do this, man. You don't have to do this. We're not calling the police. Haven't you seen what's happening outside? That's not a fucking riot!"

"No?" Tone raised his voice, bared his teeth. "Then why don't you tell me, bitch! What is it?"

Conor opened his mouth to answer, to tell him everything that he knew about the creatures. But what were the words? How did you explain the inexplicable in just enough time to save your life? His jaw hung for a moment, until Tone hit him in the side of the head with the revolver and he saw red. "Aaahhh! Stop! Please! Locusts! They're fucking locusts!"

"What the fuck you just say? Speak up, nigga!"

"Haven't you ever read the Bible?" Conor cried,

curling up in a ball and covering his head and face the best he could with his hands and arms.

"Course I read the muthafuckin' Bible!"

"Then you know what I'm talking about! Just look outside! Look at what they did out there! Turn on the news, for Christ's sake!" He realized a second too late that there was probably no TV, let alone cable in this apartment. "They're killing everybody, Tone. They started in Sedrow Woolley, then they came here."

"What?" The gun came at Conor again, this time connecting only with his shoulder. "What came here? What the fuck is you talkin' about?"

"Giant bugs, Tone. Giant fucking locusts. Just look outside and see what they did. We weren't coming in here to rob anybody, man. We just needed somewhere safe."

"Daddy, this mufucka crazy. I'm a go get you a knife. Drag his ass into the tub and get this shit over with. I'll call up Jo-jo and get a whip over here for they bodies. Shit, the po-po gone be busy— "

"Bitch! Shut the fuck up a minute! Can you do that! Do you know how to just shut the fuck up! Go look out that window'n tell me what the fuck you see."

"What? You gotta be shittin' me."

"Conor stuttered?"

After a long pause, the couch squeaked and Conor heard bare feet slap the floor, sticking to the wood as they moved, one after the other, across the room. "This shit got me fucked up, Daddy."

"If yo ass lyin' ta me," Tone growled. But before he could finish, something crashed so loud that at first Conor thought he had been hit again with the gun. That his skull had cracked. Then he knew it wasn't his head, but wood that had split and he found himself wishing it had been the former. "Oh, sweet Jesus!" Tone called. Conor looked up to see him fall over backward as a creature that he knew was Shelby walked through the door it had just kicked in. It wasn't the same as the others. Its skin was covered in a thick layer of black slime. He remembered what she had told him about waking up early, and knew it hadn't had time to fully develop. It looked down at him with a horrible smile that wrapped from one side of its head to the other.

"Told you I was gonna save you," It clicked. "Why'd you push me out of the car? Don't you want me, Conor?"

The redhead screamed. Her pipe fell to the floor and broke as Tone scrambled to his feet, pointing the revolver at Shelby. Shelby was too fast, though. It flew across the room, taking his wrist and snapping it like a piece of kindling. He screamed in agony as the gun crashed to the floor. Shelby took his throat in one clawed hand and squeezed, digging its claws behind his windpipe. When she pulled it back, air hissed from his lungs and blood sprayed out, painting the monsters face. Tone's eyes went wide. His hands came up, clutched his neck. He hit the floor and kicked and flailed as Shelby walked over and bit the redhead.

"It's okay, beautiful." It stroked the woman's hair, catching her as she fell paralyzed and setting her down lightly. Then it turned its attention to Conor, who was just getting to his feet. His head pounded harder and harder with every movement. "Conor," it held its arms out, displaying its body, "what exactly is it about me that you don't like?"

He took a step back. "Mass genocide and global extinction are kind of deal breakers, Shelby."

"Don't be like that, Conor." The monster bent down, getting on all fours. It lowered its head and he knew it was going to pounce. He took another step and his back met a wall. Shelby braced itself like a frog ready to jump.

POP!

The creature hissed, turning on Percly, who now sat upright pointing his gun at it. Black blood sprayed from its neck. It raised itself back up on two legs and walked toward him smiling as he squeezed the trigger again.

CLICK. CLICK. CLICK. CLICK.

"Fuck!" He threw the heavy revolver at the thing, but it didn't stop, just continued to walk like a T-rex, leaving a trail of black blood on the floor.

Conor scanned the mostly empty living room, until his eyes came to rest on Percly's bat, leaning against the wall next to him. Picking it up, he ran at Shelby and swung as hard as he could, connecting with its ugly head. It hissed again, turned around and flashed him a look that suggested it actually had feelings and he had hurt them. He swung again. This time, it ducked, cocked its legs and jumped impossibly fast through the window the redheaded woman had been looking out of. The glass shattered, made a noise that almost resembled wind chimes as it landed all around the paralyzed woman.

Ignoring her, Conor turned his attention to Percly. He walked over, offered his hand and pulled him to his feet. Then the sound of helicopter blades grew louder. Both men seemed to register at the same time what it implied.

"Son-of-a-bitch," Percly said.

"Load your gun," Conor went to the redhead, squatting down next to her. She stared up, clearly terrified. A single tear squeezed out of her eye, rolling down the side of her face. "You're one with us now," he whispered. "Don't be afraid." He stared down for a moment, then jumped to his feet, sprinting around a corner and into a tiny kitchen with dirty dishes stacked in the sink. Opening a cupboard, he grabbed a tin can, and ran back out into the living room.

"What the hell is that?" Percly asked as he stuffed bullets into the cylinder.

"Acetone."

"What the hell we need that for?"

"Just hurry. You'll see."

"How you find it so fast?"

"Because," he squatted next to her again. "I saw it in her mind."

"What?"

"Just load the gun, Percly!"

He glanced again into the woman's mind, stroking her hair softly, seeing scenes from her childhood that he would rather not have. Memories of an uncle that couldn't keep his hands to himself. Of a stepfather that did more than just touch. Of standing on street corners in downtown Seattle at fourteen years old. Then he had what he needed. He jumped to his feet, told Percly to follow him, and ran out the broken door.

* * *

They sprinted up another flight of stairs and through a door that led to the roof. Cold air nipped at his face, causing his eyes to water. The helicopters were so close now that they could have thrown a rock and hit them, but they were oblivious to the two men.

"Hey!" Percly yelled, waving his arms. "Down here! Hey! Come on, now! Look this way!"

There were more, now, too. At least a half-dozen, mostly police and military. They shone their spotlights everywhere, it seemed, but the roof. Conor hadn't seen any gunfire since he woke up. He went to the ledge, looked over and saw why. Townspeople seemed to come out of every dark crevice and alley, from every direction, walking quickly toward the building. Though he saw the monstrosities that they were, he knew they had reverted back to their human appearances. The soldiers and officers didn't know whether to fire on them or not. And they had spread out, taking different routes to the apartment complex. And they were coming for him.

Percly appeared beside him. "Oh shit! Why the hell did we trap ourselves up on this roof again?"

"Would you rather we trapped ourselves down there?" Conor didn't wait for him to answer. He ran to the middle of the roof and started pouring acetone in a long, winding line until the can was empty and the fumes burned his nostrils. "Give me your lighter!"

"What?"

"Your lighter! Hurry up!"

"Shit." Percly reached into his pocket fishing around for too long, then pulled out the blue Bic. "Here." His hand shook as he passed it over.

Conor leaned down, flicked the sparker. Nothing happened. He did it again, and it lit, but a gust of wind quickly blew out the flame.

"Gimme that shit!" Percly squatted next to him, snatched the lighter out of his hand. He cupped a hand around it, and lit the acetone, which burst into a flame that stretched six feet across and spelled the word 'help' in perfect cursive. Both men jumped to their feet to avoid being burned.

"Well there's that fucking rat-basket." A buzzing voice crackled behind them. They turned at the same time, to see the monster that thought it was a fully grown Phillip Harris walk through the door and out onto the roof smiling. "Been looking for you, Valentine."

Machine gun fire erupted, seemed to echo off the sky from every direction. Conor glanced to see multiple helicopters spitting flames, shooting at the sides of the building. Though he couldn't hear over all the noise, he knew the monsters were climbing up.

Behind Harris, two more walked slowly through the

door, and he knew it was his mom and stepfather. Brett Mitchell held a thick leather belt in one hand and smiled at him. "You been causing a lot of trouble around town, son. Let's see how much shit you can get into after I whip your ass black and blue."

"You know, Valentine," Harris crouched down on all fours. "They taught us in the academy to never make it personal. Serve and protect, but don't get involved. What a crock a shit, right? How the fuck am I supposed to not take it personal when some smelly fucking monkey moves into my train? It is mine, you know? But I let that go for a long time, didn't I? Have I ever harassed you? Have I ever shown up early in the morning and hooked you up for trespassing? No! But what did you go and do? You shot my dad. Now that, I can't forgive." He flew forward and a fraction of a second later Conor's parents followed, Brett wielding his imaginary belt as if ready to strike.

Conor stumbled, landing on his back, looking around frantically to see if any of them had made it up the sides of the building. Percly didn't move, though. He raised his gun and smiled right back at the beasts. They were mere feet away, when he emptied the cylinder—POP! POP! POP! POP! POP! POP! CLICK. CLICK. CLICK—and all three bugs fell twitching and hissing.

Only then did Conor see that he wasn't smiling at all, but rather snarling, his teeth bared like an angry dog. "Bet you don't call no one no fuckin' nigger, no more."

Machine guns screamed and bullets slammed into brick and metal, creating a cloud of dust that floated through the beams of light coming from the helicopters. A gust of wind caused it to dance maniacally as one of the machines finally landed on the roof. Its blades seemed to spin in slow motion, making the flames—which had begun to spread—dance. It was dark blue, and read, "POLICE" in bold white lettering across the side.

The door was propped open, and a cop wearing a helmet and clutching an assault rifle hung halfway out. He motioned them over frantically, just as the first stream of monsters poured over the edge of the roof and scurried toward the vehicle from every direction. Conor and Percly sprinted.

The cop's eyes went wide and he mouthed something Conor couldn't make out, moving out of the way. Percly jumped in first, then it took to the air.

"Come on! Come on! Come on!" the cop screamed over the sound of the blades and the engine. "Get the fuck in!"

Conor dove, landing halfway inside as a bony hand wrapped around his ankle and tugged so hard he moved back. The cop caught him by the wrist and the chopper flew higher. Conor felt like an anchor was attached to his leg. Another officer took his other hand and they pulled him in further. Then the thing climbed his leg like a fireman's pole. Claws scraped his skin as it hooked one hand into his waistband and put another on his shoulder, pulling itself up his back.

Conor glanced over his shoulder into Toby's smiling face. The insect dog barked, then its thin black tongue shot out and licked his face. Its breath smelled like rotting meat, and it took every ounce of self-control not to vomit.

"Holy Mother of God!" A gun went off inside the helicopter and the creature's head exploded. It fell from Conor's body as the cops pulled him the rest of the way in.

* * *

"Take out the damn building!" a voice called through every Navy radio in Everett. "That's an order! Over."

"Sir!" the response came instantly. "They're already moving! They're not on the building anymore. Over."

"Then follow them, damn it! Over."

"Roger that. Over."

Twenty-six seconds later, a call was made authorizing bomber jets to be deployed.

* * *

"Mother of God, are you okay?"

There were four cops in the helicopter. Two with rifles, two in the cockpit. They all wore helmets with mouth pieces attached. The ones with the rifles stood in the back with Conor and Percly, where two rows of seats faced each other.

"I'm fine," Conor yelled over the noise. "Listen to me. I can—"

"Sit back and put on a seatbelt. We had an accident earlier. Couple choppers collided head on."

"Listen to me!" Conor yelled louder. "I can stop this. I know what's happening out there and I know how to stop it."

The cop appeared to be in his late forties or early fifties. He had a white moustache that made Conor think of Charles Bronson. He eyed Conor skeptically, then glanced at his much younger partner, who just shrugged.

"Fine." He redressed Conor. "You have twenty seconds."

"It's some kind of an inter dimensional plague."

"I thought you said they was locusts," Percly yelled.

"I just said that. That guy was gonna shoot me. Wait— you were awake?"

"Ten seconds," the cop pushed.

"Listen, who says they're not locusts anyway? We don't know what the writers of the Bible were seeing. They could have had visions of all this and just called them giant locusts because it's the closest comparison they could come up with. These things, they're not things. I mean, they're not multiple things. It's just one entity, and it exists outside of time."

"Times up, kid. Put on your seatbelt."

"No! Listen to me! I'm from Sedrow Woolley, damn it! This thing came here for me."

"Oh yeah? Lemme guess, you're humanity's only hope for defeating the aliens? We need to fly back to your house so you can pick up your tinfoil hat, though?"

"I don't know if I'm the only hope, but I can help you beat them."

The cop took a deep breath, let it out slowly, shaking his head. "And how is that?"

"Because I'm one of them."

A noticeable tension spread through the helicopter. The cop bared his teeth, as the other one raised his rifle and pointed it at Conor's chest.

"No!" he threw his hands up. "Don't shoot! Not like that. Listen, I was attacked last night and I managed to survive. Since then I've been connected to it at the mind. I know this sounds crazy, but I'm not lying. I know everything there is to know about it, and trust me, that's not much."

The guns had stopped firing at some point. Conor knew this was because the creatures had once again taken on their human appearances and scurried into the shadows.

"Twenty more seconds," the cop said. "And if you don't convince me this time, I'm throwing you out of this chopper."

"It's a virus," Conor spoke quickly. "It looks like a bunch of giant bugs, but that's just because it's from another dimension, where existence isn't anything like what we understand. It doesn't have a physical appearance. It appeared the way it did because of where it started. Kind of a play on words to do with Sedrow Woolley's history." He shook his head. "None of that matters though. It's gonna wipe out every bit of life on this planet—the whole fucking universe—then move on."

"Why?" the cop snapped. "For the love of God, you're telling me this is some kind of an intelligent virus?"

"No. It's not intelligent at all. It's parasitic. It's latching onto us and using our thoughts to navigate our own extinction."

Finally, the younger officer lowered his weapon and addressed his older partner. "Gardner?"

Gardner held up a hand, silencing him, not looking away from Conor. "Your time's almost up, kid, so I recommend you tell me how you intend to help."

Conor nodded. "I need you to put me to sleep."

* * *

Walter Murphy took his wife by the hand. They huddled side-by-side against a dumpster in a dark alley smiling into each other's faces.

"I love you, you beautiful bitch," he whispered.

She didn't respond. Not with her words, at least. Instead, she leaned her head down, resting it on his bumpy reptilian shoulder. He cupped her face in his clawed hand, then stroked it lightly. If this wasn't heaven, he didn't want to go there.

Overhead, the helicopters whooshed around, shining lights everywhere, searching for townspeople. They wouldn't find them, though. Not until they wanted to be found.

* * *

"What the hell are you talking about, 'put you to

sleep'?"

"I told you, I have a connection with them. It only seems to work when I'm asleep or intoxicated, though. I know how it sounds, but I need you to trust me, or at least try it. If you put me to sleep, they'll come after me again. You can use me as bait. Get them all in one place, then take them out."

Percly was the only one sitting down. He watched silently, gripping his empty gun in his lap.

The cop growled. "And how the hell am I supposed to put you to sleep?"

"I don't know. Don't you have a tranquilizer gun or something?"

"Do we look like fucking zookeepers?"

"I don't know! Jesus. Think of—"

Before he could finish his sentence, the younger cop dropped his rifle, came up behind him and put him in a rear naked choke, pushing down on the back of his head. Percly's first instinct was to jump up and help his new friend, but he resisted it, and within seconds Conor fell limp to the floor.

* * *

Conor was in the back of a minivan. There was blood everywhere. A naked brunette girl lay under him screaming and crying, begging him to stop. Her face and breasts were covered in bloody three-fingered handprints. He thrust his claw into her chest and she inhaled, coughed, and began to convulse, pressing her hands into his face and trying to push him back.

* * *

He opened his eyes and looked up to see both cops

hanging out the open door of the helicopter, staring down.

"Son-of-a-bitch!" Gardner yelled. "They're coming out!"

Conor rolled over, stuck his head out the door and looked down to see the townspeople gathering below them, looking up. Then gunfire erupted from the other choppers and they fled again into the shadows.

"Make them stop!" he yelled. "Make them stop shooting!"

"What? Then what do we do?"

"Put me back to sleep, then lure them somewhere away from civilization."

"Like where?"

Conor thought a moment, then met the cop's eyes. "I don't know. All I know is that you need to get those things away from the city and drop a bomb on them."

Gardner's eyes and mouth opened and just hung that way for too long before he called to the pilot. "Tell the Goddamn Navy to hold their fire! Reeves!"

"Sir?" the younger officer replied.

"Administer that choke again."

* * *

Conor was back in the Heaven that the townspeople of Sedrow Woolley had created. They all still surrounded the goat, but young Phillip Harris no longer sat in his passenger seat. The crowd was still parted in front of him, but Toby and his Mom had disappeared. He put her in drive, flipped a U-turn, and everybody moved out of his way as he pushed the pedal to the floor.

In under a minute, he was back on Highway Nine, pulling over next to Shelby, where he had left her by the road. She still wore the white wedding dress, but now held a bouquet of flowers as well.

"Get in," he said.

She smiled, leaned in and kissed him on the lips long and deep. When she pulled away, she didn't go far. Her face rested so close that their breath would have mixed together, had it not been a dream. She stared into his eyes, and Conor saw something in hers that he had never noticed before. It was a sadness that seemed to beg him to make it better. A need to be loved that was easier to mask with pot, alcohol, and sex, than to face head on. The moment seemed to go on forever before she finally said, "I am *me,* Conor."

"I know," he replied. "Get in the car. I'm taking you out of here."

After another moment, her smile widened and she walked around the front of the goat, opening the passenger door and climbing in. "Do you want me now?"

"What do you think?"

"Then say it."

"Don't be silly, Shelby."

"I never cheated on you, you know. Even before we were serious, whenever that started." She shut the door. "It was so confusing sometimes because you were so distant. I wasn't with anyone else though. Yeah, I talked to other guys in the beginning. Not because I was interested, though. I did it to see how serious you were. I'd take their calls or text them right in front of you. But you didn't seem to care, so eventually I just stopped. I cut them all off.

"I know this sounds stupid, but I changed the names in my contacts. I listed all my girlfriends and family members under guy's names, just hoping you would look and get jealous."

"I know," Conor said.

"You never looked, though. You never snooped through my phone, or even asked me if I was with anyone else. Did you ever even care, Conor?"

"Yeah." His voice shook. "Don't be stupid, Shelby. You know I cared."

"Then say it."

"I love you too."

"I know."

"I know you do."

"I wanna be with you, Conor. Here. Forever."

"I know," he said.

"Is that what you want too?"

He just nodded. He closed his eyes, and when he reopened them, he wore a black tuxedo. She paused for so long that he thought his heart would beat out of his chest with anticipation. When he looked over at her, tears streamed down her face on either side of her nose. She sniffed and wiped them away with the back of her hand.

"Will you?" he asked.

Shelby nodded.

Conor put the car in gear, turned it around and drove back toward downtown so fast that the goat left tracers behind.

* * *

The helicopter floated over the surface of the Puget Sound. Percly, Gardner, and Reeves all watched as the crowd of townspeople stopped at the water's edge, staring up at them.

"Why aren't they following?" Reeves yelled.

"How the hell am I supposed to know?"

Both cops looked at Percly.

"I don't know," he said. "Maybe they can't swim."

They were about a quarter mile from the beach now, and though the monsters hadn't begun to retreat, they refused to go any further. That's when Conor sat up.

"Put him back to sleep!" Gardner snapped.

"Whoa! Whoa!" Conor threw his hands up. "Chill!

That's not gonna work."

"Then we need to bomb their ass right now, while they're all together."

"That won't work either. There's too many of them. You'd have to drop a big fucking bomb to kill them all."

"You think the Navy doesn't have one?"

"I'm sure they do." He stood up, moving to the open door and peering out at the townspeople. "But they're too close to civilization."

"Then what the hell do you suggest we do?"

"Drop that bomb. But not until they're way out in the water."

"I don't think you're hearing me. How the hell do you suggest we get them there?"

Conor glanced over at Percly and nodded. Then at Gardner. "Like this." He leapt out the door.

* * *

As far as he was concerned the dream hadn't ended. Only this was a dream in which he was falling, falling, falling, until finally he crashed into the water and sank. He sank for so long that he thought he would never come back up. Then, before he knew he was doing it, he was kicking his feet, making his way back to the surface of the ocean. His head emerged and he took a deep breath, looking up to see the helicopter retreating back toward the shore.

As it put distance between itself and him, its propellers died in volume, and he heard the splashing of the townspeople as they swam toward him. Then they were close enough to be seen, even in the dark. Soon, he was surrounded, but none of them laid a claw on him until Shelby appeared in front of his face. It stared into his eyes and he saw everything it intended to do to him. To bite him. To slice him open. To lay its eggs inside of him and bury him in the sand below the water. To make him hers forever.

* * *

Percly watched out the window as the bomber jets appeared, firing missiles into the ocean. Then the helicopter shook and the sky lit up so bright that for a moment it looked like afternoon, rather than night. The cops sat back and buckled their seatbelts as more missiles were fired, one after another. Percly tried not to look away, but then his eyes couldn't take it anymore. He buckled his own seatbelt, but it was a useless gesture because a few seconds later, the chopper landed in the middle of Broadway.

# Epilogue

The '66 Pontiac GTO convertible always had the top down. In the two years that it had sat in the middle of the lobby in the Everett courthouse, nobody had vandalized it. The security guards wouldn't allow it. The rif-raf that came through the building for misdemeanor and felony cases may, or may not have forgotten the sacrifice that Conor Mitchell made for their city, but the car put on display in his honor assured that the employees who worked around it every day never would. Neither would Percly.

Catey Mitchell was a pretty girl. So was Cindy, but in a different way. A more homely way, Percly guessed. They both stood about Percly's height and had dark brown hair. Before today, he had only talked to Conor's sisters on the phone. He had moved back to Louisiana after the initial outbreak, and hadn't returned to Washington since.

"Thanks for coming," Catey said. "I know it really means a lot to my brother."

He resisted the urge to tell her that Conor was dead, and didn't have the ability to care one way or the other. Instead, he said, "Yeah. Well, didn't seem right not to come back eventually'n pay my respects. Would a come sooner, but it was just a matter of gettin' the time off work. Your brother was a good kid."

Both girls nodded.

As an afterthought, Percly said, "You know what? He wasn't just a good kid. He was the bravest man I've ever known."

The courthouse was as active as could be expected on a Wednesday afternoon in the middle of summer. It looked like how he guessed an old Renaissance temple might appear inside, with pillars that ran from the floor to the tall ceiling and an abstract design painted on the marble floor. People went about their business, paying them no mind.

"I guess I just never pictured Conor like that," Catey said, not looking at Percly or his sister, but staring ahead at the car.

"Like what?" Percly asked.

"You know—like a hero. He was always so quiet growing up. I mean he never really did anything wrong, and he was still always in trouble. At the time I guess I didn't notice how hard Dad was on him, but—" She paused and Percly knew she was fighting back tears, because she didn't want to let herself speak an ill word about her dead father.

"I get it." Percly saved her the trouble. "Listen, I don't wanna say anyone in your brother's position would've done what he done, 'cause I don't really know. Trust me, I done thought about it a hundred an one different ways. You know, whether or not I would've done the same thing. Then, sometimes I wonder if he even had to do it. You know, could we of solved the thing any other way?

"Most of the time, I try not to think about it too much, though. Just be grateful that he gave his life for mine. For all of ours."

What he didn't say was that more often than not, he found himself feeling like the kid had given his life for nothing. Sedrow Woolley had been completely irradiated of all human life. The only residents who survived had been the ones lucky enough to have been on vacation when it all happened. They never stepped foot in the town again.

It was quarantined and for the next two days soldiers shot down every life form that crawled out of the earth. One lost her life when she refused to fire on a class of pre-schoolers. Two years later, the town was still fenced off and uninhabited. Only residents of the Upper Skagit Indian Reservation were allowed anywhere near the site, because they had to pass through to get to their homes. They were in the process of petitioning the court for the land, which had been theirs not so long ago anyway, and proceedings seemed to be moving in their favor.

The body count in Everett was never agreed upon, but known to have been in the thousands. Only portions of the city were blocked off in order to be exterminated of all alien presence.

The outbreak didn't stop, though. The engineer, who had disappeared from Sedrow turned up at his home in Denver. Less than a month later, the city was under an attack that ended with a nuclear strike and millions dead. A town in upstate New York was wiped out before they were discovered and dealt with again. Then they turned up in Europe. Conor was right about one thing; it was a disease. And like every other disease that had arisen throughout history, it wasn't going to stop trying to kill them off, and it wasn't going to just go away.

"Yeah," Catey said. "That makes sense. How's

work?"

"Same as could be expected workin' at a damn factory. Back hurt. Tired all the time. Ain't got no money. Shit, more than I had livin' on the streets, but not much more. Apartments cost money, an bills don't pay themselves." He laughed. "Been thinkin' bout gettin' me a glass eye." He moved the black patch from his bad eye and showed it to Catey. "What do you think?"

After examining it for a moment, she giggled. "It's not that bad. I don't even know why you cover it up."

"You know, me neither, really. When I was a boy, I had a accident. Fell off a bike a landed right on a stick. I mean how fuckin' likely is that? Of all the places to land. I was devastated, too. I'm tellin' you, you wouldn't believe me if I told you how sad I was. But my Nana would ask me, 'Percly, how many things work for good to those who love God?'

"And like a good Louisiana boy, I'd say, 'All things.'" Percly laughed.

"Then she'd say, 'Really? All things? Doesn't that mean not just the things that make us happy, but the things that make us sad too?'

"And I'd say, 'Yeah, Nana. Yeah, that's what it means.

"And she'd say, 'Even broken eyes?'

"And even though I didn't believe her, shit I couldn't think of one good reason God would want me to have a broken eye, I'd say, 'Yeah, Nana.'

"It wasn't 'til all those years later, when this broken eye saved my ass, then it saved your brother so he could save all those people that I finally started to get it." He moved the patch back over his eye. "You girls wanna go somewhere an get a drink?"

"Aren't you in recovery?" Cindy asked.

"I didn't ask if you wanted to watch me have a drink. I

ain't touched the shit in years. That don't mean I can't have a cranberry juice while we shoot the shit. Come on, I know a place just up the street."

Catey smiled. "You're just a charmer, aren't you?"

"Now don't you go an get any ideas. I'm old enough to be your grandad."

"What?" She mocked appall. "I'm engaged, you know!"

Percly looked again at the goat. So did the girls.

"He used to love this car so much," Cindy said. "We used to joke that he loved it more than any of us."

"It's a nice car." Percly nodded.

"Yeah. Yeah, it is."

"Come on." He turned and started for the door. "I wanna take you there."

"Where?" Catey asked.

"The bar where I had my last drink with your brother. And I sure as hell hope you can hold your liquor better than he could."

A few seconds later, both girls followed.

# END

## ABOUT YOUR AUTHOR

Michael J Moore lives with his wife, author Cait Moore, in Seattle, Washington. His books include the bestselling post-apocalyptic novel, *After the Change.* His work has appeared in Blood Moon Rising Magazine, Horrorzine Magazine, Minutes Before Six, has been adapted for theater and produced in the Seattle area by various organizations, and is used as curriculum at the University of Washington. His short story, "The House on East 46th Street" will also be released this year by Rainfall Books of the United Kingdom.

Follow him at:
https://michaeljmoorewriti.wixsite.com/website
https://www.facebook.com/michaeljmoorewriting
https://twitter.com/MichaelJMoore20
https://instagram.com/michaeljmoorewriting
https://www.amazon.com/Michael-J-
Moore/e/B07N8CS23D/ref=ntt_dp_epwbk_0

## Other HellBound Books Titles
## Available at: www.hellboundbookspublishing.com

### Follow Him

True love doesn't die – it devours.

Just outside the sleepy town of Dreury, a mysterious cult known as The Shared Heart has planted its stakes. Its followers are numerous. More join every day. Those who are lost and suffering seem to be drawn to it; a home for the broken. When Jacob finds himself in need of such a home, he abandons his dead name and gives himself over to the will of The Great Collector.

However, love refuses to let Jacob go so easily; his ex-fiancé, Nina, kidnaps him in the hopes that he can be deprogramed. As she attempts to return Jacob to the life they once had, a terrible fear creeps in: what if there isn't enough of her Jacob left?

When The Great Collector learns of his missing follower, the true nature of The Shared Heart is unleashed. Nina discovers what Jacob already knows: that hidden behind the warm songs and soaring bonfires is a terrifying and ancient secret; one that lives and breathes… and hungers.

## Tremble

Widow and single mother, Rebecca Noland, wants nothing more than to rekindle the passion with her overworked fiancé, Detective Dan Slaviche.

Expecting to surprise him by slipping into his apartment before he comes home from work, her curiosity gets the best of her when she discovers the key to unlock his desktop. What she finds there is a nightmare that sends her, along with her seven-year-old son, running for their lives.

Terrified and broke, her only option is to flee to her family's estate in Tremble, Tennessee where memories of her mother's violent death still haunt her childhood home. But bad memories aren't the only things that await her.
As Dan abandons all morals in his attempt to locate his bride-to-be, Rebecca struggles to make the house a home for her son while growing closer to her next-door neighbors. But her sanity comes into question when she realizes the entity responsible for her mother's murder is lying in wait, intent on destroying anyone who tries to come between it and the object of its deadly obsession... *her.*

## The Devil's Hour

A new and altogether awesome anthology of all things horror!

Seventeen spine-chilling tales of the darkest terror, most unpleasant people, and slithering monsters that lurk beneath the bed and in the blackest of shadows…

## Satanic Panic

An incredible homage to 1980's horror!

Satanic Panic, a mass hysteria created in the nineteen eighties, has returned to a small college town in the Midwest.

Ritualistic murders and the presence of the occult have bled below the surface of the town in the form of icy accidents and other coincidences.

And when three lifelong friends find themselves on the radar of a killer—and leader of a satanic cult—they must fight for what's good without being seduced by the evil that possesses their campus.

## The Toilet Zone
## RESTROOM READING AT ITS MOST FRIGHTENING!

Compiled and edited by the grand master of 80's schlock horror, Bret McCormick, each one of this collection of 32 terrifying tales is just the perfect length for a visit to the smallest room....

At the very boundaries of human imagination dwells one single, solitary place of solitude, of peace and quiet, a place in which your regular human being spends, on average, 10 to 15 minutes - at least once every single day of their lives.

Now, consider a typical, everyday reading speed of 200 to 250 words per minute - that means your average visitor has the time to read between 2,500 to 4,000 words, which makes each and every one of these 32 tales of terror - from some of the best contemporary independent authors - within this anthology of horror the perfect, meticulously calculated length. Dare you take a walk to the small room from where inky shadows creep out to smother the light and solitude's siren call beckons you?

Dare you take a quiet, lonely walk into… The Toilet Zone

## Invasive Species

A monster has come to Maldus, Arkansas, and the residents of the small mountain town are too busy to notice. With the monster comes something even more terrifying and threatening than gnashing teeth or razor-sharp claws.

The monster has brought change.

The residents of the small mountain town are too busy to notice at first. Busy with things such as addiction, racism, work, or land deals. Unnoticed, the change the monster brings in its insidious wake spreads like wildfire.

Unnoticed, the town of Maldus falls prey to an Invasive Species.

## A HellBound Books LLC Publication

http://www.hellboundbookspublishing.com

**Printed in the United States of America**

9 781948 318808